Praise for Nico...

After the Leaves Fall

"Baart writes compellingly about a young girl's struggle with loss, love, identity, and faith. . . . Sparkling prose makes this new novel a welcome addition to inspirational fiction."

PUBLISHERS WEEKLY

"Baart's writing is evocative and beautiful. . . ."

ROMANTIC TIMES

"[F]or readers who enjoy a sensitively written coming-of-age story about a captivating young woman, this book is well worth reading."

CBA RETAILERS + RESOURCES

"*After the Leaves Fall* is so emotionally gripping and true to life, readers will find it hard to put down and even harder to forget."

CHRISTIANBOOKPREVIEWS.COM

"*After the Leaves Fall* gathers an array of powerful emotions and gently arranges them in all their vibrancy. Each page throbs with realism. . . . *After the Leaves Fall* is a novel that soars with significance."

IN THE LIBRARY REVIEWS

Summer Snow

"Baart continues her saga of Julia DeSmit with the same careful prose and enjoyable storytelling she showed in her debut. . . . This is a treat for faith fiction readers and proves Baart is not just a one-hit wonder."

PUBLISHERS WEEKLY

"Baart's sequel to *After the Leaves Fall* is beautifully written. The prose will resonate with readers as the flawed characters speak to our humanity."

ROMANTIC TIMES

"The sequel to *After the Leaves Fall*, this novel overflows with raw emotion. The characters are incredibly true to life, and the poignant storyline . . . is equally realistic."

CBA RETAILERS + RESOURCES

The Moment Between

beneath the
night tree

beneath the
Night Tree

nicole baart

Tyndale House Publishers, Inc., Carol Stream, Illinois

Visit Tyndale's exciting Web site at www.tyndale.com.

Visit Nicole Baart's Web site at www.nicolebaart.com.

TYNDALE and Tyndale's quill logo are registered trademarks of Tyndale House Publishers, Inc.

Beneath the Night Tree

Designed by Jessie McGrath

Edited by Sarah Mason

Published in association with the literary agency of Browne & Miller Literary Associates, LLC, 410 Michigan Avenue, Suite 460, Chicago, IL 60605.

Scripture taken from the Holy Bible, *New International Version*,® *NIV*.® Copyright © 1973, 1978, 1984 by Biblica, Inc.™ Used by permission of Zondervan. All rights reserved worldwide. www.zondervan.com.

This novel is a work of fiction. Names, characters, places, and incidents either are the product of the author's imagination or are used fictitiously. Any resemblance to actual events, locales, organizations, or persons living or dead is entirely coincidental and beyond the intent of either the author or the publisher.

Library of Congress Cataloging-in-Publication Data

Baart, Nicole.
  Beneath the night tree / Nicole Baart.
    p. cm.
  ISBN 978-1-4143-2323-7 (pbk.)
  1. Unmarried mothers—Fiction. 2. Grandmothers—Fiction. 3. Birthfathers—Fiction. 4. Families—Fiction. I. Title.
  PS3602.A22B46 2011
  813'.6—dc22   2010040217

Printed in the United States of America

17 16 15 14 13 12 11
 7   6   5   4   3   2   1

To Nellie and Julia,
my extraordinary grandmothers

Acknowledgments

Many heartfelt thanks . . .

To my early readers and everyone who supported and encouraged me along the way. Your names are too numerous to mention, but you know who you are.

To the team at Tyndale for giving me the chance to write one more Julia book. What a wonderful journey it has been.

To Danielle Egan-Miller, my amazing agent. Thank you for working so tirelessly on my behalf.

To Todd Diakow. You know why.

To my family and friends. The books keep coming and yet your enthusiasm for what I do never seems to run dry. I would be lost without you.

To my readers and the remarkable people who have created a sense of belonging and kinship on my blog and beyond. Who knew community could exist even in the absence of face-to-face contact?

Always and forever, to my boys. Aaron, it just keeps getting better, doesn't it? Isaac, Judah, and Matthias, I could not love you more. My sons, may you grow in grace.

Part 1

songbird

DANIEL HUMMED in his sleep. It was an unconscious song, a midnight lullaby, as familiar to me as the sigh of my own breath. I fell asleep at night listening to the cadence of his dreams, and when I woke in the morning, his quiet melody was a prelude to birdsong.

I opened my eyes in the darkness and strained to see an imprint of peach on the horizon beyond my open window. It was coming, but when I blinked at the black reflection in the glass, dawn was nothing more than a promise, and Daniel's every exhalation seemed tuned to charm it into being. I pictured him in his bed, arm flung over the pillow and palm opened toward the sky as if God had set an orchestra before his still-chubby fingers. As if God had chosen my son to coax light into our little house.

Maybe He had.

If there was one thing I had learned in five years of being a single mom, it was that the Lord did exactly that: He used the small, the inconsequential, the forgotten to shame the wise. He worked in contradictions, in the unexpected. And I wouldn't have been the least bit surprised if He hovered over my Daniel, drawing music from the curve of his parted lips with the gentle pull of divine fingers.

The thought made me smile, and for a moment I longed to tiptoe across the cool floorboards and be a part of it all, to slip into the tiny attic nook that was my son's bedroom. I wanted to feel my way through the shadows, stretch out beside him, and kiss the sugar-sweet little-boy mouth that puckered like a perfect bow.

But I didn't. Instead, I did what I did every day. I got up, grabbed the clothes that I had laid out the night before, and headed downstairs. If Daniel was singing, then I danced: avoiding the stair that creaked, twisting around the smooth-worn banister like a ballerina, waltzing to Simon's room, where I peeked through the crack of the mostly closed door.

My ten-year-old half brother was on his stomach, bare back exposed to the unseasonable cool of an August morning. We had all the windows flung open, and the house whispered with a light breeze. It wasn't cold, not really, but the sight of his skin made me stifle a shiver. I floated into Simon's room, a part of his dreams, and laid a blanket across his shoulders like a blessing. Schoolboy shoulders, I noticed. Thin and angular, but broadening, hinting at the strong man he would soon become as if the clean line of his skin were bursting with promise. A tight bud about to unfurl. Sometimes I still couldn't believe that she had left him here to blossom.

I touched the mop of his dark hair with my fingertips and thanked God that the child below me slept in peace. That he loved me.

When I spun into the kitchen and switched on the coffee-maker, I couldn't stop the prayer that rose, a balloon lifting beneath the cage that held my heart. *Thank You,* I breathed in the silence. For Daniel, for Simon, for my grandmother, who still slipped from bed not long after I turned on the shower to whisk pancake batter or fold blueberries into muffins for breakfast. *Thank You* for the four corners of our family and the way that we folded into each other like one of my grandma's quilts. Edges coming together, softening.

Most of all, I was grateful for the stillness of the predawn hush, for the short reprieve when everything was dark and new, emerging. It was in these moments as the day was still lifting its head that I could believe everything was exactly as it should be instead of the way it was.

Not that life was horrible—far from it. But as the weeks and months circled on, I couldn't deny that our ramshackle family was often more off than on. The whole thing reminded me of Daniel's birthday present: a carved model train track. Though the sleek, red engine could pull a chain of cars around the twining loops for hours on end, there inevitably came a moment when a single wheel tripped off the track. Who knew what caused the quiet stumble? It was a magician's trick, a sleight of hand—everything bustling along one minute and struggling the next. But the train kept going; the engine pulled on. It just dragged the coal cars behind it, clacking unevenly all the way.

I felt just like that engine, hauling everything in my wake. Hauling every*one* in my wake.

When I pulled back the shower curtain, it became obvious that the DeSmit family train was already well on its way to derailment. There were worms in the bathtub, a dozen or more squirming in a mound of dirt so rich and black it made me think of cake. Devil's food.

I had specifically told Daniel not to put worms in the bathtub and had even given him an ice cream bucket in which to store his newest collection. My son needed to have his hearing checked *again*, I decided. But it was an exercise in futility. I knew that what plagued Daniel wasn't a hearing problem; it was a listening problem.

As I deposited handfuls of squirming earthworms into the bucket I rescued from the front porch, I felt the momentary bliss of my morning slackening its fragile hold. Hot on the heels of the stark reminder that Daniel was an angel only when he slept came a familiar twinge of worry for Simon, the boy who earned his wings in a thousand different ways. By the time I finally stepped into the mud-streaked shower and turned it on full blast, I could feel concern overflow my fists like worry stones too heavy to hold.

Handsome as Simon was, and growing more mature by the day, he still wore loss like a chain around his neck, heavy and awkward, dragging his head down. He loved us, I knew that, but he missed her. And why shouldn't he? Janice was a terrible mother to me, and yet I missed her every single day. I felt her absence in the shadowed corners of my heart, where longing echoed. It was a sound track of hurt—soft, but always there.

And Janice had been a *good* mom to Simon. Or at least, as good as she could bring herself to be. No wonder he bore her ghost like an anchor.

"Do you like it here?" I asked him once, in the beginning, when Janice's departure could still be considered nothing more than an extended trip. I had wanted to ask him, *Do you like us?* but I couldn't bring myself to say those exact words.

All the same, Simon's eyes sprang to mine, wide and startled. The question was innocent, but the look on his five-year-old face told me that the answer wasn't quite so benign.

"It's okay," I said then, reaching to ruffle his hair. "You don't have to—"

"I do," he interrupted me, and his voice cracked with the emotion behind the words. "I like it here."

It took years for me to realize that the problem wasn't Simon's affection for this newfound family and home; it was his own fears about our affection for him. No matter how hard we tried to make him believe that he was a part of us, I knew he continued to battle the personal pain of wondering, deep down, if he was an outsider.

And the problem was only exacerbated at Mason Elementary. Although I was quite sure that Simon was off-the-charts brilliant, the sort of student every teacher longed to shape and mold, he dreaded the start of a new school year. I knew it, even though he had never ventured to so much as whisper a word against his classmates.

As far as I could tell, the kids were decent to him. Mason was a rural community, and the area boasted a substantial population of Latin American immigrants, many of them already second or third generation. The local schools were, at least in theory, diverse and welcoming. Simon seemed to fit right in. Sometimes, when people mistook him for Mexican, he didn't even bother to correct them or point out his North African roots.

But there were other things that set him apart. Like the fact that he was parentless—I knew the pain of that particular stigma all too well. Or that he lived with his half sister, whom most of Mason considered a child herself and only fourteen years his senior. An unwed mother on top of it all. And no one could forget that the woman Simon called *Grandma* shared no blood ties with him, or that the boy he named *brother* was in fact his half nephew. In a community where families were formed along staunchly traditional lines—cue the theme song from *Leave It to Beaver*—our home was a mismatched patchwork that was more than just an aberration from the norm. It was a source of almost-morbid fascination.

I groaned and turned to face the stream pouring from our antiquated shower faucet. The water coursed over my forehead, pooled in my open mouth. *It'll be fine,* I told myself for the thousandth time. *We'll be just fine.*

"Mom! I have to go pee!" Daniel's fists on the bathroom door sent shock waves through the quiet worry that shaped my morning.

Spitting out a mouthful of lukewarm water, I called, "Almost done! I'll be out in a minute."

"A minute? That's, like, forever. I can't wait that long!"

"Give me a break," I muttered, turning off the faucet and throwing back the shower curtain. The brass hooks screeched against the metal rod in perfect harmony with my mood.

Before hopping in the shower, I had laid my towel on the back of the toilet, and when I reached for it now, I realized that the old porcelain was beaded with sweat from the steamy room. I had forgotten to turn on the bathroom fan, and even the rose pink wallpaper of the tiny room was covered in rainbow-colored droplets. I stifled a sigh, forcing myself not to think about mold and mildew and rot. We were already battling enough of that in the cellar beneath the mudroom.

"My towel's wet," I told Daniel through the door. "Could you grab me a clean one from the linen closet?"

"No time!"

Whipping the damp towel around me, I unlocked the bathroom door and threw it open. "A little patience would be nice," I chided Daniel. But even though I was annoyed, I couldn't resist reaching a hand to smooth the sleep-creased skin of his cheek.

"Get out of the way!" he screeched, yanking me by the wrist. When he could wedge himself between the doorframe and my dripping form, Daniel threw his shoulder into my side and deposited me in the hallway that opened onto the kitchen. The door slammed at my back.

"Good morning." Grandma smiled from the counter.

"*Good* is a relative term," I told her.

"The sun is shining."

I turned to look out the window over the sink. "So it is."

"You have a beautiful son."

Though I cocked an eyebrow at her, I felt my lips rise in assent.

"But you are leaving a puddle on the floor."

When I looked down to assess the damage, rivulets of water from my drenched hair deepened the gathering pool at my feet. "Sorry. I got kicked out of the bathroom."

"I heard." Grandma opened a drawer and extracted a flour-sack towel. "Here. It's thin, but it'll help."

I crossed the room and took the towel from her out-stretched hand. Wrapping it turban-style around my hair, I gave her a wry grin. "I'd go upstairs and get dressed, but I left my clothes in the bathroom with Daniel."

"They're going to be wet." Grandma's smile was apologetic. "When I got up, I could tell that you forgot to turn the fan on."

"I was distracted," I muttered, trying to defend myself. "Daniel put worms in the bathtub again."

"Remind me why the bathtub is prime earthworm real estate?"

"Who knows? Daniel's mind is a mystery."

Grandma laughed. "Right you are. Why don't you head upstairs and find some dry clothes? By the time you come down, I'll have coffee on the table."

"Sounds great." I did a quick scan of the kitchen counter and realized that she hadn't started breakfast yet. "But I'm in charge of grub this morning. You, sit. Put your feet up. I'll make French toast."

"French toast?" Simon enthused, stifling a yawn. He had materialized in the archway that led to our small living room, and I was stunned by how he seemed to fill the space.

"Yup," I told him, swallowing the feeling that I was looking at a young man instead of a boy. "Good morning, by the way."

He removed his glasses, rubbed his still-sleepy eyes, and replaced the plastic frames on his nose with a yawn. Finally taking the time to focus on me, he gasped. "Get some clothes on, Jules!"

"It's not like I'm naked."

"You're wearing a towel!"

Grandma and I exchanged amused looks as he hurried back to his room.

"I think you may have scarred him for life," she laughed when we heard his door slam.

"Only if I'm lucky." I was trying to be funny, but suddenly Grandma's eyes glazed over. It was a quick change, a transformation that I was starting to get used to. She misted over easily these days. "Hey," I whispered, tightening my towel with one hand and squeezing her arm with the other. "I was only teasing."

"I know." Grandma sniffed and patted my fingers where they rested on the terry-cloth arm of her robe. She was staring at the place where Simon had stood as if she could see the faint glow of the aura he left behind. "But I worry about him."

"Me too."

"You don't think we're . . . ?"

"Scarring him?"

"Yes," she breathed, the word so faint it was barely voiced.

"No," I assured her. "No, we're not."

"But our house is so small."

"You mean cozy."

"We're practically on top of each other, Julia."

"It draws us together."

"Simon is surrounded by women."

I laughed. "There're only two of us. And two of them, I'll remind you. The boys are hardly outnumbered."

"A little privacy would be nice. . . ."

"Tell me about it," I groaned, drawing her attention to my towel toga with a gentle hip-to-hip bop.

Grandma shook her head and covered her eyes with one hand, but I could tell that the mood had passed. "We're not exactly your typical family unit."

"It's okay," I said, bestowing a kiss on the lined knuckles that hid her expression. "We're doing the best we can."

"Is it enough?"

It was the question I asked myself every single day. But I didn't tell her that. Instead I parroted the words I had heard her say a hundred times. A thousand. "It has to be."

I made my way upstairs, leaving Daniel to his morning routine, Simon to his preteen disgust, and Grandma to her thoughts. It felt selfish, almost indulgent, that I stole away when everyone was, for one reason or another, preoccupied with their own concerns. As I gathered a new outfit from the drawers of my old-fashioned bureau, I wished for a moment that I could crawl back between the sheets of my double bed. I'd yank the duvet over my head and pretend that Daniel was obedient, Simon well-adjusted, and Grandma a decade younger. Maybe more. I could use another adult in this house with energy to match my own.

Twenty-four, I thought, yanking on a pair of khaki cargo shorts. *I'm almost a quarter of a century old.* Sometimes I felt double my age.

And maybe I was. My life seemed divided in two. There

was the mundane, the everyday, the work. The frustration and wondering and worry. The times when I felt like no matter what I did, it was the wrong thing to do. And then there were the moments that transcended it all. The laughter, the warmth, the awed understanding that in spite of everything, we were so blessed.

Sometimes I woke up and believed, really believed, that God sang over us.

Had I felt that way only an hour ago?

"What do you want from me?" I asked the reflection in the mirror on my wall. The woman in question just stared back. I wasn't even sure who I was talking to. Myself? The three people who depended on me downstairs? God? I might be failing all of them, but heaven help me, I was trying. It had to be enough.

Straightening my Asian print T-shirt, I gave the hazel-eyed girl in the mirror a nod of encouragement. "You're doing just fine," I told her.

I almost believed myself.

everything

"YOU'RE GOING TO EAT us out of house and home," I told Simon, depositing the last two pieces of cinnamon French toast on his syrupy plate. I regretted the words the instant they were out of my mouth, but for once Simon seemed unaffected. His carb high must have elevated his blood sugar to near-lethal levels, I decided, laying a motherly hand on his forehead before I sat down.

"I'm hungry," Simon explained with a shrug, "not sick." He drizzled yet more syrup over the remains of his breakfast and dug in.

"He's a growing boy," Grandma affirmed, watching him eat with a fondness that I wished I could capture on film. Maybe Simon would understand if he could only see the way that she looked at him—that we all looked at him. You can't fake love like that. I know. I've seen more than my share of people trying to conjure up love for me.

My camera was on top of the refrigerator, poking out of the bulky, padded bag where I kept my zoom lens and extra rolls of discount film I picked up at Wal-Mart. I tried to be unobtrusive as I went for it, but Daniel seemed programmed to my moods. He squealed the moment I angled toward my most treasured possession.

"Ooh! Take a picture of me! Do you like seafood?" He opened his mouth before I could assure him that I wasn't a fan of seafood or his well-worn joke. "See, food!" he giggled around a mouthful. "That's funny. Take a picture."

"No." I narrowed my eyes in disapproval. "That's gross. Besides, how did you know I was getting my camera?"

"You had that look in your eye," Simon told me while Daniel swallowed his food.

"I have a look?"

"Only when it comes to your camera." Grandma smiled. "It's a happy-thoughtful-wistful look."

"Wistful?"

"Something like that."

I perched on the end of my chair and flicked the Canon on with my thumbnail. It had been one of my dad's only extravagant purchases, a gift to himself when Janice was pregnant with me. It was still a beautiful piece of equipment, even if it was decades old. Holding the 1980s relic reminded me of the days when I was on the other side of the lens. Somehow the angles, the weight, the worn-smooth dials and knobs made me feel the heft of my dad's hand in my own. I put the viewfinder to my eye so no one would notice when I blinked away the memory. Suddenly I knew exactly why Grandma used the word *wistful*.

"Smile," I said, centering Grandma in the viewfinder and adjusting the aperture until her eyes shimmered. But I clicked before she had time to arrange her face, and I was sure that the only point of interest in the artless portrait would be the reflection of me and my camera in her clear gaze.

"I'm not sure the breakfast table is the best place for a photo session," Grandma remarked as she got up to clear the dishes.

"I was just . . ." I trailed off, not sure how to explain my need to immortalize my family, to capture them in still life where they would never change or age. Grandma might read too much into it. I didn't dare risk her tears. "I just like taking photos."

"Uh, yeah, we know." Simon exhaled in his low, muted laugh. "It's pretty obvious, Jules."

As if I needed evidence, Daniel was already off his chair and reaching for one of my prettier landscapes with a syrup-sticky hand. But Grandma was faster, and she whipped my framed rendering of a spindly spring tree off the buffet before Daniel could grab it. He moaned in protest.

"Uh-uh," Grandma cautioned, though she sounded anything but stern. "You know you're not supposed to touch those."

"I wanted to show Mom," Daniel complained.

"I don't need to see it. I took it." I waved my son over, enticing him with the outstretched camera. "Want to take one? I'll hold it for you."

The camera was too heavy for Daniel to manipulate, but at the prospect of pushing the weighted button, at the thought of producing that deliciously smooth and satisfying click, he catapulted himself around the table. He scrambled under my arms and onto my lap with a happy grunt. "Simon," Daniel announced. "I want to take a picture of Simon."

"No way. Get yourself a willing subject," Simon warned.

I pointed the camera at my half brother anyway. Any ten-year-old who talked like that needed to be reduced to a giggling child. He was in there; I knew it.

"Come on, Si. Give the camera a little love." I held the camera as steady as I could and let Daniel position his finger over the shutter release.

Click.

"Work it. Work it . . . ," Daniel said, mimicking me when I was in one of my sillier moods. "The camera loves you, baby."

Click.

Simon stuck his tongue out.

Click.

It was the photo I had been waiting for: Simon, looking like the child he was instead of the young man he often seemed to be.

"We're done," I assured him, trying not to smirk. "The torture is over."

"Not until you give me that film."

"Don't be ridiculous. That last one should make a nice poster."

Simon knew I was teasing, but he lunged at me anyway, springing out of his chair as if he had been coiled like a helix in his seat.

I shrieked and launched off my own chair, clutching my camera in one hand and pressing Daniel to my chest like a human shield with the other. His legs dangled against my knees; his laughter bubbled beneath my hand.

"Take the kid!" I shouted, backing around the table with Daniel between me and my flinty-eyed brother. "He snapped the shutter! It's him you want!"

Daniel struggled, squirming to loosen my grip. But his indignant grunts were shot through with a glee that he couldn't contain or hide. The truth was, my son lived for this. For the thrill, the pursuit, the fall-down game of *please don't chase me anymore* that really meant *please do*.

I didn't grow up with brothers. I wasn't schooled in the ways of men. If I was honest with myself, what I knew about boys

could be summed up on a Post-It note. But this came naturally, and as I dropped Daniel—making sure he landed lightly
on his feet—I caught a glimpse of the grin that Grandma
tried to conceal behind a cotton napkin. It was good, it was
healing, to hear the laughter of children.

"Can't catch me!" I goaded them, fully aware that they
could and they would. But I spun on my heel and ran all
the same.

The laminate floor was cool on my bare feet, but I didn't
even pause to kick on my flip-flops before I flung open the
front door and sprinted across the porch. It was still early,
and the warm mist of an August morning was just rising off
the fields in a fog of damp that shimmered in the low-flung
sunlight. I skipped the last three steps of the wide porch and
landed on the dew-soaked grass, hair flying.

"Gotcha!" Simon exulted when he caught a fistful of my
T-shirt.

I hadn't realized he was so close. But I didn't lose my balance. Yanking away from him, I lifted the camera over my
head and kept running. "You've got nothing, kid!" I hooted
when I felt his hands slip away.

It was a lie. Simon had everything. Simon and Daniel
and Grandma—they had my whole life in their hands. I
loved them all as dear as my own heartbeat, my breath, my
thoughts and emotions that circled untouched into the space
around us like ripples without end.

The next time I felt his hand brush my back, I slowed. It

was a small thing, imperceptible, and Simon didn't notice. He caught me around the waist. I felt him go limp—the easiest way to take me down—and I fell with him, a slow-motion tumble to the lawn, where I gave the dew my back and waited in expectation for Daniel to catch up.

I still had the camera suspended over my head, away from the sparkling grass, and though I knew the position left me utterly defenseless, I didn't care. I groaned when Daniel jumped on me, but I was laughing too hard for him to register the small sound of pain. Instead of backing off, he tickled me mercilessly until I was panting, begging for him to stop.

"That'll teach you," Daniel said when he slid off my chest. He crouched on the ground beside Simon, looking down at me with all the amused contempt of a reigning conqueror.

"Teach me what?" I moaned. My ribs ached and my T-shirt was damp, but I raised myself onto my elbows and regarded my boys with a thin smirk.

Daniel looked to Simon for help. He had forgotten what had instigated the chase.

Simon rolled his eyes. "I don't like having my picture taken," he reminded us both. Then, remembering that Daniel had been in on it too, he put his nephew in a head-lock and mussed his already-unruly hair. "That means you, too, Danny."

"Daniel."

"Danny."

"*Daniel.*"

"Stop it, you two." I wiggled between them and turned on my camera. Holding my arms out as far as they would go, I rotated the Canon and pointed it at the three of us. "No more fighting," I said. "We're one big, happy family. Smile."

They did.

I had no idea if our faces were even in the borders of the frame, but I hoped for the best. "Come on. We should go help Grandma finish cleaning up the kitchen."

Simon stood and offered me his hand. He pulled me to my feet and then hooked his arms under Daniel's and lifted him from the ground too. I slung the heavy camera over my shoulder and stretched my own hands to both of the boys, optimistic for a single moment that they might reach out and let me hold their fingers as we walked back to the house. No such luck. Simon ignored me, and Daniel batted my arm away with a puppy growl that I assumed was supposed to be tough.

"Won't anybody hold my hand?" I lamented. "I don't have cooties; I promise."

"Michael can hold your hand."

I pouted. "Michael's not here."

"Yes, he is." Daniel pointed toward the road, and when I spun around, I saw Michael's car turn in to our long driveway.

"What's he doing here?" I was startled at how my voice suddenly seemed breathless, light as air.

"He probably came to say good-bye," Simon guessed. He

didn't turn toward Michael or stop to watch the car's slow progress on our gravel drive like Daniel and I did.

"He already said good-bye. Last night. Remember? You were there."

Simon shrugged and kept going. By the time he reached the steps of the porch, Michael was pulling up at the cement pad in front of our derelict garage.

I didn't mean to grin like an idiot whenever he was around, but it was hard for me to contain myself in the presence of Michael Vermeer. I was well aware that my hero worship of my longtime boyfriend bordered on pathetic, but I didn't care. He was handsome, kind, funny, and studying to be a doctor of internal medicine. I loved telling people that particular detail, even as I loathed that it meant our relationship was conducted long-distance. Mason was a good six-hour drive from Iowa City—more on icy roads—and though Michael came home to see me, to see *us*, as often as possible, it was never quite enough.

"Hey," I called as he stepped out of the car. "What are you doing here?"

"That's a nice greeting." Michael feigned a hurt expression, but even as his mouth turned down, he lifted his hand to my face and traced my jawline with his thumb. Laying a light kiss on my mouth, he murmured, "Good morning."

"Ewww!" Daniel groaned from his position at my side. "Kiss alert! If you guys are going to smooch, I'm going inside."

"Hi, buddy." Michael grinned and raised his fist to my son.

Daniel bumped knuckles, grinned back. "Wanna play football? I've got my new ball in the chest by the door."

"I'd love to, but I'm in a bit of a hurry. And I need to talk to your mom alone for a few minutes."

I watched Daniel's face fall, but when Michael extracted a roll of Smarties from his pocket, my five-year-old was temporarily placated.

"Next time," Michael promised.

As we watched Daniel race back to the house, I stepped closer to Michael and wound my arm though his. "Did you just bribe my son?" I whispered against his ear.

"I most certainly did." Michael was unabashed. "I was hoping we could talk alone."

I shivered when he pulled me into a tight embrace, but just as quickly as he drew me to him, Michael pushed me away. "You're wet!"

"We were wrestling in the grass."

"Apparently."

I shrugged. "Sorry."

"You should be." My eyebrows shot up, but before I could defend myself, Michael continued. "How dare you play with your kids? You are, without a doubt, the World's Worst Mom."

It was our private joke, a rib that meant Michael thought I was the exact opposite of what he so loved to call me. If

I punished Daniel and he cried, Michael called me World's Worst. If I threw a birthday party for Simon and he was embarrassed, I was WWM . . . *"and you know what that means."*

I punched Michael in the arm for the backhanded compliment, but I let him hold my hand when he laced his fingers through mine.

As I had sprinted across the grass only minutes before, I had thought, *Everything. This is—they are—my everything.* But with Michael beside me, I knew I hadn't been quite honest with myself. He was a part of it too. A bigger part than I dared to admit.

"Walk with me."

"Grandma's in the house cleaning up breakfast all by herself," I said, feeling guilty that I had left her to tend to the kitchen on her own.

"Simon and Daniel are in there," Michael argued. "Come on. Just this once. She'll understand."

Normally I would have put up more of a fight, but Michael was supposed to be on the road to Iowa City, not standing in my driveway. A twinge of curiosity made my eyes narrow. "Don't you have an important meeting this afternoon?" I asked as I let him pull me gently in the direction of our grove.

"Yes, I do. That's why I have to make this quick."

"Make what quick? If you needed to talk to me, you could have called from the road. There's this wonderful new technology called the cellular phone."

"Hardy har har," Michael said drily.

I could tell that I wasn't going to get anything out of him until he was good and ready, so I gave up and let him drag me toward the dark line of trees.

The grove was my favorite place on our farm. It was wide and old, filled with gnarled bur oaks that littered the ground with acorns every fall. I used to tell the boys that the knobby tops were fairy cups, and if you filled them with water, the fairies would watch over our farmhouse since rain was often scarce in the fall. It wasn't hard to convince them that fairy protection was an act of gratitude. I must have separated hundreds of nuts from their bumpy little hats and dripped water into the tiny vessels one drop at a time. It took a couple of seasons for the boys to figure out that I was the one who emptied the cups of their offering, not magical woodland sprites. It was sweet, while it lasted.

Several yards into the thick of the grove, there was a small clearing where my grandpa's ancient John Deere tractor sat in a grown-over heap of rusted neglect. I had scrambled all over it when I was a kid, and now the boys used it for their imaginary games. I loved this spot, and it was here, in the shadow of a sugar maple that would blaze crimson by autumn, that Michael stopped.

He let go of my hand and leaned against one of the tractor's giant metal wheels. Now that we had achieved our destination, Michael seemed suddenly hesitant, even shy. Moments alone were few and far between, and usually we filled them with furtive kisses, private whispers, fingers, arms, bodies twined. But he pulled away from me and cupped his neck with a slender surgeon's hand. Looking off into the trees, away from my curious stare, he cleared his throat once. Twice.

My heart tripped over itself. "Michael?" I asked, taking a step toward him because I was sick with a sudden panic. But as I watched, his eyes snapped to mine and then just as quickly away. There was no apology in his gaze. No indication that he was on the verge of saying a different kind of good-bye—the kind that was much more permanent. Instead, his eyes were cloudy with something that made him fearful and hopeful at once.

And just like that, I knew.

I stepped back. Not because I was afraid. But because I couldn't believe that after five years, after all this time, he was finally ready to ask the thing that I had hoped for after our very first date.

That night was clear in my memory, the emotions bright and smooth-edged like little seeds I carried in my pocket and still fingered from time to time. I took them out now, those raw hopes that had planted themselves in my life when Michael curled his hand around mine. As we sat side by side on the steps of the porch all those years ago, my fledgling wish for us was simple, immediate: *Stay.* I wanted him to linger, to sit back beneath the stars for another hour, maybe two. But it didn't take long for me to want more. *Stay forever.*

"Julia . . . ," Michael began.

"Yes?"

He sighed hard and looked me full in the face. Then, dropping his hand, he crossed the space between us in a single stride and caught me about the shoulders. His grip was firm, unwavering, as if he knew that he had to hold me up or I would find myself sitting among the wild bergamot that sprang like pink confetti from the tall grasses at my feet.

I closed my eyes. Waited for the words I had imagined him saying a hundred different ways.

"Julia," he whispered, "come with me."

"Come with me"? I squinted at Michael, sure that I had heard him wrong. Wasn't he supposed to say, *Marry me?* Wasn't he supposed to be on one knee? I snuck a peek at the breast pocket of his vintage plaid shirt and couldn't stop my nose from crinkling when I realized it was flat. Empty. No jewelry box.

I swallowed, tried to talk.

"No." He put a finger to my lips. "Just listen, okay? I want you to come to Iowa City with me. Well, you and Daniel—and Simon if he wants to. I've arranged for you to house-sit for a while. One of my professors is in Cambridge doing continuing ed, and I told him about you—about us. You can live in his house until Christmas."

I managed to squeak out, "You want me to move to Iowa City?"

"Yes."

The desperation in his gaze was so intense, so earnest,

that for a moment I actually considered the possibility. What would it feel like to leave? to just pack a bag and go? From there, it wasn't much of a leap for my mind to imagine the impossible: What if it were just the two of us? No worms in the bathtub, worries about Simon, or working long hours for a measly paycheck that barely allowed us to make ends meet. I could act my age. Drink coffee at some corner Starbucks and talk about politics, religion, the world beyond the walls of my suddenly stifling home.

I took a shaky breath. Those were dangerous, deceptive thoughts that pulled like quicksand. I couldn't entertain such illusory demons. Ever.

"Iowa City," I repeated. "Why?" The question escaped my lips before I had a chance to gauge how he might hear it.

Instantly Michael's face fell. "Because . . ." He floundered. "Because I want you near me. I think it would be good for us to figure out if . . . if this long-distance thing can be done . . . closer." He fit himself around me and brushed his lips against my forehead.

"A trial?"

"I don't see it as a trial. I see it as a prelude. Maybe we'll come home at Christmas with a ring. A reason to celebrate."

Michael had said it: a ring. But somehow it felt second-rate, cheap. *Maybe*. I struggled to keep my composure and had to cough before I could trust my voice enough to say, "Simon and Daniel are already signed up for school. They start in a week."

"There are schools in Iowa City. I can call the district today. They'll be on the class rosters by this afternoon."

"I can't leave my job."

"You work at Value Foods, Julia. It's no big loss. Besides, maybe you could pursue your dream. You know, take some photography classes at the university." He tapped the camera that still hung from my shoulder.

"I'm already taking classes."

"At the tech school." It seemed to me that there was an edge of disdain in his voice.

"I like my program," I said through my teeth.

"Early childhood development? You can work at a day care or teach preschool. Is that really what you want?"

Though I had wondered that myself a hundred times, I bristled at his casual dismissal of my choice in education. "Yes," I stated decisively.

Michael's arms slackened. He pulled away. "I thought you would be happy about this. We could be together."

"I can't leave Grandma," I told him because I couldn't tell him the truth: *I can't come with you under these circumstances. Not like this. Not without a promise, something more than* maybe.

The grove seemed unnaturally quiet. No breeze stirred the leaves; no songbird trilled in the trees. I shifted on my feet and heard the soft crunch of broken grasses, bent stems that would turn brown because of my careless trampling. It made me unaccountably sad.

"I'm sorry," I whispered. "I love you." It was what I had wanted him to say to me.

"I love you, too," Michael echoed, too late. He checked his watch and ran a sun-browned hand through his hair. "Tell you what. Think about it, okay? I know I just dropped this on you. You haven't had any time to process, to think of the possibilities. . . . Just promise me you'll give it some serious thought."

"Okay."

Michael straightened and stretched as if the conversation had exhausted him. Then he smiled at me like there was no tension between us. But I saw the lingering shadows in his eyes. He kissed me hard on the mouth. "Think about it. I've gotta go, but I'll call you from the road."

"Okay."

"You going to be all right?"

"I'm fine."

"Okay."

"Love you."

"Love you, too." And without waiting for me to follow, Michael turned from the clearing and loped back toward the house, his car. I waited until I heard his engine catch and his tires crunch gravel on their way back to the highway.

It was only then that I let myself cry.

dreams

I DIDN'T SLEEP THAT NIGHT—or for many nights thereafter.

When Michael called me from the road like he promised, and when he phoned every evening following that, we acted like the conversation in the grove had never happened. He didn't ask me if I had made a decision and I didn't offer one. It was as if I dreamed up the whole encounter. But I knew that it was real. I could feel the tension between us in the pauses between words, in the moments when he took a breath and I opened my mouth to say something at the exact instant that he did. There was a subtle awkwardness between us that made my heart ache.

I wanted to talk to Grandma about it, but I couldn't make my tongue form the syllables, the phrases and sentences that would change everything. They were hard words, cut from metal that had the potential to reshape our lives in ways that would inevitably feel violent. *Leave?* To me, that one small verb had many synonyms: *divide, split, sever.*

So instead of wrestling with Michael's bewildering offer, I buried it in some corner of my mind and tried to ignore it. Of course, it was like trying to disregard the proverbial elephant in the room, but at least I could deal with it alone. It was me against myself. My own feelings warred in silence.

I was grateful that no one seemed to notice my personal combat. Daniel was protected by the cheerful oblivion of early childhood, Simon seemed absorbed in his own mild angst as school approached, and Grandma bustled through her day with little time for herself, much less occasions to observe the struggle behind my polished exterior. And I kept my armor as spit-shine sparkly as I could. It was something I had become very good at.

Thankfully, the final week of summer freedom before Simon entered his fifth-grade year and Daniel became a kindergartner was so busy, I didn't have much opportunity to agonize over Michael's offer. Our days were filled with work, last-minute excursions, and photography appointments.

I had made a modest name for myself as an amateur

shutterbug, and a few people called me regularly to do on-location portraits of their kids. Some families liked to use their own backyards or homes, but I had also accumulated a list of great sites for photo shoots that included an abandoned barn, an old train bridge, and a little-known corner of the local park. I lugged an ever-growing pile of junk with me and used my imagination to position the kids in charming, unusual ways. I loved it.

Simon, on the other hand, claimed that he hated every minute of it, but that didn't stop me from dragging him along to my photography sessions. He was a huge help, and the kids loved him even though he didn't solicit their attention or affection. Simon was simply magnetic that way.

"You're coming with me tomorrow, right?" I asked him the night before I had my least favorite clients scheduled.

He sighed dramatically, but twelve hours later I was watching out of the corner of my eye as Simon inched a little closer on his knees and jammed the sticky wand back into the purple plastic bottle for another go-round.

"I need more bubbles, Si!" I called before disappearing behind the bulky camera. My Canon was outfitted with an impressive zoom lens, even though I was up close and personal with my young subjects. "I want it to look like they're swimming in bubbles."

"You need a machine," Simon sighed, blowing carefully into the saw-toothed circle. A flood of iridescent froth surged from the wand and cast dozens of rainbow-sparkled bubbles across the cheeks of the little girls in front of him. The younger one, a curly-haired carbon copy of Thomas at two, giggled and reached for the magical spheres. The camera made a series of rewarding metallic clicks.

Simon blew again.

Click-click-click-click-click.

"Come on, Angelica," I coaxed, drawing out every syllable of the older girl's name. "You look so pretty in your dress. Aren't you having fun?"

"No."

"Carlye's having fun."

"She's two. I'm *four*."

Simon blew another long string, then leaned on one elbow and peered around the jubilant toddler who was blocking his view. Angelica, the sulky preschooler whose almost-comical scowl threatened to ruin my attempt at portraiture, was standing with her arms crossed, her expression so sour that Simon couldn't stop himself from laughing. But a lightning-fast look from me wiped the smile off his face. He dipped his wand with a dutiful flick of his wrist and whispered more bubbles to life.

"Are you too old to play with bubbles?" I asked, twisting the camera in my hands to change the angle of the shot. Off center, at a slant, with the parchment blue sky framing the soft halo of their child-fine hair. *Click-click-click.* "You can't be too old to play with bubbles. Look at Simon. He's ten and he still plays with bubbles."

Simon snorted and broke the perfect film of liquid that would have been another deployment of soapy orbs.

I turned from the viewfinder long enough to toss my brother a playful wink. "You're never too old to play with bubbles, right, Si?"

He fixed me with a vicious glare, but instead of distressing me, he made me laugh. Angelica, who was watching the exchange, let the corner of her lip pull up into the slightest of smirks, a little edge of indication that she was, despite her every effort to convince us otherwise, having fun.

Simon caught her look and scowled at me, making sure that he was so caught up in our mock battle that he let his hand tip just enough to spill a fine drizzle of liquid in his own lap. "Look what you made me do!" he cried, his voice lush with artificial horror.

Angelica giggled.

Click-click-click-click.

"Keep 'em coming," I muttered between my teeth, loving Simon for his selflessness, for his willingness to go above and beyond the call of duty to help me out.

He obliged, filling the air around the girls and veiling a grin when Angelica reached out a tentative finger to see if her skin would pop the glossy membrane or hold it. It popped.

Click-click-click.

"Perfect. I think we're done here." I lowered the heavy camera and stood up from a crouch amid the audible crack and moan of knee joints. I pressed a fist to the small of my

back. "You girls are gorgeous. But you're a little too short.
Oh, my back!" I hunched over and ambled toward them
with a Quasimodo limp. "I'm too old! I can't bend like that
anymore!"

Carlye squealed in delight and ran from me, straight into
the arms of her mother, who was crossing the lawn with her
daughters' extra outfits in hand. Francesca smiled a bland,
tight-lipped smile and smoothed Carlye's dark curls. "Did
you get some good ones?" she asked.

I nodded. "Your girls are beautiful. It's hard to take a bad
photo of them."

It was exactly what Francesca wanted to hear. She tipped
her chin in acceptance and held out her free hand for
Angelica. "Come on, sugar," she called. "You have dance
in less than an hour. We've got to get you in your leotard
and to the studio."

"I don't want to go to dance!"

"You have to. Daddy and I paid good money for your
ballet lessons."

"I'm hungry!" the little girl whined.

"I have a sandwich for you in the car."

"I don't want a sandwich!"

"Too bad."

Angelica screamed her protest and stomped off in the
direction of their waiting car.

The entire exchange made me feel tense and uncomfortable, and I tried to busy myself with the camera so that I

didn't have to acknowledge that I had ears and could hear every word Francesca muttered. I peeked at Simon from under my lashes and realized that the situation was awkward for him, too. "Hey, Simon," I called, "could you start loading the props into the car?"

He fired me a grateful look, then began throwing lengths of gossamer into the oversize basket that I had cradled the girls in only minutes before. "Be back in a sec," he said with a salute. Simon hefted the basket into his arms and disappeared beyond the row of trees that lined Fox Creek Park.

It didn't strike me until I was alone with Francesca that I had set myself up for the inevitable. Time alone with her, even a minute or two, was never a good idea. My relationship with Francesca Walker was never easy. And maybe that was to be expected. After all, we had loved the same man. But what she didn't seem to grasp was that any love I felt for Thomas was past tense—a child's fantasy, a little girl's dream because he was the closest thing to Prince Charming I had ever known. But I grew up. Learned better. Knew better. I knew that Thomas was no prince. And I was no fainting princess, locked in some tower, waiting for rescue.

Yet Francesca persisted in believing that any flame I'd held for Thomas still burned bright and true. It didn't help that Mrs. Walker, Thomas's occasionally overbearing mom, was always finding ways to force me into their lives. After Angelica was born, I was enlisted as her part-time day care provider when Francesca had to go back to work. It was a miserable few months. Angelica never bonded with me, and I had to work odd hours to keep my job at Value Foods. The extra income helped, but in the end I seriously doubted if any amount of money would make that sort of headache worthwhile.

Though her attempt to bond our families through day care failed, Mrs. Walker didn't stop there. She pushed Francesca and me together, coordinating playdates for the "two young moms" at her house on a regular basis. And she kept inviting our messy family to infrequent Walker holiday functions. I considered my longtime friend and surrogate auntie a keen woman and an astute observer of people, but she didn't seem to grasp that Francesca and I would never be best friends forever.

But whether or not I hit it off with her daughter-in-law, I knew that Mrs. Walker would always be proud of her great discovery: my talent for photography. It was after I snapped a few photos of her grandkids at a Thanksgiving get-together that my gift, as Mrs. Walker perceived it, was officially revealed. A week after the holiday, I brought her a handful of snapshots that made her already-perky eyebrows curl into unbelievable arcs.

"You took these?"

I nodded, chastened, though I didn't know why. "With my dad's old camera."

"Julia, honey, they're beautiful."

Mrs. Walker declared my work better than any local studio's, and she enlisted my services once a year—every summer—to document her granddaughters' growth and development. I couldn't complain about the hundred-dollar paycheck, but interacting with Francesca only got harder as time went on.

One look at Thomas's wife told me that today would be no exception.

"So," Francesca drew out the word, studying me with her head at a condescending tilt. "You'll get the photos to us in a week?"

"Same as always," I said, trying to be patient. "I'll send the rolls to my developer, and you'll get the proofs and the negatives in five working days. I've already signed the waiver. You're free to do whatever you want with the photos."

"Seems to me it would be easier if you had a digital camera."

I shrugged. "I'm sure it would be. But I think that 35mm film adds a certain vintage quality you just can't mimic with modern technology."

Francesca grunted, and I almost heaved a disappointed sigh. She had always been condescending, but why did she still hate me so much when there was nothing at all to fear? She had Thomas, and she had his children. I didn't want any part of it.

As if to prove my level of detachment, I directed my attention to the furniture and knickknacks I always hauled along on photo shoots. There was a jumble of low benches and dried grasses, felt hats and lengths of fabric. Maybe if I acted busy, Francesca would grab Carlye and leave—and avoid the uncomfortable moment when her youngest daughter insisted on a good-bye hug and kiss.

For reasons that I probably would never understand, Carlye had attached herself to me with the sort of childish abandon that accompanies blind devotion. She adored me without rhyme or reason, and I believed that her willingness to grin at me no matter the situation deserved more credit for my reputation as a good photographer than any so-called talent I possessed. Every picture I took with Carlye in it boasted the same infectious, gap-toothed smile that made people sigh. She really was a sight to behold. And I would have expended much love on her still-pudgy toddler frame if it hadn't galled Francesca so that her daughter thought I hung the moon. As it was, I demurred, tried to redirect the little girl's attention.

Which was what I was trying to do as I stacked antique fruit crates and folded lengths of burlap into neat, portable squares. But Francesca lingered. *Masochist,* I thought when I caught a glimpse of Carlye squirming out of her arms.

"Carlye!" Francesca warned. "Stay here!"

But it was too late. With her mother's admonition still ringing around us, I felt Carlye's chubby arms go tight around my neck.

"Hey, sweet pea," I breathed so that only she could hear. "I think it's time for you to go. Your sister is already in the car."

"No!" Carlye half shouted, pouting.

"Yup." I stood, bracing her against me for a short piggy-back ride. She squealed in delight, and I tried to hide my own enchanted smile. "Here you go," I told Francesca, angling so she could pluck Carlye off my back.

But the lovely woman across from me didn't reach for her daughter. Instead, she regarded me with a cool, assessing stare, her lips parted slightly as if she had something to say.

"What?" I asked because I didn't feel like playing games.

Francesca raised one shoulder in affected nonchalance. "I just heard a rumor about you. I was wondering if it was true."

A rumor? I went cold. "I don't hold much stock in rumors," I said tersely.

"Normally I don't either, but it came from a reliable source."

I rotated Carlye to my hip and didn't try to stop her when she nuzzled her cheek against my neck. Francesca looked angry for a split second, but joy at the juicy tidbit of gossip she possessed overruled her jealousy.

"Do tell," I muttered since she seemed determined to make me beg.

"Well . . . a little birdie told me that you're moving on to greener pastures."

"Excuse me?" I had to stop myself from rolling my eyes. Francesca's "little birdies" existed all over town, and she made it her business to stick her nose everywhere it didn't belong.

"You don't have to pretend with me, Julia. We're . . . friends, right?"

She seemed to stumble a little over her own characterization of our relationship, and I was gripped by a sudden, childish urge to call her Franny. But I held my tongue and merely nodded.

"I know you're moving to Iowa City with Michael," she said lightly.

"What?"

"Oh, I know he didn't propose—" Francesca's eyes glinted—"but there's a certain romance in his offer, don't you think?"

I was too stunned to speak.

"Well," Francesca continued, "I hope you're not agonizing over this decision. The way I see it, there is no decision to make. You have to go."

"Why?" The word slipped out unexpectedly before I could censor or stop it.

Francesca looked exultant. "Because this is it, honey. If you don't take this chance at a family, I doubt you'll get another."

She couldn't have hurt me more if she slapped me. "I have a family," I whispered. Then, because I rarely allowed myself the luxury, I cradled Carlye tight for a moment and kissed her baby-soft cheeks.

Francesca pulled her from my arms. "Think about what I said," she advised over Carlye's animated protests. "I think this is just what you and Daniel need."

I watched her walk away, Carlye reaching over her mother's

shoulders to extend open hands toward me. I should have turned away, but I felt rooted to the ground. Stuck in the exact spot where she left me with a load that bent my shoulders beneath its implications. In the five days since Michael and I had stood in the grove, his question had tormented me. I loved him—I had for years—but when I dreamed about our life together, it never took this perplexing shape. And what about Grandma? I couldn't leave her. Then there was Simon. . . . I had no real claim to him. He was my brother, not my son. What would he want?

Simon.

With a gasp, I spun and searched the clearing where we had set up our little photo shoot. There he was, only part of his face visible as he made a halfhearted attempt to hide behind a paper birch. One dark eye regarded me with a clear, stark pain that made me moan.

"Simon . . . ," I said, taking a step toward him. "What did you hear?"

He didn't have to say a word for me to know that he had heard everything. Sensitive, perceptive Simon would fill in every blank, every subtle, unanswered question with conjectures I couldn't begin to imagine.

"She doesn't know what she's talking about," I rushed to reassure him. "She's just trying to hurt me."

"Did Michael ask you to move to Iowa City?" Simon asked so quietly I had to strain to catch the words.

I couldn't lie to him. "Yes," I said, narrowing the distance between us to one long stride. I didn't dare to go any closer, but I was quite sure that if he bolted, I could catch him before he got too far. "Yes, Michael did ask me to move to Iowa City with him. And he wants you and Daniel to come too."

"I don't want to go."

"I know."

"Why didn't you tell us?"

"I guess I wasn't ready to talk about it," I confessed.

"Do you want to go?"

I shook my head sadly. "I don't know."

Simon nodded at that, took a deep breath. Squeezing his eyes closed as if to summon his courage, he stepped away from the tree. Fists balled at his sides, he said, "You should go. You and Daniel. Grandma and me will be just fine here."

It was hard to tell if he meant what he said or if he was putting up a strong front. I hoped it was the latter. He didn't give me a chance to find out.

"We've got a lot to pick up," he mumbled, rolling the words together like they were too big for his mouth.

I considered my brother for a minute, watching the sure way he stacked and carried, arranging my collection of junk in a couple of easy-to-carry piles. Although I had studied Simon's every feature, memorized each expression and what it meant, with his words like a prophecy in the air between us, I felt like the boy before me was a stranger.

The sob that rose in my throat was so unexpected that I choked on the breadth of my grief. Simon whirled to look at me, and I longed to cross the space between us and fold him in my arms. *We're not going anywhere,* I wanted to say. But my mouth wouldn't form the words, and in the end I pounded my chest with the heel of my hand and shook my head to indicate that it was nothing. A body malfunction instead of my heart breaking. A moment of insignificance instead of the dissolution of my dreams.

He nodded and turned away.

wanderer

"YOU SEEM OUT OF SORTS," Grandma said after Simon and Daniel were settled in their rooms for the night.

I could hardly argue with her. When Simon and I returned from the photo shoot, it was pretty obvious that something had gone wrong. He was moody and even quieter than normal, and I couldn't seem to force myself to muster the subtle cheer that I wore like an accessory these days. Never leave home without it.

"It's hard to photograph Francesca's kids," I told her. It was the truth, but I didn't know if it would be enough to pacify her.

"I thought you loved Carlye."

A smile danced across my lips because she hadn't bothered to mention Angelica. Grandma knew me too well. "I do," I said, "but that doesn't make the job easy."

"A cup of tea," Grandma declared, pressing herself up from the table and going to put the kettle on. "You need a hot cup of tea and a few minutes to yourself."

I didn't want to be alone. I wanted her with me and I almost said so. But she seemed frail as she lifted the kettle, the palsy in her hands making the water slosh around like waves on a restless sea. I had to sign her checks for her these days. And separate her tiny pills from the army of bottles that stood guard on the windowsill above the sink. I snuck a peek at the clock on the wall and realized that at nine, Grandma was ready for bed.

"Let me get that," I said, reaching around to steady her hand with my own. Her skin was warm and soft, as insubstantial and flimsy as a knotted tangle of old lace.

"Sorry," she murmured. "These hands . . ."

"Are beautiful," I finished. I squeezed her fingers gently so as not to leave a bruise.

"Are old," Grandma laughed.

"You're not old. You're immortal."

She looked at me for a long moment, her warm eyes like melted caramel, and smiled at what she saw. "No," she told me, "I'm not immortal. But I am eternal. I just have to face my mortality first."

I didn't mean to tremble at her words, but soon Grandma's hands were gripping mine in a hold that was part steadying, part palliative. "You have to be immortal," I whispered. "I can't imagine life without you."

"I'm an old woman," Grandma said. "I have lived a life of abundance. My cup overflows."

"It's not your cup I'm worried about."

Grandma clasped my hands for a second more; then she took a step back and studied me as if to cement my every feature in her mind. "I'm very proud of you," she said finally.

It was something she said often, but I had never felt so undeserving. *If you only knew,* I thought. In the depths of my heart, where I could still pretend that the unfolding map of my life was charted by different choices, I wanted to pack for Iowa City. To be with the man I loved, unhindered, unburdened. There was nothing to be proud of in that. Especially when I was so needed here.

"What does that have to do with anything?" I asked.

"It has everything to do with everything. Julia, I'm not worried about you anymore. I don't fear for your future or wonder if you'll wander forever. Lots of people do that, you know. Wander."

"I'm a wanderer."

"No, you're not."

It was hard not to roll my eyes, even though I knew she was only trying to shore me up, encourage me so that one day I could stand alone. The thought made my heart whimper.

"All I'm saying is you're going to be just fine. Even when this old body proves its fragile humanity."

Fragile humanity . . . Weren't we all breakable? And yet, all at once it wasn't hard for me to imagine her gone. This woman who had been my constant, the mighty wind that kept me upright through every storm of my life, had somehow faded before my very eyes. Grandma was a whisper, a quiet breeze, a soft sigh that would someday weaken and disappear. I didn't even realize that I was blinking back tears until she chuckled and cupped my face in her hands.

"No tears."

"You cry all the time."

"That's different. I'm allowed."

"And I'm not?" I cried, incredulous.

"Not over me. And not today. I'm not going anywhere today."

"You'd better not be going anywhere tomorrow either. Or the next day."

Grandma turned back to the kettle and set it on the stove for my solitary tea, switching the burner on high. "I'm off to bed. A little time alone will change your perspective."

I wasn't much in the mood for a shift in perspective—I was more eager to wallow—but I forced a smile and let her go. The kitchen felt empty with her gone, dim and shadowy because dusk had fallen when we weren't watching and we hadn't bothered to turn on any lights. I flicked on the lone bulb above the stove and leaned against the counter to survey the whole of my domain.

It had changed a little in the years since Daniel was born. When I got a bonus check after working at Value Foods during one particularly lucrative season, we put new flooring in the kitchen and living room. It was cheap laminate that was textured and colored to look like real wood, but it ate holes in all our socks and was cold in the wintertime. Though I swore I wouldn't miss the outdated shag we hauled to the dump, I did. And there were different pictures on the walls now. Grandma had been a sucker for samplers, and while she never got into cross-stitch herself, many of her friends loved nothing more than to painstakingly sew Bible verses and trailing flowers that they framed and gifted. Where the poem "Footprints" once hung, Grandma had mounted one of my better portraits—a photo of Simon and Daniel when they were still little, holding hands as they walked down the gravel road near our house. Their backs were to the camera and their heads were bent together, the sunlight on their hair making them radiate as if from within.

The other changes were more subtle. I could see a toy peeking out from beneath the buffet. One of Daniel's Imaginext pirates, if I wasn't mistaken. And Simon had left a paperback novel on the side table—a Hardy Boys mystery that looked dog-eared and much loved. Grandma's Bible was still the single decoration on our kitchen table, and it had only become more filled and worn with time. She had given it to me all those years ago, but I still thought of it as Grandma's Bible. The truth was, it was all of ours now. It belonged to our family. I knew that she was hoping I would pick it up when she went to bed, that I'd scour it for wisdom, comfort, and advice. I didn't have the heart. Instead, I averted my eyes from the cracked leather cover and the many things I knew I should do.

By the time Grandma was in her robe, false teeth in a pink melamine cup that had been a part of her bridal set, the kettle was whistling merrily. I took it off the stove, waving good night as my sweet grandmother closed the door to her bedroom, and realized that the last thing in the world I wanted was a cup of hot tea. Or to be surrounded by the thinly veiled disorder of our threadbare lives. What had been so dear to me only moments before, so quaint, suddenly seemed tarnished and shabby like a piece of elegant furniture that had been repaired with duct tape.

For all intents and purposes, I was a prisoner in my own home.

Trapped.

I had never thought of it like that before, never allowed myself the luxury of examining my situation closely enough to see the truth. Instead of bemoaning the particulars of my life, for five years I had done everything in my power to rise to the occasion, to be an exemplary mother, sister, and granddaughter. After all, the circumstances of my existence were born of my own choosing. My mistakes—and the mistakes of others—had charted a path for me that I never imagined or hoped for.

In the months and years after Daniel was born, Grandma spoke so earnestly about God's design for my life that I couldn't help but soak in every word as if her quiet proclamations were water for my parched soul. A plan for me. A good work that would surely be brought to completion. Hope and a future.

Right now, those words rang false. Maybe for me, God meant something very different. Like despair and a holding pattern—my life was nothing more than an endless cycle of monotony.

"I gotta get out of here," I muttered to myself. Grabbing an ice-cold Coke from the fridge, I tiptoed to the bottom of the steps and listened for signs of life from Daniel's bedroom. All was quiet. The same was true for Simon's room, though by the sliver of light that escaped from beneath his door it was obvious that he was reading by the glow of a flashlight. I shrugged. He was ten, after all. It had been my hope to get him in the school routine before a strident schedule was upon us, but a couple of late nights wouldn't kill him.

I left the house as quietly as I could, squeezing out a one-foot crack in the screen door because I knew it would squeak if I opened it any farther. Once on the porch, I breathed a little easier. At this one moment in time, I had no obligations, no responsibilities. Nobody was expecting me to do something or go somewhere. Nobody needed me. I popped the top on my Coke and drank half of it in one long swallow. I'd be up for the better part of the night since caffeine always did a number on me after supper, but I didn't care.

The sun had set while I was putting Daniel to bed, but the remnants of a late summer twilight still smoldered against the far horizon. As I watched, the fields that had been flush with crimson faded into a fierce, living obsidian. All was quiet, but the world seemed strangely animate. The fireflies that had decorated our midsummer nights were long gone, and the cicadas that had screamed their unearthly tune were silent. Yet the air around me lived. I breathed it in and took off down the steps.

I wished I were the running type—or at least the sort of girl who had a goal in mind. Sometimes I felt if I could only decide on a destination, the journey would come easily. But I wasn't nearly so farsighted. More myopic, focused on the now, the day-to-day. So instead of lacing up a pair of tennis shoes and sweating out my frustrations on a long, punishing jog, I slapped across the lawn in my worn flip-flops and took off down our gravel driveway at a snail's pace. I wandered.

The thought that Grandma was wrong about me made me sad, but it didn't stop me from ambling down deserted gravel roads with aimless abandon.

There was a farm about a mile from our property where the land cut away as if God had taken a scythe to the soil. It was the high point before the little river valley of the

Big Sioux, a muddy, winding waterway that separated Iowa from South Dakota in my forgotten corner of our often-overlooked state. I felt like I could see forever from the ridge at the edge of Mr. Vonk's property, and if the curve in the distance was merely the rolling of the prairie landscape, I never failed to pretend that it was the bend of the earth as it bowed away from me.

Iowa City was at my back, the place where Michael lived and waited. My future home, if I wanted it to be. And yet, as I stared off into the shadows that still waltzed along the farthest reach of my cloudy vision, I had no desire to turn around and search the darkness for hints of my future. Maybe I was just stuck in the middle. Michael behind me; Grandma before me. And I was suspended in between. Alone.

Wasn't that exactly what I had always feared? When Janice left, when Dad died, when the father of my baby proved himself to be a coward and a deserter, the same track played over and over in my mind, a scratched CD repeating the tired refrain: *You are alone; you will always be alone. . . .*

"That's ridiculous," I said out loud, startling myself. But it felt good to talk, and there was no one around to hear me raving like a lunatic. "You have a son who loves you, a brother who was returned to you, a grandma who sacrificed everything for you, a boyfriend who . . . wants you to move away with him . . ." I trailed off. The way I felt, Michael might as well have asked me to move to the moon.

I looked up as if to find him there and realized that the

only light left in the sky came from a waning moon that had been full only days ago. It was disappointing to see that pale sphere like a ruined fruit, its perfect symmetry destroyed by the slice of a razor's edge. But it reminded me all the same that I should get home. That Daniel might have a nightmare or Simon might get up for a drink and want to talk. I needed to be there for them.

As I turned to retrace my steps through the darkness, it hit me. I wasn't alone. I never would be. It was a long, hard road, but I would walk it because of them. We'd make it. It was dim comfort, but I cupped it in my hands and protected it, hoped that if I breathed it into life, it would continue to glow, to grow. I had learned to cling to fragile hopes long ago.

"You are not alone," I whispered to myself. "And you are not a wanderer." My nose crinkled in disbelief at my own words, but I determined to make them true no matter what I felt. I would make a plan. I would stick to it. What other option did I have? I had to focus on what was best for Daniel and Simon, on the path that would offer them the sort of life they deserved.

When I got home, the house was still. The light beneath Simon's door had been extinguished, and as far as I could tell, everyone slept in peace. All was as it should be. For a moment I was tempted to call Michael, to tell him that as much as I loved him, I couldn't move away with him. Not now. Maybe someday, but for now my place was here. He would understand. Or he wouldn't. And I'd lose him.

Just the possibility of his good-bye was enough to steer me far clear of the telephone. I might be accepting my situation, but I wasn't ready to lose the man I hoped to marry.

The caffeine had made me restless, just as I'd known it would, but for once I didn't mind. I had taken a week off from Value Foods so that I could enjoy the last dog days of summer with my boys, and it wouldn't kill me to oversleep in the morning. Not that Daniel would let me. But if I promised Belgian waffles and strawberry syrup, there was a slight possibility that he'd allow me to cuddle him in bed for an extra minute or two.

I wasn't much in the mood for TV, so I turned on our ancient laptop, a donated relic that the local high school had outgrown. It wasn't good for much besides writing papers and checking e-mail, but that was all we really needed it for anyway. Someday, if I got a digital camera like Francesca openly wished I would, I'd like a new computer to go with it. A Mac, maybe, with all the cool photo software that everyone seemed so excited about. I could edit my own pictures, crop and zoom and play with color. I used black-and-white film in my camera from time to time, but there was something enticing about the thought of switching from sepia to natural light to color saturation at the click of a button.

As the computer whirred to life, I set aside my technology daydreams and tried to be content with what I had. The word processor worked great when I was writing papers on the social development of toddlers, and the truth was that once bad weather hit, my photography dabbling would be cut short. I didn't have an indoor studio, and no one seemed too eager to pose outside in below-zero weather.

I had an e-mail account at the local tech school, an assigned address that delivered messages from my professors and student services. There were two items in my in-box: a "Welcome to the Fall Semester" newsletter that I deleted without reading and a course syllabus from my child psych professor. I scrolled through it halfheartedly, counting on picking up a hard copy my first day in class, but before I could click out of the message, something caught my eye.

Under the heading *Written Reports/Activities*, an item toward the end made me catch my breath.

> Activity 5: Autobiography. Students are to write an autobiography of their first twelve years of life. This is a subjective report and should not be longer than 2,500 words. Topics to include are family interactions, relationships with siblings and parents, most memorable grade school year and why, peer connections, major life events, and overall memories of childhood.

I wondered if it was too late to drop the class. Wasn't I supposed to be assessing other kids? I had no desire to perform an autopsy on my own late childhood. I shuddered and quickly closed the Internet tab so I didn't have to see the other horrors that the class contained. Maybe I didn't need child psych for my degree. Or maybe I could switch degrees. I was only one semester invested in a four-semester program. The credits might transfer.

My other e-mail address was personal. I had signed up for a Hotmail account in a high school computer class, and since I rarely used it and never seemed to deal with annoying spam, my user name and password hadn't changed in nearly a decade. It still made me giggle to type my password—*camelmenthol16*, my choice of cigarettes and the age when I smoked them. *Little rebel*, I thought, my mind skipping to Simon and his upcoming teen years. What would I do when he came home smelling like smoke? I forced the thought from my mind and turned my attention to the screen in front of me.

There were a few more e-mails in this in-box. A forward from Michael. A note from a coworker wondering if she could have a couple shifts off next week. A reminder from the school that classes started at 8:15 on Monday morning. Another note from Michael, this one more personal. A quick *I love you. I miss you.*

I clicked on the Junk tab just to clear out the extra baggage and glanced at the list of unknown senders with a trained eye. A couple of Nigerian moneymaking scams and some newsletters that I was sure I had never signed up for. I was just about to hit Delete All when a name that looked different from the rest seemed to jump off the screen. My cursor paused over the sender's name and my fingers turned to stone above the keyboard.

Patrick Holt.

Was this some kind of joke? Had some spam engine managed to string together the two names that had changed my life forever? The subject line said simply, *Hello*. It wasn't enough to assure me that this wasn't some cruel mistake, but it wasn't an off-putting offer for free Viagra either. Click on it? Or delete it?

It wasn't really a question, for from the moment I saw his name, I knew without a doubt that I would click on the e-mail, even if it was undoubtedly a virus that would make my computer spontaneously combust. What was a little conflagration when the father of my child could have sent me an e-mail?

How long had it been since I'd seen Parker? I hardly knew him as Patrick, but his names, all of them, were like tattoos on my skin—forever, indelible. If I heard someone call out to a Patrick in the grocery store, it was hard not to turn and look. And when I'd considered giving Daniel up for adoption, Holt was one of the many agency names that popped up—and the only one that made my heart skip a beat. But no matter the titles his parents bequeathed him, Daniel's dad would always be Parker to me—the insolent, arrogant grad student who left me without a single look over his shoulder.

"Is it you?" I muttered to the computer screen, squeezing my eyes shut as I clicked on the message. There was no audible pop, no indication that the mysterious Patrick Holt who found his way to my Junk folder had infiltrated my computer and fried the hard drive. I opened one eye and then the other. It wasn't meaningless scrawl or a plea for funds or an advertisement for a drug I didn't need or want.

It was a note.

tightrope

"Julia! Honey, it's breakfast time!"

Grandma's voice floated up the stairs and penetrated the snarl of sheets that tangled around my head. I pushed myself up groggily and fumbled for the alarm clock that sat on the table beside my bed. Eight thirty? I never slept this late.

Twisting out of my sagging mattress, I flung the sheets off and grabbed the cotton robe that I kept hanging from a hook on my wall. I took the stairs two at a time, my heart pounding with . . . what? anxiety? guilt? shame at letting the rest of the house rise and shine without me? When I reached the kitchen, I was breathless and no doubt a sight to behold. I stopped in my tracks at the peaceful scene of everyone around the table and pulled the belt of my robe tighter with a self-conscious tug.

"Your hair is sticking up, Mom!" Daniel giggled at what I could only imagine was a bird's nest of tousled waves.

My hair had been long for years, but when Daniel was two and insisted on twining it in his fingers as he fell asleep, I decided enough was enough. I asked my hairdresser for something cute and stylish, and she left me with a long bob that fell just past my chin and curled softly around my face. I loved it, but I never quite got used to the fact that I had to actually do something with it. Long hair I could ponytail or clip back and ignore. Short hair I had to style.

"Is it that bad?" I asked, running my fingers through my hair to muss it even more. "Are you embarrassed of me? Should I bring you to school like this on Monday?"

"No! Wear it to church like that!" Daniel shouted.

"Church?"

"Did you forget that it's Sunday?" Grandma laughed. "That must have been one heavy sleep."

All at once my night came flooding back. I had hardly slept at all. It felt like I had hardly breathed. Had my heart continued to beat through the witching hour? I didn't remember much past 3 a.m.

I swallowed hard and tried to force a smile. "Just tired, I guess. And no, I won't wear my hair like this to church. I'd better hop in the shower."

"But we're having cereal for breakfast," Simon reminded me, pointing to the three boxes lined up on the table. Grandma was a staunch believer that breakfast should be hot, but on Sunday mornings when everyone was in a rush to get dressed and out the door, we were allowed bowls of our favorite cold cereal. Cheerios for Grandma and Simon, Cocoa Puffs for Daniel, and Alpha-Bits for me. I loved Alpha-Bits. But just the sight of the unmistakable blue box turned my stomach this morning.

"I'm not very hungry," I assured him. "Maybe I'll grab a bowl later."

Grandma gave me a funny look, but she didn't argue. "If you're going to shower, you'd better hurry. We have to leave in just over half an hour."

Technically, we could have squeezed an extra twenty minutes out of our morning routine and slipped into church as the opening hymn was playing. But Grandma liked to be early. She had a blueprint for Sabbath mornings, a carefully constructed pattern that she followed each and every Sunday. I wasn't even 100 percent sure what activities filled her precious prechurch moments because when we arrived at Fellowship Community, I usually took the boys and sat right down. But whatever Grandma did, when she joined us in our regular aisle, she always radiated contentment as she passed me the stack of notes and newsletters from our mailbox.

I knew it was important to her that we left by 9:05. "I'll shower fast," I assured her and hurried to the bathroom. I was motivated by a deadline, but I was more worried about sticking around too long and giving Grandma the opportunity to realize that something was really wrong.

As I showered, dressed, and went through my regular morning motions, I couldn't stop myself from replaying every word of Parker's startling note. Though I wished I could forget his message entirely, I had memorized it in the long minutes that I sat staring at the computer screen. Now different phrases and words rose to haunt me. To taunt me.

> Dear Julia,
>
> I have thought about you every day for the past five and a half years. I don't know what to say except, I'm sorry. I'm sure you've moved on from that night in the parking lot, but it haunts me. I believed that I could just forget everything and live my life without the distraction of you or what happened between us. I'm a grown-up now, a thirty-one-year-old chemical engineer at a successful biomedical corporation. You'd think I could leave the past behind, but I can't.
>
> Anyway, you have every right to hate me, and I understand if you do. I don't expect anything from

you. But if you still use this e-mail address, and if you can bring yourself to write back, will you answer one question for me?

Do I have a child?

Parker

By the time we left for church, I felt drugged, detached, like the first hour after Daniel was born, when exhaustion and hormones and shock and love all mingled together to make the entire experience feel out-of-body. I went through the motions with admirable composure, but I was sure that no one in my little family was much fooled. Grandma knew me as well as she knew herself, and Simon had always been perceptive. As for Daniel, we were connected; what else was there to say?

My son sat curled against me during church, his head beneath my arm and his fingers laced through mine as if he couldn't quite get close enough. It was a rare experience— he normally squirmed, wiggled, and whispered his way through church, but it wasn't hard for me to overlook his uncharacteristic behavior. I loved him snuggled close. Especially since I felt so unhinged. Daniel grounded me through songs that I didn't sing and a long-winded sermon that I didn't hear.

I have thought about you every day for the past five and a half years. . . . I'm sorry. . . . Do I have a child?

What did he expect me to say? *Me too. You should be. Yes.*

What I wanted to say was: *You're a jerk. A loser. A bum. You don't deserve to know what happened to me or that you have a perfect, beautiful son. Your pathetic e-mail is too little, too late.*

Or maybe I could just pretend that I never got his message. His words could be forever lost in cyberspace.

It was when the service was over and we were all turning to file out of the pews that I realized I couldn't simply ignore Parker's long-overdue plea. Daniel had finally unraveled himself from my arms, and he was several feet ahead of me, excited to find his friends in the fellowship hall behind our quaint sanctuary. Church services were still held in the old part of the building, a modest-size room with wooden floors and benches and stained glass windows that were lovely to the point of distraction. But a new addition had recently been tacked on to the antiquated chapel, a modern hall with a kitchen full of stainless steel and more than enough room for the under-ten set to run themselves into a froth.

Usually, the first words out of my mouth when the morning service was over were *No running, Daniel. You're going to knock someone over.* But today I was distracted, and when he was nearly free of the benches and poised to race down the aisle, my five-year-old tossed a quick glance over his shoulder.

His chin was tilted away from me, and he looked up through faintly narrowed eyes. There was a smirk on his lips, a grin that he tried to hide because it was obvious that he was convinced he was about to get away with murder. It was that look, that mischievous I-have-the-world-by-the-tail expression that reminded me the most of Parker. Daniel was indisputably the spitting image of his father. He had been from the day he was born. But I was the only one who knew it.

Parker was a nonentity in our home. Once, just once, I had slipped and mentioned his name, but I couldn't be sure that Grandma had caught it or that she even realized what I was saying. She never pressed me for information, and I never offered any. The father of my baby was a ghost, as nameless and anonymous as a stranger. Yet I lived with a piece of him every day.

Now what? Did he want to meet Daniel? be a part of our lives? After all this time he had no claim over me, over my son. And yet his very likeness stood before me, a gorgeous little boy with piercing blue eyes, features that were chiseled and distinct even at the age of five, and hair the color of wet sand.

I tried not to moan when Daniel spun away from me and took off toward the teeming fellowship hall, but I must have made some noise.

Grandma put her hand on my back. "You okay?" she whispered.

"Fine."

Simon was on Grandma's other side, and he gave a little grunt at my less-than-honest answer. I would have flashed him a warning look if Grandma hadn't been between us.

"Something stuck in your throat, Simon?" I asked, trying to sound casual.

"No, I was just thinking that you were probably upset about your conversation with Michael."

He couldn't have shocked me more if he told me Janice was on her way home. My expression must have communicated every ounce of my distress because Grandma's eyes filled with concern.

"What's going on?" she asked, looking between the two of us as if we were keeping something important from her. Which we were.

"Nothing," I lied.

Simon raised an eyebrow in disbelief.

"Fine," I muttered between clenched teeth. "There's something going on. But I don't want to talk about it here."

"Let's go home." Grandma linked her arm through mine and turned to Simon. "You go find Daniel and bring him to the car. Julia and I will be waiting."

She led me out of the sanctuary and through the throng of people crowding the fellowship hall. The scent of bad coffee and a dozen disharmonious perfumes mingled in an offense of unbearable odor. I felt choked, trapped. Almost desperate in my desire for fresh air.

"You going to be all right, honey?"

I couldn't meet Grandma's worried gaze. "I don't know," I whispered.

By the time we got home, even Daniel knew there was something big going on. He had sensed my anxiety in church, but now that Grandma and Simon were also tight-lipped and tense, Daniel looked downright solemn. He held my hand on the way upstairs and even allowed me to help him out of his Sunday clothes as if he were still a very little boy instead of an almost kindergartner.

"Hey," I said as I unbuttoned his starched, white shirt, "don't look so serious."

Daniel ignored me and eased his arms out of his short sleeves, raising his hands obediently as I lifted a T-shirt over his head. It was on in one smooth movement, and I took advantage of his uncharacteristic compliance by dropping a kiss on the tips of his gelled hair. He let me do it without complaint.

I assumed my comment was already forgotten, but as I turned to head back to my own room and slip out of my sundress, he asked, "What's *serious?*"

Mothers were supposed to be pros at answering those sorts of questions, but I was terrible at fielding them. I never knew what to say, how to make the complexities of a perplexing world make sense to my five-year-old. "Ummm . . ." I faltered. "I guess *serious* means 'grave,' 'somber,' 'stern.'"

Daniel gave me a weird look.

"It means 'not happy,'" I said, trying again. "It means you look like you're thinking about something very important and it's making you sad."

"I'm not thinking about anything important," Daniel assured me. A smile zipped across his earnest face and then just as quickly disappeared. His brows furrowed; his mouth formed a grim line. "I look like Simon. See?"

Torn between laughter and tears, I bit my lip and pulled Daniel close. He endured my embrace for a moment before backing away to grab a handful of Matchbox cars from the little desk beneath his window. I stood in the doorway and watched him cram the detailed trucks and sports coupes in the pockets of his shorts. He took toys with him wherever he went, as if he had already learned at such a young age that you should never be caught unprepared.

What else had my son discovered about life? That Simon was serious? That there isn't a daddy for every family? That Mommy clutched at things, trying to hold people close so they wouldn't slip through her fingers?

I didn't want Daniel to absorb all the junk, all the dysfunction and baggage that the rest of us seemed doomed to inherit. But how could I stop that from happening? Especially now, as I was about to drop a bomb on my unsuspecting family?

When I finally descended the steps, clad in a pair of cargo shorts and another of my cheapo T-shirts, I found Grandma in the kitchen with a picnic basket on the table.

"Grab a knife," she said, indicating the bag of raisin buns on the counter. "They need to be cut and buttered."

There was a Tupperware container in front of her, and she was peeling carrots with a paring knife, quartering them, and dropping them inside. I peeked into the basket and spied a bunch of freshly washed grapes, a sleeve of Simon's favorite wheat crackers, and the last of the cupcakes we had made a few days ago.

"We're going on a picnic," Grandma told me unnecessarily. "I think it would do us all good to get out of the house."

I nodded and took a bread knife from the butcher block. The bakery put eight buns in a package and I sliced them all, spreading both sides with real butter and putting a square of cheddar cheese in the middle. By the time we got wherever we were going, the sandwiches would be the tiniest bit warm, the cheese soft, the butter on the verge of melting. I could close my eyes and imagine how they would taste. It reminded me of my childhood.

"Where're we going?" Simon asked, coming into the kitchen and inspecting the contents of the picnic basket.

"The Black Hills, the Rocky Mountains, the beach . . . ," I muttered, wishing that one of those dream destinations was exactly where we were headed.

"Somewhere a little closer to home." Grandma popped the plastic top on her container of carrots and deposited it in the basket beside the grapes.

"Thought so." Simon gave me what I considered a dirty look.

"Ooh! A picnic!" Daniel thundered into the kitchen and climbed on a chair so he could examine the provisions for our spontaneous outing. "Can I have a cupcake now?"

"No," I exclaimed at the exact moment that Grandma said, "No."

She caught my eye and a knowing smile passed between us. It was nice to be reminded that we were a team, no matter how unconventional.

"I think we're ready to go," Grandma announced, taking the bag of buns from my outstretched hand and adding it to the growing pile of food. She closed the picnic basket and handed it to Simon. "We need a strong man to do the honors. Julia, if you'd grab some bottles of water from the fridge, I believe we're set."

"A picnic, a picnic!" Daniel shouted as we trailed out of the house single file. He took the lead, careening over the lawn toward the car, but when he threw open the door to the backseat and started to hop inside, Grandma stopped him.

"We're not taking the car, sweetie!"

"But we can't walk to the park!"

"We're not going to the park."

"Where are we going?" He seemed completely mystified, but Grandma just marched past him wearing a secret smile.

"Come on," I said, motioning for him to come. "Might as well follow the lady."

Grandma led us to the east edge of our property, past the old chicken coop, the stable that had once held half a dozen horses, and up the hill where a sagging barn stood like a proud, elderly gentleman still clinging to his dignity. I had spent hours playing in the hayloft when I was a kid, but now the outbuildings were all in a sad state of disrepair. I felt bad banning the boys from the rotting ladders, but I couldn't stomach the thought of one of them falling through the decaying floor.

"Tell me about when you were little," Daniel asked as we approached the barn.

There was only one story that he wanted to hear, and though I regretted ever voicing my ridiculous—and danger-ous—childhood tale, I repeated it in an effort to calm my nerves.

"When I was a girl," I began, "I wanted to be a tightrope walker."

"In the circus," he cut in.

I shrugged. "In the circus." In reality, I don't know if I ever wanted to run away with the circus; I was merely addicted to the rush of doing the one thing my dad prohibited me from doing. But Daniel loved to embellish, so I let him. I imag-ined he pictured me in sequins and feathers, though I never wore anything beyond my uniform of faded denim and hand-me-down shirts. "So I wanted to be a tightrope walker, and Grandpa's barn had the perfect place for me to practice."

"A tightrope?"

"Nope, a beam. A great, big wooden beam that stretched from the north end of the barn to the south."

"But there was hay beneath it."

"There was hay beneath part of it," I agreed. "But at the south end of the barn, the hayloft opened up over the animal stalls."

"But you didn't walk there."

"I did," I said, giving his ear a little tweak.

"You were naughty," Daniel laughed.

"I was adventurous."

"You were naughty," Grandma agreed with Daniel and gave me a stern look. Addressing my son, she said, "Your mother should have never done such a foolish thing."

"Yeah, 'cause she could have fallen and hit her head and *died*."

It was a warning that I had used just once when Daniel climbed on the counter to swipe a cookie from the cookie jar. I was petrified of what the hard floor would do to his sweet, soft head, and I shouted the first thing that came to my mind. Daniel never forgot it. Now, if anyone did anything even remotely unsafe, they were surely going to fall and hit their head and *die*.

The first chuckle came from Simon, a wet burst of laughter that told me he had been holding in just such a giggle for a long time. Then Grandma was laughing and finally Daniel and I joined in, though Daniel asked, "What are we laughing at?"

"Nothing, honey."

"You know," Grandma said, "I could tell you lots of other stories about when your mom was little. There was one winter that Grandpa got a new batch of chicks, and your mom—"

"Thought they were cute," I burst out, placing a warning hand on Grandma's arm. She grinned at me but let it drop.

We walked past the barn to the very peak of the sloping

hill that stood sentinel over the length of our property. At the top, Grandma stopped in the shade of a gnarled oak tree and spread out the blanket she had snagged when we passed through the mudroom. From the square boundary of our makeshift table, we could see to the farthest edge of the DeSmit farm. Eighty acres spread before us, rising and falling as if the breath of God swept over the ocean of green. Grandma rented out the land, and the man who farmed it had planted soybeans just beyond the barn and corn in the second parcel. I was grateful that there were no tall plants to block our view. On a bright, clear day like this, we could practically count the leaves on the trees that bordered the creek between sections.

"Who needs the park when we've got a vista like this?" Grandma asked.

We ate quietly, with a certain attentive diligence as if we were spellbound by the world around us. But my thoughts weren't nearly so peaceful, and when Grandma finally broke out the cupcakes and announced, "I think it's time to talk," I startled as if I had been deep in a trance.

"Daniel—" Grandma wiped the corner of her mouth with a napkin—"why don't you go explore behind the barn? It's cool and shady there, and when your mother was little, she could always find frogs in the tall grass."

"Frogs?" He stuffed the last of his cupcake in his mouth and took off at a sprint.

"Thank you," I said, grateful that Grandma didn't see this

as a family affair. "I'm not ready to tell him yet. Simon, I think you should leave too."

"But I already know."

"Know what?" Grandma murmured.

"That she's moving to Iowa City," Simon muttered, gazing at the uneaten cupcake in his hand.

Grandma didn't say anything, but I could see the shock in the downward slant of her mouth.

"Simon," I warned. "That's not true. And this isn't your story to tell."

His head drooped lower.

"No one is moving to Iowa City," I said, trying to placate both of them. "Michael asked me to come with him . . ." I caught myself and added, "And Simon and Daniel, too, but I said no. Well, I haven't said no yet, but I haven't said yes. And I'm not going to."

Grandma nodded slowly. "Did he . . . propose?"

It hurt so much to say the word, I found that the only thing I could do was shake my head. "One of his professors is on leave, and Michael asked him if I could move into his house for a couple of months. It would be a . . . trial."

"A trial? A trial of what, exactly?"

"I don't know," I whispered, overwhelmed by how hurt I was that his offer hadn't been one of marriage. "It's terrible, isn't it? I mean, he should know, right? If he wants to be with me—with us—or not."

I expected to feel Grandma's arms around me, but when

she didn't move to comfort me in any way, I looked up to find her cool and unemotional. "I don't know, Julia," she said carefully. "I don't think it's such a terrible idea. It might be good for you to see if this is what you really want. Michael is the only person you've dated since Daniel was born. What if you spend more time together and realize that it isn't meant to be? What if God has something else in store?"

Her words stunned me. Something else in store? For me? Who was she kidding? "I love Michael," I said quietly.

"Then you have to go."

"But—"

"But nothing," Grandma interrupted. "Have you heard of the phrase 'leave and cleave'? What about, 'For this reason a man will leave his father and mother and be united to his wife, and they will become one flesh'?"

"We're hardly one flesh," I muttered.

"Maybe you will be. Either way, I don't think this—" she spread her arm wide to encompass the whole of our land—"is all God has planned for you, Julia. It might be time to dream bigger than our little farm."

This wasn't the way I had hoped this conversation would go. I thought Grandma would be surprised, maybe a little saddened, and then ultimately supportive. I didn't need her second-guessing my decision or the motives behind it.

"I can't leave," I said, staring at my empty hands as if the answers that were supposed to be hidden inside had slipped through my fingers.

"Why not?"

Because of you. Because Simon doesn't want to go. Because this is the only home I've ever known. . . .

We didn't say anything for a long time. Unspoken words drifted between us like the debris of a phantom conversation, one that didn't go quite according to plan. Simon picked at his cupcake, Grandma gazed off over the fields, and I stole glances at both of them, loving them in silence and wishing I could say all the things that I felt. When Daniel finally came back, a fat, green and brown frog squeezed in the death grip of his dirty palm, Grandma sighed and reached to pat my knee.

"We have much to think about," she said, mustering up a smile for Daniel as he approached. "Lots of decisions to make."

She didn't know the half of it.

little gifts

I DROVE THE BOYS to school on Monday, even though my shift at Value Foods was supposed to start at six. It was an extra two hours of vacation, time that I had worked hard for and—my manager assured me—I deserved. Though it meant starting my workweek a little behind, I was grateful for the opportunity to ease into my fall routine. The questions and uncertainties that collected in our house like a fine layer of dust were making a muddle of my already-confused mind. It didn't help that after our picnic confrontation, no one said another word about Michael's proposed trial. I wondered how they would react if they knew about Parker. The thought made me shudder.

Grandma tried to make the first day of school special by baking her famous cinnamon rolls and letting Daniel smear his with lots of real butter *and* peanut butter. And I caged my worries and chatted cheerfully, filling the hour before school with mindless conversation that was intended to put my boys at ease. My little plan seemed to work wonders with Daniel; by the time I told him we needed to leave, he was already wearing his backpack, waiting at the door. But Simon wasn't quite so malleable. I put my hand on his shoulder as we left the house and he abruptly shrugged it off.

"Nervous?" I asked.

"No."

"Good. There's no reason to be. You're talented, smart, fun to be around—"

"You don't have to baby me," Simon muttered.

"I'm not babying you."

He rolled his eyes and slid into the backseat of the car. I almost told him to come in the front with me, but one look at the way his slender arms crossed his chest in defiance warned me that I should let it go.

"So . . ." I forced a smile and started the car with a flourish of jangling keys. "Who's ready for their first day of school?"

Daniel's hand shot up. "Me! I am!"

"I don't know why you're bringing us," Simon mumbled.

"Because I thought you would want me to. After today you

two are going to have to ride the bus. And it doesn't leave at 8:00—it'll pick you up at 7:25."

"Whatever."

I gave Simon a stern look in the rearview mirror, but he was staring out the window at rolling pastures and missed my reprimand. When had he become so irritable? so glum? Of course, I knew exactly when the shift had happened. I could mark his attitude change almost to the minute—his world had tilted in its orbit the day he overheard Francesca spill my secret. But hadn't I assured him that we weren't going anywhere? that nothing was going to change? What was he so afraid of?

In spite of the taut mood in the car, Daniel filled the seven-minute drive to school with stories and speculations about his upcoming year. His teacher was a seasoned veteran, a lovely lady with a graying bun and earrings that betrayed her quirky sense of humor. She wore tiny lassos for kindergarten roundup, dangly silver spoons and forks for the parent dessert night, and miniature stuffed teddy bears for the new student meet and greet. Daniel was completely in awe of her and more than eager to commit himself to her tutelage five days a week.

When we pulled up in front of Mason Elementary, he had his door half-open and one foot on the street before I could utter a protest.

"Hey!" I called, reaching over the back of the seat and catching his wrist. "You can't leave without a good-bye!"

"Oh." Daniel grinned. "Bye, Mom."

"No hug? A kiss, maybe?"

He peered out the crack in his door at the shuffle of kids and teachers crowding the long sidewalk in front of his new school. "Nah. You can hug me tonight."

With that, he slipped out of my grip and was gone.

"Don't forget Grandma is picking you and Simon up this afternoon!" I shouted, hoping he could hear me through the open passenger window. Stifling a sigh, I turned to wish Simon a good day. My backseat was empty. He was gone too.

"Maybe I should go to Iowa City," I grumbled to myself. "Apparently I'm not as needed here as I thought."

It took me less than two minutes to get to Value Foods from Mason Elementary. My heart was still in the drop-off lane with Daniel and Simon, and my head must have been in the clouds because I drove to an empty spot at the very back of the lot before I remembered that there was a space next to the back door just for me. It didn't have my name on it, but it did have my title: assistant manager.

Value Foods was a pretty small operation, so my new job didn't carry the same sort of prestige that it might at a larger chain. But the pay was better, and I liked working under Mr. Durst. He was fair and honest and straightforward— many of the same traits that he claimed made me perfect for the job. Since accepting the promotion in June, my days had consisted of a lot more desk work and a lot less on-the-floor melodrama. There was always some soap opera going on between the clerks, shift managers, and bag boys, but I felt impervious in my ivory tower. Actually, my office more closely resembled a windowless dungeon, but I had brightened it up with photographs of my family, a few pieces of art that I had scrounged from summer garage sales, and a stuffed green and blue snake that Simon had won at the county fair. He gave it to me as a gift when I was named assistant manager.

Michael had seemed less than enthusiastic when I told him about my new title, and though I hadn't understood it at the time, I realized as I grabbed my purse off the floor of the car why my position caused him alarm. He thought that it would be harder for me to leave Value Foods if I was anything more than a clerk. I bit my lip when it struck me that he was right. At least a little. There was more to it than that, but I couldn't help taking pleasure in a job that I had never hoped would be anything more than a way to earn some money. I had never imagined myself assistant manager material.

Sure, the scheduling and record keeping were mundane, but Mr. Durst also let me do some of the purchasing and sales, and after the first month he completely handed over control of the weekly Value Foods flyer and promotional discounts. I quickly discovered that I loved unearthing wholesalers who could provide items we'd never stocked before. It was like finding treasure.

At first, my manager had been skeptical that we'd be able to move items like garam masala or the fresh raspberries that

I contracted from the farmer who lived just down the road from us. But I had provided a recipe for spicy pork curry with the masala coupon in our flyer and made a Local, Homegrown sign out of old barn wood to post by the woven tubs of gem-colored berries. Both had been a huge hit, with jars of masala disappearing off the shelf and people begging for more raspberries. Mr. Durst just laughed in wonder and told me to keep at it.

In spite of being more or less abandoned by my boys, I couldn't stop myself from smiling as I wrenched open the heavy back door of Value Foods. The storeroom was cool and my favorite worker was filling a grocery cart with cans of tomato sauce to restock the shelves.

"Good morning, Graham," I said, offering him a little wave. He had grown up so much in the years that I had known him. The scrawny boy who had stood a whole head shorter than me when I started working as a stock girl was now a star athlete who towered so high that I worried about neck cramps when I looked at him. He had even gone to a major university on a basketball scholarship. "Aren't you supposed to be on your way to college?" I asked, confused that he was handling tin cans instead of basketballs and books. "I didn't schedule you for this week."

"Yeah, but I actually don't start until next week. I commandeered a couple of shifts. Textbooks aren't cheap, you know."

"You could always quit and keep working here."

He knew I was teasing, but he seemed to give my suggestion serious thought anyway. "You're easy to work for, Jules, but I think I might still like to get my degree."

"You'd better," I told him, leveling a finger at him like the mother I was.

He winked and went back to work, but just as I was about to disappear through my office door, he called, "Hey, Julia! I thought we had something special."

I gave him a puzzled look.

Graham's smile was crooked and endearing. "I'm just jealous that you're getting flowers from some other guy."

Spinning a finger around my temple to let him know he was crazy, I edged my office door open with one hip. Suddenly I got Graham's strange joke. In the middle of my desk was a vase of flowers so big, it stood nearly as tall as I did. Flowers had never really been my thing, but these were exquisite—not your typical bouquet of red roses. I recognized the tall spires of purple delphiniums and the smaller clusters of white freesia. There were magenta spider lilies and pale yellow chrysanthemums the size of dessert plates. When I looked closer, I saw that there were roses, too, but they weren't red—they were the color of tangerines and sunrise, of a warm summer flame.

My breath was caught in my throat, and when I finally grasped that I was suffocating and took in a wheezing breath, the scent of all those flowers was nearly overpowering. *Michael,* I thought. It had to be Michael. But somewhere in the back of my mind, I paused. If Parker had my e-mail address, it wasn't a huge leap to imagine he'd tracked me down. But the bouquet before me was too personal. He wouldn't, I assured myself. He wouldn't dare.

I lunged for the credit card–size note that was wedged between two waxy leaves. The envelope betrayed nothing more than my name, written in a curlicue script that was anything but masculine. So a florist wrote the note. No hint there. I ripped it open and found one line in the same handwriting. *Call me.* It was signed *M.*

All at once I felt winded and dropped into my office chair with a moan of relief. In comparison to Parker's loaded e-mail, Michael's unexpected gift of flowers felt safe, almost homey. I was overwhelmed by the reminder that whether or not Michael had proposed to me a week ago, he loved me. I loved him. He was my best friend and confidant. He made my pulse race. Somehow I had lost sight of that in the midst of my disappointment that everything had not turned out exactly as I dreamed it would. I had lost sight of us.

I fumbled in my purse for my cell phone and dialed Michael's number with trembling fingers. "Pick up," I whispered. "Pick up."

It rang only once.

"Hey, you." Michael's voice was soft and familiar. It sounded as if he had been expecting my call.

"Hey, you," I echoed.

"Got the boys dropped off at school?"

"Yeah."

"And you're at work now?"

"Yeah."

"So you . . ."

"Are staring at the amazing flowers you sent me."

"I hoped you'd like them."

"I do. And I'm not the sort who goes all wobbly at the sight of flowers, but . . ."

Michael laughed. "You're wobbly?"

"It might have more to do with you than the flowers."

His low exhalation spoke volumes, but I was surprised when he whispered, "I'm sorry."

"You're sorry? For what?"

"For putting you in such an awkward place. How could I expect you to just pack up and leave everything? Your job, Nellie, your home . . . And all I offered you in return was a social experiment."

I giggled. "You've been in med school too long."

"Yet I'm nowhere near done," Michael said, his voice low and serious.

"I know." It broke my heart a little that what had started out so innocent—a moment of renewal, of reconciliation even—had turned into something somber in the span of a second. "So . . ."

"So we forget my ridiculous—my insensitive proposal."

I wondered if he realized the way that word stirred my soul. A proposal was a promise, a pledge, the assurance of forever.

His offer in the grove hadn't been a proposal. Far from it. And yet it was something. "You want to just go back to the way things were?" I asked, my words light as the air it took to voice them.

"No." Michael's answer was immediate. "No, I think we've come too far to turn back now."

Hope pricked at my heart, made tiny holes where everything I felt for him began to leak out, slow and warm. It filled me, made me believe for the first time since his awkward proposition that we could still make this work. "What do you mean?" I whispered.

"I have an idea."

"You do?"

"But I'm not going to tell you over the phone."

"What?"

"This is more of a face-to-face sort of a thing." Though I couldn't see him, I could imagine the smirk that graced Michael's lips.

"You're kind of a jerk," I told him.

"You're kind of quick to jump to conclusions."

I clutched the phone, pressed it to my forehead for a moment, and wished that I could wrap my arms around Michael instead of the small piece of plastic in my hand. "When do I get to see you?" I asked.

"Well . . . I just started eight weeks of microbiology, and it's pretty intense."

"Eight weeks? I can't wait that long!"

"What are you talking about? Our entire relationship has been long-distance."

"You don't have to remind me. Holidays and summer break are like endless appetizers. I feel like I never get to eat a full meal."

"I'm a snack to you?" Michael snorted.

"Bad analogy. But you know what I mean. We've never been together for more than a couple of weeks at a time."

"So eight weeks should feel like nothing. The syllabus eases up a little at the halfway point. I might be able to squeeze in a quick trip home then."

I worried my bottom lip, doing the mental gymnastics necessary to calculate if I could fit in a visit to Iowa City. It just didn't seem plausible. I let go of a shallow breath. "Okay. Just make sure you grow some nice microorganisms for me."

"We're dealing with bacterial meningitis and pathogens. You wouldn't believe the—"

"Too much info, Dr. House."

Michael laughed. "Okay, okay. I'll see you soon."

I thought his definition of *soon* was a little loose, but I didn't tell him so. "A month," I declared, trying to put a time frame on it so I could start counting days.

"A month," he agreed. "But more likely two." He sounded rueful, almost despondent, and my heart trembled at the realization that he hated the distance between us just as much as I did.

"Fine," I whispered. "Two."

We were silent for a moment, the only sound between us the measured exchange of our quiet breaths. As he breathed out, I breathed in. "Thank you," I finally said. "For the flowers. They're beautiful."

"I love you," Michael told me.

"Love you, too."

I clicked the phone shut, laid it on my desk, and stared at it as if it contained Michael's secret. He had an idea. . . . What in the world could he be planning?

But as much as I wanted to waste hours daydreaming about Michael, I simply didn't have time to think about him. About us. Guilt at coming in to work late, and then spending my first five minutes on duty glued to the telephone, drove me into warp speed as I officially started my day. I was grateful that Mr. Durst came in at nine, and no one but Graham was around to suspect that I was doing anything other than work in my office.

Moving the flowers to a side table, I plunged into my daily workload. I reconciled the sales receipts from the day before in record time, filled the final holes in the new September schedule, and made a disciplinary phone call to a sales clerk who continually showed up five to ten minutes after the start of her shift. She was contrite, and I was in a gracious mood, so I didn't give her the tongue-lashing she deserved. Instead, I asked about her daughter's first day of high school, and we commiserated as lonely mothers of independent children. It was a brief moment of connection, and when I hung up, I felt confident that she wouldn't be late again.

I took my lunch break with Graham and sent him to Subway with a twenty-dollar bill and instructions not to come back until he had purchased a feast worthy of his bon voyage party.

"It's Subway." Graham's sloped eyebrow assured me that there was no such feast to be found at the sandwich mecca.

I shrugged. "Do what you can. I'll uncork a bottle of our finest."

Although Graham laughed when he realized that our finest consisted of a $2.99 bottle of nonalcoholic cold duck, he seemed willing enough to go along with my impromptu celebration. I poured it into mismatched mugs from my office and we settled ourselves on the picnic table outside. Napkins served as plates, Doritos a delectable side dish that perfectly complemented our matching meatball subs. Of course, the sandwiches weren't quite matching. Mine was a six-inch; his was a footlong plus the other half of my truncated sub.

By the time we had laughed our way through the half-hour lunch break, I was in such an expansive mood that the loose ends of my life seemed less like frayed edges and more like bright ribbons. They were a bit tattered maybe, but cheerful too. Full of possibilities instead of dead ends. I was revived by the assurance that Michael had an idea, that he could somehow make everything work when only yesterday I was certain that our relationship had turned the final corner. It was like the sun had broken from behind a cloud, and though the light was thin and indistinct, it cast coins of color where shadows had crept.

I was in such a good mood that when I unpacked a box of startling new stock, I found myself laughing uncontrollably instead of groaning in disappointment. It was probably my first foolish purchase, though the seller had assured me that the postcards adequately captured the "pastoral beauty of our lovely Iowa." If by "pastoral beauty" she meant barrels of pink piglets and a gigantic ear of corn in a rusty wagon, the postcards were a smashing success. But I had hoped for twilight landscapes and vistas of endless Midwestern horizons. On any other day, I would have been dismayed at the sight of an eighty-year-old farmer in gumboots with manure up to his armpits and a jaunty caption proclaiming, *Wish you were here!* Today, I found it funny. Endearing, even.

As I prepped them for a display near the checkout lanes, I ended up choosing one postcard of every design for myself. Little gifts for Michael. He would find them hilarious. Or he'd be embarrassed by our quaint, backwater state and insist we move somewhere more chic the day he graduated from med school. I grinned when I realized I had envisioned *us* moving.

My workday was over at four, and I was anxious to go home and find out how Daniel and Simon had fared their first day of school. I arranged my desk carefully, wondering how in the world I would get the flowers home without smashing them and plotting special things to do with my boys. I'd take Daniel exploring around the creek at the back of our property, and if we found a frog or—heaven help me—a snake, I'd put it in a jar and let him take it for show-and-tell. And I'd persuade Simon to take a walk with me. I'd explain to him that everything was going to be okay, that we absolutely were not moving to Iowa City right now, and that he had nothing at all to worry about. He'd believe me; I knew it.

I was just about to switch off my computer when I realized that there was one more person I could bless on this banner day.

My junk box was empty save for the one note that had caused me such heartache. In a few days the message would be erased from my account permanently, and I would never have to confront it again. It was a comforting thought, and I almost let myself shut down the computer without acting on my foolish impulse. Almost. But deep down I knew that whether or not the note existed in cyberspace, it would always exist in my heart, in a private place where I clung to those fathomless emotions that I couldn't begin to explain or understand. A place where secrets and questions and what-ifs stirred with every inhalation.

I paused for a moment before clicking the message to life, then quickly hit Reply so I wouldn't be forced to reread Parker's words. There was no need to revisit his plea. I knew what he wanted to know.

Do I have a child?

I typed three letters before hitting Send.

Yes.

words

I DIDN'T KNOW that three letters would change my life.

Of course, I should have. Throughout my twenty-four years I had been forever altered by such trios. *Bye. Boy.* And someday soon, I hoped, *I do.* It was irresponsible of me to imagine that my small act of benevolence wouldn't ripple forward like waves on a pond. *Yes* was a tiny pebble to throw, but it wrinkled the fabric of my days all the same, shaping my future in ways I couldn't begin to fathom.

But I didn't know that at the time. It took me a good week to realize that e-mailing Parker was quite possibly one of the most self-destructive things I could have ever done.

For seven days after my one-word response, life at the DeSmit farm settled into a predictable routine. The boys seemed to embrace school, Grandma flourished amid the daily peace and freedom in her quiet home, and I found myself enjoying the hours at Value Foods with a sort of contentedness that I hadn't imagined possible in a dead-end grocery store job. The truth was, my staff felt more like a family, and our customers part of a close-knit community. Even the gray brick walls of the outdated interior seemed to take on a patina of silver, as if the store itself were a modest treasure—a place that deserved respect for both its generous service and its steadfast longevity.

As for Michael, although we hadn't seen each other since his failed suggestion in the grove, our relationship defied common sense and deepened. His unexpected gift of flowers, our subsequent telephone conversation, and his startling, earnest apology launched us to a new level of intimacy that convinced me all over again that the man I had loved for five years would be the man I loved for fifty more. When we spoke on the phone, it was as lovers—we finished each other's sentences, communicated through silence, cherished one another in spite of distance. It felt like we had recaptured the immediacy of our first months of dating, that almost-heartsick longing to know more, learn more, be more. But this was different. It *was* more.

Looking back from even the close proximity of mere days, I could see that one lone week in August as a respite, a small haven of peace before my world split open at the seams. *I did this to myself,* I thought when I opened my e-mail one day and found a reply from the father of my son. *I have no one to blame but me.*

It shocked me to find Patrick Holt's name among the notes from friends and family in my private in-box, but as I sat staring at the screen, I remembered that I had e-mailed him back. My online account would automatically assume he was a safe contact and reroute him to the inner sanctum of my carefully guarded and privacy-protected in-box. The thought leveled me. He had inched his way in.

"Okay," I whispered to calm myself. "Of course he wrote back. What did you expect?"

I steeled myself, clicked on the recycled message title, and found one word hiding in the upper left-hand corner of the screen.

Yours?

My breath left me in a cough of anger and disbelief. What did he mean, *yours?* Did he presume ownership, as if Daniel could be *ours* after all these years of silence, detachment, impassivity? Or even *his?* Like he had any claim at all. Daniel was mine; it said so on the birth certificate—the line where I was supposed to fill in his father's name was left painfully, conspicuously blank. Nothing could change that now.

But as I heaved in and out, glaring at the computer screen like it bore the blame for delivering such an indiscernible message, Parker's carefully chosen question flickered as if caught in the mirrors of a kaleidoscope. All at once I understood. He hadn't meant to question my claim on Daniel. He meant, *Is the child yours, or did you give it up for adoption?*

But it didn't matter what he had intended to say. It mattered how I felt about it.

Mine. I typed avariciously, unaffected by the faint understanding that I had more or less turned my son into a pawn. And though I should have paused to consider the consequences, I clicked the Send button with an almost-vicious abandon.

A few days later there was another lone word in my inbox.

Healthy?

I sent back, *Perfect.*

The very next day he asked, *Girl?*

For some reason I took great pleasure in typing the three letters of *son.* Daniel wasn't merely some boy; he was my flesh and blood, my offspring, my son. It was a lot more than Parker had a right to say.

Although the back-and-forth exchange with my long-lost boyfriend was utterly serious, it felt like a game of sorts to me. He asked questions that only I could answer, and for a couple of days I relished the power of holding every card in my hand. What did he have to offer me? Nothing. And yet I believed with all my heart that if I simply stopped responding, he'd feel as if he had lost everything. I didn't know what he wanted from me, what he wanted from Daniel, but each e-mail convinced me a little more that his interest was more than a passing curiosity.

Parker was silent for a while after he learned that he had fathered a son, and a part of me harbored the wild hope that that would be the end of it. I remembered all too well the grad school student who ran like a frightened child when I refused to abort his baby, and I couldn't stop myself from wishing in some dark corner of my soul that the Parker I knew back then still existed. Maybe he'd run away again, and I could go back to life as normal. Marry Michael—eventually—and let Daniel's biological father forever be some nameless bum who had taken advantage of an eighteen-year-old girl.

But it couldn't be that simple.

One day it hit me that I knew what Parker's next question would be. He was biding his time, working up the courage to ask me the most intimate detail yet. It was what I would ask if I were him, and suddenly I dreaded checking my e-mail for fear that today would be the day he mustered the nerve.

It was hard to believe that I had already let him in this far—I wavered between loathing myself for giving away information about my child like dime-store candies doled out one by one and feeling a sense of relief that the man who gave Daniel the slope of his nose had finally taken an interest in his amazing son. Daniel deserved to be known, to be adored. But I didn't know if I wanted Parker to be the one to do the adoring.

By the time I received his e-mail, I was a mess of contradictions. For my own sake, I wanted to push Parker away. But for Daniel's sake, I wanted to draw him close. Instead of reading Parker's question, I pressed my hands over my eyes, trying to hide from the reality of the road I found myself on. It was uncharted, a bewildering, foreign land, and I was scared of what I would find around the next bend. There were so many uncertainties, so much at stake. Who was Patrick Holt? Did he want to be a part of Daniel's life? Did I want him to be a part of Daniel's life? Was it wrong of me to even contemplate preventing it?

I took a shuddering breath and peeled my fingers from my eyes like a little girl watching a scary movie. The question was there, exactly as I knew it would be.

Name?

Before I could doubt myself further, I thrust my hands to the keyboard and quickly typed, *Daniel Peter.*

It was the first time I had responded with more than a single word.

I longed to talk to someone about Parker's sudden appearance in my online world, but the person I would normally run to was the last one I could ever tell. Though I shared everything with Michael, I wasn't ready to baptize him with the full reality of loving a single mom. It seemed cruel, an unexpected splash of ice water in the face. Of course, we had endured our share of trials already—nap schedules when Daniel was little, jealousy issues as he got older, and blank stares from people when they heard my son call the man whose hand I held "Michael" instead of "Daddy." But that sort of trouble seemed pale in comparison to the sudden appearance of Daniel's deadbeat biological father.

If Parker wanted to worm his way back into our lives, it changed the landscape of everything. Michael, who had been a father figure to Daniel—and Simon, too—would be relegated to merely my boyfriend, a man who had no claim on the boys he had grown to love. And Parker, a virtual stranger, could enter our lives out of the blue and profess the title of birth dad. It wasn't fair.

And it certainly wasn't fair that I had to shoulder this alone.

I prayed for wisdom, for guidance, but God seemed tight-lipped. Or maybe He was just biding His time, following a schedule that I couldn't access no matter how earnestly I begged to catch a glimpse of His agenda.

There was a time in my life when I would have waited. I would have worried, chewed my fingernails down to the quick, and obsessed about what people were thinking of me. But much had changed. I had faced my mother, forgiven her, and lost her again all in a span of a couple months. I had become a mother myself. I had more or less parented my brother through the same heartache I faced as a child—the abandonment of the woman who gave us birth. In some ways, Grandma was right. God was working in me, and I was no longer the sort of girl who just let life happen to her.

I decided that whether or not it would break my heart, it was time to tell Grandma about Parker. We were a family. We existed, for better or worse, together. And I had failed us by keeping Michael's proposition to myself. I wouldn't make the mistake of keeping secrets again.

My classes at the local tech school began the second week in September, and before I abandoned myself to the dash and scurry of work, family activities, and night class, I carved a couple hours out of my week for some one-on-one Grandma time. Mr. Durst was willing to let my schedule at Value Foods be flexible as long as I got everything done, and after I e-mailed Parker the final detail that had the potential to unleash the unknown—my son's name—I worked through several lunch breaks so I could leave early on Friday. Grandma and I would have the rare chance to be alone before the boys got home from school.

Grandma wasn't expecting me when I pulled into our winding driveway. She looked up from her roost in the garden, where she was plunging a narrow spade into one of our potato hills, and gave me an uncertain wave. I expected her to return to the task at hand while I parked and walked across the browning grass, but instead of thrusting her shovel back into the black soil, she folded her hands over the wooden handle and watched me come.

"What are you doing home at one?" she called when I was within earshot. "Are you feeling okay?"

"Fine." I smiled, hoping that the sentiment reached my eyes.

"I thought you had to work until four."

"I've been skipping lunch breaks, putting in some extra hours."

She buttoned her lip on one side in an expression that I had learned long ago meant she was skeptical of my actions. More likely, she questioned my motives. "What for?"

I laughed. "What is this? twenty questions?"

"Something like that. It's just unlike you to be home in the middle of the day."

"I'd like to talk to you," I said, skipping the trivialities so that I could get straight to the point. "I want to take you out for lunch."

"I already had lunch."

"You did not! You rarely have lunch when we're not home. Maybe an apple or a leftover muffin from breakfast . . ."

"Fine." Grandma leaned against the spade with a resigned sigh. I would've been bothered by her less-than-enthusiastic reception if it hadn't been for the sparkle in her eye. "Let's have lunch. But I don't want to go out. We have finger-lings."

I followed her gaze to the woven basket at her feet and marveled at the modest crop of diminutive potatoes. "I thought we needed to give them a few weeks yet," I mused, bending to select one of the delicate yellow tubes. It was heavy for its size and crusted with a fine layer of dirt as dark and moist as used coffee grounds. I rubbed it off with my thumb.

"I decided to check this morning, and it turns out there are a few ready." Grandma thrust the spade into the hill and came up with a fibrous root system and a harvest of potatoes that clung to the tangled vines like fat fish on a line. "This plant was more decayed than the others, so I dug here. For some reason it matured faster. Must be in just the perfect spot."

"Must be," I parroted, dropping to my knees so she didn't have to. I loosed the potatoes from their moorings and placed them in the basket beside me. "I think that's everything this plant has to offer."

"Good enough. We'll give the rest a bit more time."

In the house, I sent Grandma to go clean up while I prepped the potatoes. They were small, golden cylinders, covered in knots and bumps like the fingers of an arthritic centenarian. I wondered for a brief moment if that was why Grandma loved them so. Maybe they reminded her of my grandfather. Maybe she couldn't hold his hands anymore, but she could harvest little reminders of him every fall.

I scrubbed the potatoes gently and placed them in a pot of cool, salted water. They didn't need much to dress them up—a quick boil and a dollop of Dijon mustard was more than enough to make them delicious. While the water began to simmer, I scoured the fridge and came up with some left-over chicken and enough spinach for two small salads.

By the time Grandma emerged from the bathroom, arms rubbed pink from fingertip to elbow and a bemused look on her face, there were two plates on the table all dressed with a piece of cold barbecue chicken and a pear and spinach salad drizzled in a vinaigrette I had whipped up in less than a minute. In spite of the solemn nature of our impromptu lunch date, I couldn't help but admire my own domesticity. It was impossible to pinpoint the moment I grew up, but it had happened little by little, and I knew that no matter where life took me from here, I would always be equipped to care for my family. Grandma had taught me much.

"The potatoes will be done in a couple minutes," I told her. "They're pretty slender; they shouldn't take long."

"I'm still wondering why you're home," Grandma murmured so softly I wondered if she intended me to hear her or not. She seemed tired to me, as if we were sitting down to a late dinner after a long, exhausting day instead of a quick lunch in the early afternoon.

"I need you," I whispered back.

She either didn't hear me or chose to ignore my comment. I let it pass because I wasn't even sure myself of what I meant by it and moved around the table to pull out a chair for her. At the last second, I found I couldn't let go and ended up holding on to her arm as she lowered herself. My hardy grandmother had never needed assistance before, but this time she didn't shoo me away or cluck at my overbearing attentiveness. In fact, I was troubled by the way she leaned into me, by the sudden give of her knees when she was inches above the uncushioned seat. The tiny sound that escaped her lips when bone hit wood was enough to nick a hole in my heart. I made a mental note to add chair pads to my next Wal-Mart list.

We didn't say much as I drained the potatoes and separated them onto our plates. I grabbed mustard, salt, and pepper and poured tall glasses of cold milk. The entire time I bustled around the kitchen, I watched Grandma out of the corner of my eye. Her blinks were long, her head heavy. I almost wanted to skip lunch altogether and tuck her into bed.

I held her hand as I recited the Lord's Prayer, feeling the fragility of her bone-thin fingers and wondering when my invincible grandmother had gotten so old. "You shouldn't have been out in the garden," I chastised her after I said *amen*.

"Why not?" She extracted her hand from mine and picked up her knife and fork. The first bite that she brought to her mouth was a sliver of new potato, bare and unadorned, still steaming.

"You seem really tired today."

"I'll take a nap after lunch."

"Do you usually nap in the afternoons?"

Grandma's timid shrug was enough to tell me that regular naps weren't the only secret she was keeping from me.

"I'm glad you sleep," I told her. "If you're tired, I want you to rest."

"I don't sleep for long."

"Of course not."

I almost broached the topic of her health then and there, forsaking my reason for coming home early. But Grandma didn't let me. "So," she said, touching the corner of her mouth with a napkin, "to what do I owe the pleasure of your company this afternoon?"

For days I had been planning what I would say, practicing the words so that they would slip over my tongue like warm tea. It would be easier for her, I reasoned, if I was calm, confident. But the house was unnaturally quiet, and Grandma's gaze inescapably weary. It scared me. I didn't mean to, but I blurted out, "I don't know what to do."

"About Michael?"

And then I had no choice but to say his name. "No. About Parker."

I expected her brow to tighten in confusion, but the way my lips formed the syllables of his nickname—as if I were holding shards of glass in my mouth—told her everything she needed to know.

"Daniel's father?"

"Yes," I whispered.

"But I thought—"

"We've been in contact," I interrupted, my words coming in a sudden rush. "He e-mailed me, and it was . . . not awful. It was nice. He apologized, and I felt sorry for him, so I wrote him back. Then he sent me another message and I sent him one, and it's been going on for almost three weeks."

"You've been talking to him for three weeks?" Grandma's appetite must have left her because she pushed the plate away from her and put her hands on the table palms down. I assumed she did it to steady herself, but she began to run her fingers over the worn wood grain, tracing patterns and fitting her fingernails into divots where life had scarred our gathering place. If I didn't know better, I would've thought that she hoped to divine answers from the knots and whorls.

"Not talking, not exactly . . ." I trailed off, but she didn't prod me further, and I found myself rambling on. Telling her everything. Who Parker was, how we met. Why I thrilled at his attention in the beginning, and why I loathed him by the end. How Daniel reminded me of his dad every day. "But Parker has no right to Daniel," I said, shaking my head as if to clear it. "He's no daddy."

"Yet he is Daniel's father," Grandma reminded me. Her first words in several minutes were the five-pointed tips of a throwing star. I had read once that the Japanese called their tiny weapons *shuriken*, "sword hidden in the hand." And though I knew that my grandmother meant no harm, it pierced me to hear her say the very thing I feared.

I had known the truth before, pressed it down deep and

tried to ignore it, but I could disregard it no more: Patrick Holt was about to reenter my life.

"I don't know if I can do this," I breathed.

Grandma raised her hand to my face and let her fingertip trace my hairline, the curve of my jaw. She said simply, "You have to."

all this time

GRANDMA AND I AGREED on one thing when it came to Parker: I would never offer more than he asked. It wasn't my responsibility to draw him in, to convince him that Daniel needed to know his biological father. It wasn't my place to facilitate a loving father-son relationship. That one small concession was like a burden lifted; it gave me a reason to hope.

After our lunchtime conversation, I found myself praying without ceasing. Wasn't that the sort of devotion I longed to achieve? And yet I knew that my desperate entreaties weren't exactly the sort of communication God wanted from me. *Don't let Parker ask; don't let Parker ask . . .* hardly constituted meaningful interaction.

It didn't work anyway.

Parker e-mailed me one more word on Saturday afternoon. *Please?* I knew precisely what he meant.

I endured a sick, gut-twisting feeling that left me breathless and dry-mouthed while Parker and I worked out the details. He offered to call me, had the gall to actually ask for my phone number, but instead of giving him the satisfaction of such an intimate connection, I insisted on continuing our pithy e-mail exchange.

In response to his monosyllabic plea, I wrote, *Next week Saturday, 10:00, Fox Creek Park, Mason, Iowa.* I had no idea where Parker lived or if it was even possible for him to make such a set rendezvous. Frankly, I didn't care. If he wanted to make it, he would. If not, I had my answer.

He wrote back, *Where's Mason?*

Google it.

Does Daniel know?

I wasn't entirely sure what Parker expected Daniel to know, but since my innocent five-year-old was in the dark about both his biological father and our developing plans, I answered, *No.*

Can we talk about this? May I have your phone number?

No.

Parker was silent then for nearly twenty-four hours, and I

started to believe that he would simply call the whole thing off. Claim that he was busy or too far away or not quite ready to take such a huge leap. But when I checked my e-mail at work on Monday morning, his final reply was waiting.

See you then.

The rest of the week was a nightmare of paradoxes. One day flew by so fast, I felt as if I suffered from vertigo—my whole world seemed to spin off-balance. But the next day dragged, each minute heaving itself forward in lurches and stops that made me certain time was an old man indeed. A decrepit old man, walker-dependent and arthritis-ridden.

Even looking at Daniel was an agonizing experience. A single glance at my towheaded son was enough to ensure my heart broke down the same hairline fissure that had carved my soul in two all those years ago. One side argued with the other, assuring me that my son would never forgive me if I kept him from the man who gave him life. But the very same heartbeat produced a toxin of fear and anger, a poisonous cocktail that made my blood run hot at the nerve of this shiftless, irresponsible, good-for-nothing deserter. What right did he have to infringe upon our lives?

It was hard for me to mask my emotions, and Michael noticed the change in my attitude the very first time we spoke after my plans with Parker were finalized. As the weekend loomed nearer and nearer, my boyfriend seemed unable to talk about much beyond my obvious distraction during our daily telephone conversations.

"Are you sure you're okay?" he asked, the wearied question beginning to sound like the refrain of a broken record.

"I told you, I'm fine. Just busy."

"Do you really think school is the best thing for you right now?"

I rolled my eyes, thankful that we had never figured out the Skype thing and he couldn't see me. "School is exactly right for me. Child psychology is fascinating so far."

"You've only had one class."

"And already I feel like a better mom to Daniel and Simon."

"After one class?"

I mustered up a laugh but it was choked and short-lived. "I have an amazing professor."

Michael sighed. "If you think you can handle it all . . ."

"I can."

"Just don't overdo it, Jules. You don't have to do everything. You don't have to be Superwoman."

"I'm not trying to be Superwoman."

"Hey." Michael's voice was soft, appeasing. "You don't have to get all defensive. I'm just worried about you."

"I know."

"You seem tense. Preoccupied. I'm trying to help."

"I know you are." I flopped back on my bed, draping an arm over my forehead to muffle the dull throb that had started in my temples. "I don't mean to be short with you."

"It's okay. We haven't seen each other for a while."

"Too long."

"I wish I was there."

"Me too."

"I'd give you a back rub."

That made me smile. In one of Michael's anatomy courses the professor had given his students an impromptu primer on therapeutic massage. How to loosen pressure points, where a firm, slow hand could release all the tension in tight shoulders. I had wanted to send the thoughtful professor a handwritten thank-you note. With flowers and chocolates.

"That sounds amazing," I sighed. "I could use a back rub."

"I'd love to be of service."

But Michael was hundreds of miles away, and I had to face Parker alone. Without a stress-relieving backrub or even a quick hug of solidarity, of encouragement.

While the week before my meeting with Parker was long and unseasonably hot, Saturday dawned crisp and cool, the very first day that actually felt like autumn. Summer had been hesitant to release its grip, but there was a freshness in the air when I woke on Saturday morning that made me think of pumpkins and bonfires and the sweaters I had packed away in a cedar chest at the foot of my bed. I embraced the drop in temperature, the brittle edge to the morning that left beads of dewy condensation on the inside of my slightly cracked window. I loved the way my skin prickled in the cool air, the way my muscles tightened to resist a shiver. I loved the way it all made me feel invigorated, alive.

I figured I needed that sharpness, that clarity, to face Parker.

The light breeze coming in from my window convinced me to undo the latches on my cedar chest and retrieve a sweater for my meeting with Daniel's dad. I dug around for exactly the right one, a charcoal cable knit with three-quarter-length sleeves and a small row of buttons from the collar to the left shoulder. It was a designer brand, perfectly formfitting and flirting with the fine border of sexy. I had purchased it on clearance in the off-season, but it made me feel worth every penny of the original price tag. I paired the sweater with vintage-washed jeans, a secondhand store find that had tiny, intentional rips in all the right places. Jeans and a sweater: my version of a power suit.

I put my makeup on in the quiet of a sleeping house, taking extra time to try to mimic the smoky-eye look I had seen perfected on the pages of a magazine. It wasn't a terrible attempt, but nothing to write home about either, and I decided to go with carefully tousled hair to match my darker-than-usual eyes. The end result was a little surprising. I looked ageless somehow, attractive in a beguiling, almost-mysterious way. It was my intention to shrug off the soccer mom impression that I was sure I emanated like cheap perfume. My efforts were undeniably successful. The woman who emerged from the bathroom was striking. Maybe even alluring.

It occurred to me as I stared at my reflection in the mirror that I wanted Parker to find me attractive. Not because

I longed for his attention now, but because I wanted him to regret what he had done. I wanted him to see me and instantly know that I had survived without him—and managed well, thank you very much. Though I had nothing to base my insecurities on, I imagined that he pitied me, the poor, single mom who had to slug it out on her own. But I didn't want his pity; I wanted his admiration. I wanted his respect.

Turning to survey the fit of my hand-me-down jeans, I decided Parker would have no choice but to appreciate who I was. What I had become. Or at the very least, he'd have to admit that I had aged well.

When I emerged from the bathroom, my family was gathered in the living room watching Saturday morning cartoons. Simon claimed he was too old for such silliness, but even Grandma liked to watch the kids on *The Electric Company* spin literacy facts and concepts against a hip-hop, urban backdrop. For weeks after an episode about silent letters and how they work, we all walked around the house singing, "'Silent E is a ninja . . .'"

Grandma looked up from the opening scene just as a curly-haired character yelled, "Hey, you guys!"

"You going to watch with us?" she asked, a glint in her eye. But as her gaze took in my outfit and each carefully fingered strand of hair, the lines of her brow hardened. She remembered.

"Not today," I told her. "We have to be at the park by ten."

"Are you still planning on me coming with you?" Grandma pushed herself up from her chair, assuming the answer before I voiced it.

"I was hoping so."

"I'll just take the boys to the pond for a while?"

"That's the idea." I led the way into the kitchen and began rummaging through the refrigerator for breakfast fare. We had plenty of time, but for some reason I felt rushed, uptight. "Cereal?"

Grandma shook her head. "Let's go to Lily's. The boys will enjoy getting out of the house." She continued as if our discussion of the morning's events hadn't dissolved. "And you want me to stay at the pond for . . . ?"

"I don't know. A half hour or so? Just keep them occupied until I'm ready for Daniel. I want to talk to Parker before he meets our son." I coughed a little, almost choking on the unexpected pairing of the words *our* and *son*. It was such a small thing, two insignificant syllables that seemed meaningless apart but hinged together had the potential to transform our lives. I wanted to take a screwdriver to the axis, the place where the words fit into one. But the link was fixed.

"I'll watch for you," Grandma said, reassuring me with a nod. "I'll know when you're ready for him."

"What about Simon?"

"We'll have a little alone time." A soft smile lit Grandma's face at the thought.

"Are you going to tell him?"

"About Patrick?" Grandma insisted on calling Parker by his given name. "Maybe. It depends on whether or not Simon asks."

"He'll ask."

"Maybe. Maybe not. He's not one to pry."

I gave her a quizzical look.

"Perhaps *pry* isn't the right word. But I think you know what I mean. Simon sees things that other people miss, and yet he's not pushy or aggressive. He holds his cards close."

Grandma was right, but it still concerned me that the sudden advent of Daniel's biological father might prove difficult for Simon. My brother, the boy whose mother left him and whose father he barely knew. The young man who couldn't help feeling like an outsider in our family, no matter how hard we tried to convince him he belonged.

"Simon is strong," Grandma assured me. "If we need to, we'll work through it together."

I tried to be optimistic, but as we ate thick slices of sweet bread in the warm comfort of Lily's tiny dining room, I couldn't deflect the insidious thoughts that crept through my mind. *Daniel won't understand* was the first phantom whisper to make my heart pound with nauseating irregularity. Then, *This will ruin Simon. Parker will be the end of us.*

By the time I glanced at my watch and realized it was too late for me to change my mind and back out, I was so queasy with dread, I was ready to go home and leave Parker empty-handed. Wasn't that exactly what he deserved?

But Grandma was my backbone when my own resolve failed me. "Everything is going to be just fine. Things will work out for the best," she declared as if claiming it could make it so.

"What's going to be fine?" Simon piped up.

I opened my mouth to say something, anything—to lie if I had to—but Grandma cut in before I could do any damage.

"Julia is meeting an old friend this morning. They're going to spend a little time together at the park, and I'm taking you boys to play by the pond."

"Did you put my nets in the trunk?" Daniel chirped, ecstatic at the thought of digging around in the stagnant, shallow pond that bordered the northwest edge of Fox Creek Park. I thought it was overgrown and disgusting, but the dirty pool harbored all manner of insect, amphibian, and boy-beloved creatures.

"I've got the nets," Grandma said. "And some canning jars and your magnifying glass, too."

"Yippee, plankton," Simon muttered.

"I know!" Daniel howled. "Maybe we'll find a water bear this time!"

"More likely we'll pick up a couple dozen flatworms."

"You think so?"

I watched as Simon turned his sour expression on Daniel. But my little boy's face radiated nothing but hope, and in the end, Simon gave his nephew's shoulder a shove and grinned. "I'll help you find a tardigrade."

"What's a tardy-gray?" Daniel asked.

"A water bear. If you're going to be a scientist, Danny, you've got to know the terminology."

"Terminology?"

"Whatever."

We drove the few short blocks to the park in a flurry of excitement. Daniel couldn't stop plotting his water excavation, and Simon offered his brand of sage, brotherly advice. My own heart was a riot of emotions, and I was grateful that the boys were so enraptured with their adventure that they didn't have time to notice my distress.

As we pulled into the circular driveway of the park, I scanned the blacktopped parking spaces for signs of an unfamiliar car. My breath left me in a hiss when I realized Parker was already there. His vehicle wasn't the rusted-out pickup truck I remembered, but the new-looking sports coupe reeked of Parker. Who else would drive an immaculate silver Audi with out-of-state plates?

I pulled to the side of the one-way road and leaned over the backseat. "This is your stop, boys," I croaked, praying my voice didn't betray me.

"You can't park here," Daniel chastised me.

"I'm not going to park here; I'm just letting you out. It's closer to the pond—you won't have to walk so far."

"Grab your stuff, boys," Grandma called, opening her door and stepping out.

Simon and Daniel slammed their own doors and raced

for the trunk. I popped it and heard their mad scramble for supplies.

"It's going to be just fine," Grandma whispered, leaning down through her open door. "I'll be covering you in prayer the whole time."

"I'll need it." My voice was barely audible, less than a whisper.

Grandma didn't argue.

The short drive to Parker's car was an infinity of speculation. My mind skittered through a dozen different scenarios, a hundred, and I even entertained the hope that I was wrong and it wasn't Parker's Audi. But as I pulled up a few spaces from the shiny, metallic bumper, I could see a man sitting behind the driver's seat. Watching me.

It was him.

I switched off the ignition, took a long, steadying breath, and forced myself to step from the car.

He was already out of his seat, closing the space between us. "Julia," he said.

It was a blow to see him. A mind-numbing, skin-tingling jolt to my soul. Parker hadn't changed much in the years since I had known him. He was still tall, still angular, still arresting with eyes the color of an iceberg beneath the water. But his hair was shorter, shaded with caramel instead of sand. His step was as sure as I remembered, but he seemed burdened somehow, like he carried extra weight beneath the straight line of his fine suede jacket. Maybe he was wearing a bulletproof vest, a line of defense between the frailty of his humanity and the depth of my anger.

And I was angry. Angry-scared. A bewildering mix of panic and regret and worry. I wondered if he could see it in my face.

"Julia," he said again, stopping a pace away. It looked for a moment like he was going to reach for me, offer a handshake or maybe even a hug, but instead he lifted his hands as if he didn't know what to do with them. It was a gesture of surrender, a shrug that encompassed all that had happened yet accounted for none of it. Parker looked at his palms, the guilt I imagined etched there, and then tucked his fists self-consciously in his pockets. It seemed there was nothing more to say.

I stared at him, shocked at his inability to speak. Wasn't this what he had wanted? a meeting? a chance to talk about what had happened? to meet his son? I wasn't going to give up anything until he asked for it. Begged for it.

The silence stretched taut between us, a thin line of unease that made my bones ache from the strain of waiting. I almost turned around and got back into my car. Almost. But something in Parker's face—the downturn of his mouth, the way his eyes couldn't quite hold mine, the smile lines that had begun to soften the hard planes of his chiseled features, to gently age him—held me back. Whatever he couldn't bring himself to say, I wanted to hear it. And though my hand itched with the desire to slap his perfectly formed cheek, from somewhere hidden deep inside rose a fleeting wish to cup it. To lay my fingers against the warmth of his skin.

I trembled at the thought. Crossed my arms over my chest.

Finally, Parker sucked in a mouthful of air and gulped it down with the relish of someone who hadn't breathed in many long moments. It must've emboldened him because he pulled his hands out of his pockets and leaned toward me. He didn't approach me, didn't seem quite brave enough to diminish the gap between us, but he did attempt a smile.

"After all this time . . . ," he whispered. "It's good to see you."

origins

My legs were beginning to tremble, a subtle shiver
of motion that matched the breeze lifting the soft fringe of
leaves above us. It seemed like the whole world was dancing
a waltz, a gentle, rising sway that made me feel off-balance,
dizzy.

"Would you like to sit?" Parker asked, inching yet a little
closer.

I didn't say anything but turned and carefully led the way
to a bench tucked in a copse of paper birches. The small stand
of trees looked old and tired, the white sheets of their bark

yellowed and curled like the pages of a discarded manuscript.
A sad story, irrelevant and useless, not worth the breath it
would take to repeat it. But hadn't I believed that our tale—
Parker's and mine—had reached an end? Yet here we were
unearthing a worn narrative, dusting it off, starting anew.
The thought made me want to touch the thin scrolls of bark,
to press the long fragments back against the trunk where they
belonged. Or to take an axe to each narrow base, leaving
nothing but stumps. Some stories were best left untold.

The bench seemed small to me, and I sat as far to one side
as I could get without slipping off the hard edge. Parker took
his cue from my stiff movements and gave me space, allowing
just enough room between us for another. For Daniel.

"So . . ." Parker cupped his hands as if he was cold and
stole a glance at me out of the corner of his eye. "How have
you been?"

It was a strange question. Too innocuous, too normal. But
where else were we supposed to start? "Good," I said, testing
my voice. To my surprise, it worked. I sounded like myself.
"I've been great, actually. I have a good job. An amazing family. I'm back in school."

"I'm glad to hear that. You always were bright."

Parker's faint praise felt patronizing. As if he had any right
to assess my intellect. In his first e-mail he had made a point
of telling me about his successful career as a chemical engi-
neer at a biomedical corporation. It felt like a little stab, a
small way of rubbing my face in the fact that he had achieved

his dream while mine was tossed out with the hundreds of diapers I'd changed. I might not have realized my university goals, but surely I had other things he didn't. Of their own accord, my eyes fastened on his powerful hands, studied the long fingers, the clean, pale palms of a white-collar worker. There was no ring.

I tried to squelch my petty desire to hurt him, but I found myself blurting out, "And I have a wonderful boyfriend. I'm sure we'll be married soon."

I regretted the words the second they were out of my mouth. *"I'm sure we'll be married soon"?* I sounded like a child, a grasping, desperate little girl. I might as well have stuck out my tongue and said, *Nah-nah.*

"That's . . . great," Parker muttered. He looked me in the eye and smiled weakly, but I thought it was forced and insincere.

For a moment I believed his obvious disappointment was about me—about the reality that I, his former friend and lover, was off-limits. But then his gaze slid beyond me and he squinted in the direction of the pond, past the small grove of trees that blocked our view. Understanding washed over me. Parker had caught a glimpse of Daniel as he left the car with Simon and Grandma. And he was saddened by the thought that the child he fathered already had a dad—or almost did—not that I would soon have a husband.

I expected Parker to broach the topic of our son right then and there, but he held himself in check. Abandoning the futile search for his long-lost offspring, he sat back and slapped his hands on jean-clad thighs. "Well, I'm glad to hear that you've done so well. That you're happy. And I'm sorry to barge into your life like this. My e-mail must have been a shock."

"That's a bit of an understatement."

"I'm grateful you agreed to see me. Really, I am. You didn't have to."

"I know."

Parker's chin tilted as he studied me, throwing his head back just enough to remind me of the arrogant twentysomething he had been so long ago. Much of that conceit seemed muted now. The truth was, there was something subdued and almost quiet about him as he sat beside me. Older, wiser, maybe even gentle in a learned, practiced way. The Parker I had known would not have been so patient and apologetic.

"Thank you," he said, surprising me.

At first I wondered if my thoughts had been voiced aloud, but then I realized that he meant, *"Thank you for agreeing to see me."* Grandma had taught me to be polite, and "You're welcome" slipped out before I could imagine how silly it sounded.

"I'm sure you'd like to know a bit about me," Parker offered, shifting in his seat. His tone changed just enough to alert me that what he was about to say was a practiced monologue. I wondered whom else he had given his spiel to. "It's a bit of a long story," he continued, "but I won't bore you with all the gory details. Suffice it to say, I started a company about a year ago that develops purified research proteins for pharmaceutical markets. It's a fairly small operation right now, but the demand is great and we're expanding rapidly."

I nodded and hoped he wouldn't realize that I had no idea what he was talking about. Biomedical engineering was once my major, after all. The thought made me cringe. It was hard to grasp that the man before me was the boy who had once been my statics TA. Someone I trusted. Someone who was supposed to have my best interests at heart.

"It's really exciting stuff." Parker smiled, and this time it was sincere. "We're isolating and purifying animal proteins for use in human pharmaceuticals. The industry is limitless. It's mind-boggling."

"Absolutely," I agreed. But I cared little about his professional life. "Where do you live?" I blurted out, startling myself with the mundane question. And yet his answer mattered much to me.

"In Minnesota. About two hours from here. It's a little town called New Elm."

"Seems like a strange place for a biomedical company."

"Not really. We're in the heart of agricultural America. Since we work primarily with porcine, bovine, and equine hormones, we have easy access to our supply source. Really, I could set up a lab anywhere."

Anywhere. It was an ominous thought. Mason was anywhere. What if he wanted to set up a lab here? to be close to Daniel? I shivered.

"Are you cold?"

"A little," I lied because I didn't want him to know that he was making me quiver.

Parker's coat was off before I could raise a finger in protest.

"No," I rushed to deter him. "No, keep it. I don't need a coat." I almost said, *I don't need your coat,* but I stopped myself in time.

"It's no problem," Parker said, settling the expensive jacket over my shoulders. "I have a sweater on and I'm hot anyway."

I didn't see any way I could shrug off the coat without seeming totally petty and ungrateful. So I left it where it was, the smooth collar against the skin of my neck, the scent of his earthy cologne rising from the luxurious leather in a light cloud of masculinity. He had reverted to his earlier, distant position, but I couldn't shake the feeling that Parker was touching me, that his hand was against the arc of my warm collarbone.

"No significant other?" I asked, praying my voice wouldn't falter over the three simple words.

"No." Parker's answer was absolute, rimmed by something that smacked of bitterness.

We sat there for a minute or two in silence, our disjointed conversation lying in ruins at our feet. Our words seemed like the spent arrows of a tired battle, the sort of war that no one cared to wage. We had thrown listless gauntlets down, but it was already over. We had done our part and I could think of nothing else to say to prevent the inevitable. Any moment he would ask to see Daniel, and I felt like I had no choice but to acquiesce. Hadn't I implied as much in my e-mail? Didn't Grandma think it was the right thing to do?

"Daniel doesn't know who you are." The confession spilled off my tongue, delivering a final, devastating blow.

"I didn't expect him to," Parker admitted, but he sounded sad anyway. "Who should we tell him I am?"

"A friend. You're an old friend."

"But I'm not just a friend, Julia."

"It's enough for now," I said definitively. There was no room for discussion on this matter. "He's five years old. You can't just magically appear one day and expect to be his daddy. He's lived a lot of life without you."

"I know."

"What do you want?" I demanded, desperate to finally know. "Do you want to see him and leave? Do you think you have a claim to him? a shot at partial custody or something like that?"

Parker looked taken aback. "No, nothing like that. Like either of those things. I'm not here to satisfy some morbid curiosity. And I don't have any intention of taking your son away. I'm no father."

I wanted to shout, *Amen!* but I merely stared at him, looking for a reason to believe what he was saying.

"I just want to meet him." All at once Parker seemed lonely. Sad. "And if it's okay with you, I'd like to see him again. And maybe again. And someday, if you're ready for it and if he's ready for it . . . I'd like him to know I'm his dad."

"I'm not ready for that."

"I don't think I am either. But we can take it a day at a time."

I narrowed my eyes at him, dialed up my mommy meter to high. "Are you a good man, Patrick Holt? Do I even want you in my son's life?"

Parker shook his head, but his gaze never left mine. "What do you want me to say? that I don't gamble, smoke, or womanize? that the only drinking I do is the occasional beer with the guys? I wash behind my ears, Julia, and I've never stolen a thing in my life. I even believe there is a God. I don't know if I'm good. But I try."

It was the most honest answer I could have hoped for.

"I'll go get him," I whispered.

I tingled all over when I pushed myself off the bench, but it was an empowering feeling. A shot of pure adrenaline. I had no idea how Daniel would react or if Parker planned on keeping his word, but I sent an insistent prayer heavenward as my feet swept through the grass, and I believed that my plea was heard. Parker wasn't the monster I had envisioned he would be, and in many ways I felt as if I had the upper hand. If I could handle this, I could handle anything.

"Lord willing," I whispered.

Grandma spotted me long before I ever made it to the pond and raised her hand in greeting, in blessing. I wasn't quite ready to talk to her, so I stopped where I was and wrapped my arms around me to watch Daniel come. From the droop of his shoulders I could tell that he was arguing with Grandma, that he was more interested in continuing his search for water bears than abandoning the swampy mess so he could spend time with Mom's old friend. I didn't blame him. But for some reason he was more apt to obey his grandmother, and in no time at all, Daniel was scrambling up the hill from the water's edge.

"Hey, buddy," I said, pulling him into a tight hug when he was within arm's reach. "Did you have fun?"

Daniel wiggled out of my embrace and gave me a scathing look designed to send me on an extended guilt trip. "I don't want to meet your boring friend."

I should have reprimanded him, but the poor kid had no idea what he was getting into. "How do you know he's boring?"

A one-armed shrug was Daniel's only reply.

I should have told my son to be nice to Parker, to be polite, but a part of me wanted my son's absentee father to see him exactly as he was. No special manners, no affected niceties that would fade the moment we got in the car and pulled away from the park. Daniel was a kindergartner, a little boy who belched at the table, thought farts were hysterically funny, and more often than not forgot to say please and thank you. Parker was about to get a dose of reality—life with children was never easy or neat.

Daniel sulked all the way back to the bench where Parker

and I had fumbled our way through introductions and casual revelations. I was both relieved and disappointed to find that Parker still perched on the uncomfortable seat, his back ramrod straight and his head held high. Even from a distance, I could see that anxiety emanated from his every pore—there was a fine mist of tension around him that was almost palpable.

"That's him," I said when we were still far enough away to speak without being heard.

"Why are you wearing his coat?" Daniel asked.

I had forgotten that the suede jacket still covered my shoulders. Slipping out from underneath the lightweight proximity of *him*, I caught the coat in the crook of my arm. "I was cold. I'm not anymore."

Parker either heard us or sensed our approach because he rose from the bench and turned to face us. We were mere feet away, and I could see something rush across his features, a mutiny of emotions, a tangle of hopes and dreams and fears and regrets. It looked for a moment like he might cry; the corner of his mouth shook for a split second, but then he composed himself and stepped forward with a smile.

"You're tall," Daniel said.

It was two words, but by the way Parker reacted, you'd think Daniel had shouted, *"I love you."* Parker's eyes lit up and he laughed out loud. A resonant, genuine laugh that was like nothing I had ever heard from his lips. He stared at Daniel, taking him in with long, hungry gulps of concentration as if he were memorizing every hair follicle, every nuance of movement and personality. "I am tall," he eventually agreed. "And so are you. You must be, what, seven or eight?"

Daniel grinned. "I'm five."

"Five? I can hardly believe that. You look much older than five."

As I watched my son swell with pride, I tried to reconcile my preconceived notions about Parker and his qualifications for fatherhood with reality. He was good with kids. I knew it in less than a minute. Innate child appeal is one of those things you either have or you don't, and Parker had it in spades. Already I could see that Daniel was forgetting about the pond and his quest for water bears.

"I'm pretty smart, too," Daniel told his new friend. "My teacher says I have a big imagination."

"I'm sure you do." Parker closed the chasm between us and extended his hand to Daniel like a true gentleman. "My name is Patrick Holt," he told his son with all the formality of a stranger, "but you may call me Parker."

"Hi, Parker. I'm Daniel Peter DeSmit, but you can call me Daniel. Simon calls me Danny sometimes, but I don't like it."

"Daniel it is, then," Parker said amiably, but his brow furrowed in confusion at the mention of Simon. "And Simon is . . . ?"

"Simon is my younger brother," I cut in. "He's ten. He lives with us." It was enough of an introduction for now. I wasn't willing to let Parker in any farther than need be.

"Yeah, Simon is my uncle, but really he's like my brother."

"You're a lucky boy," Parker declared. "I'd like to meet your brother sometime."

"You can right now," Daniel said, taking Parker by the hand. "He's down by the pond with Grandma."

The pure shock on Parker's face was altogether authentic. I didn't know if he was moved by the feeling of Daniel's hand in his, by the innocent trust of a little boy who had nothing to doubt or fear, or if he was afraid of offending me, of wading in too deep on his very first meeting. In all honesty, I was just as stunned as he was. I hadn't expected Daniel to be so friendly, nor had I planned on introducing Parker to the entire family on our very first awkward meeting. I floundered for something to say, some way to discourage Daniel's ingenuous idea.

"Honey," I called, jogging a little to catch up, for they were already several paces away. "I don't think that's such a good idea. Parker has to leave pretty soon and we don't want him to get his nice clothes dirty."

"We're hunting for water bears," Daniel informed Parker as if he hadn't heard me. "I've never seen one before, but I brought my magnifying glass just in case."

"Tardigrades?" Parker asked. "Oh, you can't see those with a magnifying glass, I'm afraid. They're microscopic."

Daniel whirled to face the man whose hand he still held. "What?" he screeched. "I've been hunting water bears for nothing?"

I tried to get Parker's attention so I could put an end to this runaway train of scheming and bonding. But he was wholly fixed on Daniel; I wasn't entirely sure he knew I was even there.

"You can see some phytoplankton in pond water, like clumps of algae," Parker explained, "and there are a few platyzoa that are easy to find. Have you ever seen a flatworm?"

"Yes, lots of them," Daniel sang, obviously happy that at least he could claim some knowledge of his adored pond life.

"Did you know that if you cut a flatworm in half, each half will grow into a new worm?"

Daniel looked awestruck. He dropped Parker's hand and gaped at him with the sort of wonderment that he usually reserved for superheroes and Grover. It was unsettling. I went to stand behind him and placed my hands on his shoulders protectively.

"Mom," he gushed, "did you know that you can cut flatworms in half?"

"Yeah, sweetheart, I did know that. But I don't think that now is the time to—"

"Mom." Daniel spun in my hands and wrapped his fingers around my wrists. He gave me his best puppy-dog eyes and said, "Please, can Parker help me find some flatworms? He knows all sorts of stuff about . . ." He searched for the complicated vocabulary that Parker had used and came up blank. "About water stuff."

I shifted my gaze to Parker and saw the hope in his eyes, the raw longing to connect with his unknown son in this particular way. It had never occurred to me before that Daniel was a scientist in the making. The constant parade of worms and frogs and snakes and pond life . . . He took after his father in more ways than his appearance.

"Okay," I murmured, the word falling from my lips like a sour pit. I said it quickly—spat it out, really—before I could change my mind.

Parker looked as if he could kiss me, but he tore himself from my troubled stare and bent to address Daniel. "I have a microscope in my trunk."

"You do?"

"I'm a scientist," Parker said, clearly savoring the word and loving the effect it had on his son.

"A scientist?"

"Yeah, I study this stuff. And you'll never believe this, but I have slides and dyes and all sorts of stains in a box, and we can use them on the critters we find."

"Critters?"

"Critters, creatures, pond flora and fauna . . . you know, like water bears."

"Think we'll find a water bear?" Daniel's joy was almost uncontainable.

"We'll try."

Without a backward glance, Daniel raced off in the direction of the pond, whooping as he went. There was a vacuum in his absence, as if Parker and I were left in the afterburn of our son's excitement, singed by the ferocity of his delight and the thrill of young discovery. But it was more than that, and we both knew it.

"Wow," Parker whispered. He looked deflated, emptied of every secret wish and expectation he had harbored at the thought of finally meeting his son. But he didn't seem spent, merely lovesick and poured out, ready to be filled up.

I wanted to ask him what he meant by *"Wow,"* but I already knew. I imagined he was feeling the same thing I felt when they delivered that tiny infant into my arms over five years before. Back then, Daniel was a stranger to me, an unknown entity, a mystery. But I loved him the moment I laid eyes on him, and I knew without a doubt that Parker could now say the same. It was written all over his face.

"I guess you'd better go get your microscope," I whispered around the knot in my throat. But Parker didn't notice. He was already on his way to the silver Audi.

I stood by myself in the middle of the park and clutched Patrick Holt's suede coat to my chest as if it were an anchor, a weight that pulled me beneath the surface of water so vast and deep that I feared if I went down, I might never be found.

Part 2

trust

"I LIKE HIM," Simon said out of the blue.

We were sitting across from each other at the kitchen table, doing homework on a school night like a typical sibling pair, even though we were anything but. Every once in a while I glanced at him and realized that our youth could have been like this, that we could have been children around the same table, working math equations and reading primer books with our index fingers as a guide beneath each boldfaced word. In a different life. Now I was more his mother than his sister, a woman already rocketing past her prime. A woman who found herself doing the schoolwork of an eighteen-year-old and the housework of a middle-aged mom. I rubbed my eyes with my knuckles and stifled a groan. Abandoning my chart of Maslow's hierarchy of needs, I tried to focus on Simon.

"Pardon me?" I asked.

"I like Parker."

"You do?" I tried not to sound too surprised, but Simon's smirk reminded me that I wasn't very good at hiding my emotions.

"I do. He doesn't treat me like a kid."

Since our initial meeting at the park, Parker had made the trek to Mason two more times, and each visit only endeared him more to the boys I considered my own. I had protested his sudden overinvolvement, but it was hard to prevent his visits when Simon and Daniel longed for his attention. It galled me. One pond-side encounter and Parker was a hero in my home. Granted, his on-the-spot laboratory setup and kid-friendly experiments were pretty cool, but I wasn't convinced that scientific know-how should inspire unabashed worship.

And my boys' overinflated opinions were only the beginning of my long record of grievances against Parker. Next on my laundry list of complaints was his second, completely unannounced trek to Mason. He simply showed up on our doorstep exactly one week after he breezed his way back into my life, holding a wrapped package in one hand and wearing a sheepish grin.

"What are you doing here?" I demanded.

"I have a present for Daniel and Simon," he said, rounding his shoulders in what could be interpreted as embarrassment.

"You should have called."

"I know, but I wanted it to be a surprise."

"How did you even find us?"

"Phone book."

Duh. I wanted to snatch the blue-beribboned gift out of his hand and send him home, but before I could drive him away, Daniel realized that we had a guest at the door.

"Simon!" he shouted from the doorway to our drafty mudroom. "Parker's here!"

I didn't stand a chance. Even Grandma seemed somewhat pleased to see him and almost immediately invited Daniel's biological dad to stay for supper. She either didn't see my look of horror or chose to ignore it.

The rest of the afternoon unfolded with all the delight and excitement of a trip to the county fair for my starstruck boys. Parker had brought a special gift indeed, a set of framed digital photographs that showcased the microscope slides the boys had made that day in Fox Creek Park. He regaled us with stories of his artist friend, a man who was intent on making scientific tedium and other so-called thrilling discoveries the foundation of his art. Then Parker helped Daniel and Simon each hang two carefully chosen photographs on the walls of their bedrooms and took them outside to play football on the front lawn while Grandma and I peeled potatoes for a meal I dreaded.

And though I had expected supper to be the epitome of awkward, there was laughter around the table. Then games and stories before bed. Of course, I played games with my boys and read them books, but even *Stuart Little* couldn't compete with the fantastic tales that Parker made up on the spot with promptings and cues that he elicited from the boys. Simon relished throwing wrenches into the story, introducing errant knights in the middle of a baseball narrative and killing off the princess before she could be rescued. Parker laughed at it all, rolling with the punches and earning an uncharacteristic hug from Daniel before he made his way upstairs to bed. Even Simon softened enough to give Parker a pound with his closed fist.

"He's cool," Simon said, dragging me from the memory of that unexpected night to the present reality of my open books, my brother before me.

"Cool," I repeated because I couldn't quite get my mind around the fact that Simon thought Parker was anything but just another guy. Simon had never really warmed up to Michael; in fact, he seemed to avoid contact with older males altogether. As I glanced down at the child psychology book before me, it occurred to me that Simon seemed stuck on the third tier of Maslow's famous pyramid: social needs. Some of the necessary relationships in my brother's unpredictable life had never fully developed. Or even developed at all. Who was a father figure to Simon, to Daniel? I had assumed that it was Michael, but watching Simon across the table made me realize for the first time that maybe my hopes were unfounded.

"Is he coming this weekend?"

It took me a moment to understand that Simon was talking about Parker, not Michael. "No," I said too quickly. "He can't make it down."

"That's too bad." Simon deflated a little and returned to his books with an unenthusiastic air.

"What are you working on?" I tried to change the subject.

"Social studies."

"What are you learning about?"

"The *Mayflower*."

"That sounds interesting."

"Not really." Simon appeared to be immersed in his textbook, but just when I was about to settle back into my own homework, he murmured a question I was wholly unprepared for. "Why don't you like Parker?"

I swallowed. "I do."

"No, you don't. And he's *your* friend. I don't get it."

Sighing, I closed my book with a thump. I had at least another fifteen pages to read and a five-hundred-word summary to write, but I was ruined for homework now. It felt strange to study child psychology out of a book when it was flaunting its many facets and hues right in front of me. I wished Simon had brought all this up at the end of the semester, when I was better equipped to deal with it.

"Parker was my friend," I admitted, choosing my words with such precision, I felt like I was talking in slow motion. "But I haven't seen him in a very long time. We've both changed a lot."

"I haven't seen Janice in a long time, but I'd be happy to see her if she came home."

The contradiction in Simon's confession stopped me cold. I had never before heard him refer to his mom, our mom, as Janice. Even after all the years, the enduring silence, and the gradual sense of abandonment, she had always remained *Mom* to Simon. I had assumed it was his way of keeping her close, of ensuring that her disappearance would remain a temporary state of affairs. At least, in his mind. *Mom just had to step out . . . she'll be back soon.*

But calling her Janice carried a certain weight, an otherwise-unacknowledged admission that maybe, just maybe, she wasn't coming back. It struck me that Simon was beginning to distance himself from her memory. From the hope that she would ever find her way home.

It saddened me somehow that he was ready to give up.

"It's not the same," I said softly. But I didn't know how to make him understand. "For better or worse, Janice will always be your mom. Parker was just a friend. Someone I had only known for a very short time."

"If you love someone, does it matter how long you've known them?"

"I never loved Parker," I clarified, but I knew what he was

thinking: if time was the glue that held people and families together, he had a few more years to log with us before he could be considered part of the DeSmit clan. After all, our histories spanned decades of celebrations and heartbreaks, joys and sorrows. Daniel might be new, too, but he was born into the family. Simon, on the other hand, was a tagalong, like a puppy we had added to our home as an afterthought.

Simon's question was a land mine, the sort of inquiry that I hated fielding as a young mom and purportedly wise older sister. I drew a shaky breath, knowing I had to answer, that I had to come up with something more than *It's not the same.*

"Time is relative," I began, but that was simply too oblique. "No, Simon," I started over, "I don't think it matters how long you've known someone if that person is honest with you. Do you know what I mean? You were a part of my heart from almost the first moment I saw you, and it was because you were yourself—you didn't hide anything from us. It was so easy to fall in love with you. It seemed to happen overnight."

I studied his face, watching his eyes for signs of comprehension. But Simon's features were blank, waiting. I struggled on. "Parker was different. We pretended to know each other, but the truth was we were both hiding things. And because we weren't real, our relationship fell apart when it hit . . . a rough patch. Does that make sense to you?"

"What was the rough patch?" Simon demanded.

He had no idea what he was asking. But what could I

say without sounding like I was shutting him out? *I'll tell you when you're older? You wouldn't understand? It's a secret?* Weren't secrets exactly the thing that brought us here in the first place?

"I'm sorry," I finally said. "That's between me and Parker."

Simon shrugged.

"Look, it's really hard to explain, but I think that love—true love—has a lot to do with vulnerability. Do you know what that means?"

He nodded a little, but I didn't believe him. Intelligent as he was, the concept of laying oneself bare was a notion that I was only just beginning to wrap my own heart around. How could I expect a ten-year-old to know what it meant to be undone before another person? "It's like being really open," I continued. "Not trying to hide who you are—the good stuff and the bad stuff. When you can be that unguarded with someone, I think you can start to form a real relationship."

"And you and Parker didn't have that," Simon finished.

"No. But that doesn't mean I don't like him."

"It just means you don't trust him."

I stared at my little brother, gape-mouthed. *Exactly,* I thought. But I didn't say anything.

"I don't trust Janice either," Simon whispered as if he was sharing the deepest secret of his heart.

"Why not?"

"Because she didn't come back for me."

His voice didn't crack on the words, but I could see his heart break in the reflection of his dark eyes. I didn't know if he wanted me near him or not, but I was drawn to him as surely as if he had reached out to me. Daniel was sound asleep upstairs and Grandma was knitting in her bedroom, so I was sure that no one would interrupt our moment alone, and I didn't stop to think as I rounded the table and pulled a chair next to him. I slid my arms around Simon's waist, half-expecting him to resist, but instead he curled into my embrace, allowing me to transfer his slight, seventy-pound frame to my lap.

We hadn't sat like this since the summer after his first-grade year, when he randomly decided that he was too old for such nonsense. I was bereft of the sweet burden of his little-boy body, the angles and lines of knobby arms and legs and the wild scent of the wind in his hair. But it all came back to me in a rush as Simon bent his head over my shoulder and held on for dear life.

"Oh, honey," I breathed. "I'm so sorry. I'm so, so sorry."

He didn't respond. Didn't cry. Didn't do anything at all. He just held on, and I let him cling to me as if I could keep him afloat.

I wondered if we both would drown.

When Simon was spent, his arms weary of binding us together in the midst of our shared loss, our grief, he just let go. He let his arms drop and stood up, not bothering to glance back at me or even say good night. His head hung as he left the room, and though he tried to hide them, I saw him swipe away the tears that had begun to fall. I ached for my brother with the sort of soul-wrenching sorrow that left me winded and worn.

"I love you, Simon," I said to his stooped back, but I couldn't be sure that he heard me.

Left alone in the kitchen amid the ruins of our impromptu study date, I felt a slow rage begin to simmer inside of me. I might have forgiven Janice for leaving me all those years ago, but I burned with a righteous indignation for the pain she was causing her only son now.

I didn't understand her. I never would. And though I had to just accept the reality of her complete detachment and admit that she would likely never come back for him—for us—the injustice of it all hit me as if I were facing her betrayal for the very first time.

My blood boiled. My heart raced. I had to do something.

I should have resurrected chapter 3 in my textbook and attempted to absorb more about psychosocial development and its emotional and behavioral impact, but I didn't have the heart. Instead, I gathered my notebook, pencils, and the heavy psychology manual in my arms and thrust the entire messy lot into the worn messenger bag I toted to and from class. Then I cleared Simon's side of the table, briefly wondering if I could do his homework for him. But I settled for a quick note to the teacher, a two-line explanation that would hopefully excuse Simon for any work he hadn't completed. It was the least I could do.

The kitchen was clean in a couple of minutes, and I was

left standing in the silent house with no one and nothing for company but the steady tick of the clock above the sink. It was enough to drive me mad.

I wanted to grab Janice by the shoulders and shake her. I wanted to fix everything that was broken in Simon's life. I wanted to be all my boys needed so they wouldn't have to look at Parker with adoration in their eyes. I wanted Michael to marry me and Grandma to live forever and everything—for once—to unfold against the backdrop of a symphony instead of the discordant notes that comprised our DeSmit family sound track. I wanted so much, it felt like an explosion inside me, a relentless breach of self that continued to spill my hopes and dreams and desires like so much debris from all the places I had been torn.

"One little happily ever after," I muttered, my words an angry prayer. "Would that be so hard?"

Heaven was silent.

But I wouldn't be.

It took me a while to remember where I had put it, that fat stack of ridiculous postcards that I had intended to send to Michael one by one. They had slipped my mind until now, but suddenly the Pepto-Bismol–pink pig seemed the perfect way to reach out to Janice, wherever she was. What had started as a joke felt all at once very serious.

The truth was, I couldn't call her. I couldn't visit her or count on her to ever come back to see what had become of the family she left behind. But I had to do something, and when my fingers finally found the smooth cardboard pages in the folds of my purse, I felt a certain rush of satisfaction that my words would find an outlet. No matter how vain or senseless or futile.

You're killing him, I scribbled, not bothering to open with a greeting, some formal salutation. What was I supposed to write? *Dear Mom?*

It's not fair.

You're being selfish.

For once in your life, think about someone other than yourself.

I filled the small space with tiny words, dark scrawls on the white sheet like deep scars that wouldn't fade. I poured out all my frustration and longing and resentment on behalf of a little boy who needed his mommy. On behalf of a grown woman who—though she hated to admit it—still did too.

It was all over in less than ten minutes, but the postcard bore my wrath like a scapegoat. A sacrificial lamb. I stared at it for what felt like forever, memorizing the words and trying to accept that Janice would never read them. But I wrote an address in the appropriate box anyway and hoped that somehow my message would make a difference. That it would find its way into hands that actually cared.

Lord willing, three lines would be enough.

Janice Wentwood
Minneapolis, MN
USA

crash course

"Not this weekend."

"But I have—"

"I'm sorry," I told Parker, pinning the telephone between my chin and shoulder so that I could have two hands free to help Daniel zip up his coat. "It's just not going to work this weekend. I have plans."

"You have plans? Well, maybe I could come and take the boys—"

"No," I interrupted quickly. "Grandma has something special in the works for them. Some other time, okay?"

There was silence on the other end of the line, then a barely concealed sigh. I rolled my eyes. What I wanted to do was give Parker a good tongue-lashing, remind him that he was still in the process of earning his way into Daniel's life. Three quick visits had not secured him a permanent place in our home or our hearts. Well, at least not in mine.

Daniel was looking at me with his best pouting face, bottom lip stuck far out to show me how much he disapproved that Parker would not be visiting on Saturday. I grabbed my son's protruding lip and gave it a little tug.

"Not this time," I reiterated.

"Maybe next week," Parker said.

"Maybe."

Parker said good-bye, but I simply hung up, preferring to keep him dangling on a short string. A small part of me knew that I was being a bit of a sadist when it came to Patrick Holt, but I didn't much care. I wasn't fooled by his bumbling, cap-in-hand routine, as if he were some heart-worn traveler who had been traumatized by the road behind him. He acted as if all he needed was a glass of cold water, a little understanding. I simply didn't buy it.

"Why can't Parker visit this weekend?" Daniel asked the moment I had flipped shut the phone.

"Because Michael's coming!" Though my son was peevish and sulky, I couldn't restrain the joy in my voice. I hoped the reminder of my boyfriend's company would elicit an equally excited reaction from Daniel. But he just looked at me. "Aren't you excited to see Michael?"

Daniel pulled a face. "I guess so. But Parker said he was going to bring a surprise."

"Michael always brings you surprises too."

"Candy or a Matchbox car."

"That's bad?" I lifted Daniel's backpack and slid it over his shoulders. Clicking the chest strap, I bent to give him a kiss on the forehead. "I thought you liked the things Michael brought you."

"I do. But Parker's science stuff is really cool."

"You know, Michael is sort of a scientist too. He's a doctor."

"Not yet," Simon said, ambling into the mudroom as if he had all the time in the world.

"I thought you were outside!" I cried, assessing his unkempt form. His hair was sticking up in a million different directions and his shirt was half-tucked in, half-hanging out over the waistband of his jeans. He was still clutching a pair of clean, balled-up socks in his hand. I stifled the urge to tuck in his shirt for him and spit-style his hair and settled for a verbal warning. "Get a move on, mister. The bus is going to be here in a couple of minutes!"

Simon plopped down in the middle of the floor and proceeded to put on his socks one toe at a time. I tried not to let myself get too irritated as I grabbed his jacket off the hook, fished his tennis shoes out of the box by the door, and located his backpack in the corner by our deep freezer. The frayed bag was unexpectedly heavy, full of books, and my stomach clenched as I turned to confront my brother.

"You said you didn't have any homework."

Simon wouldn't meet my eyes.

"Why did you take all these books home if you didn't have any homework?"

He shrugged.

"Answer me!"

"It's no big deal." Simon yanked his shoelace into a tight knot and stood to grab the backpack from me.

I held it out of reach. "This is unacceptable."

"I forgot."

"How could you forget about a bag full of books?"

"I'll do it tonight."

"It's too late, Simon!"

"I'll tell my teacher I didn't have time."

"You'll lie to her? like you lied to me?"

He stared at the ground, his jaw so tense I could see the thin line of a vein pulsing against his skin. I half expected a trail of steam to slip from between his clenched lips.

"What is going on with you?" I didn't like the way my voice trembled, a mixture of disappointment and incomprehension, bordering on the sort of anger I rarely felt toward my boys. "Simon? Simon! I asked you a question. I expect you to answer me!"

I felt Grandma's presence in the doorway before I saw her. I didn't want to face her, not after she had just caught me yelling at Simon, but she cleared her throat quietly and I had no choice.

"Maybe this conversation is best left for later. The boys are going to miss the bus," Grandma said. Everything about her exuded a sense of calm, of peace.

I exhaled—deflated, really—and realized that I was still holding Simon's bag above my head. Lowering it, I thrust the bulky pack into his hands. "You'd better run," I told them both, avoiding Simon's glower and Daniel's accusatory glare. Grandma's soothing presence made me feel sheepish somehow, but I clung to a sense of self-righteousness. It was my right, my duty, to punish my children, wasn't it? Hadn't Simon lied to me? How in the world did I end up feeling guilty?

A rush of entitlement swept over me and I stepped forward to stop Simon before he slipped out of the door. "We'll talk about this tonight," I told him in my best no-nonsense tone.

He gave a curt nod that I could have interpreted a hundred different ways. Then he was out the door and racing down our driveway at a flat sprint. Daniel struggled to keep up.

"I should have gone to work," I muttered, lamenting the fact that I had banked extra hours so I could take the day off. Although I had wanted the house to be perfect for Michael's visit, a spotless home wasn't worth the headache of clashing with Simon in the early hours of the morning. "Aren't Fridays supposed to be fun? relaxed?"

Grandma laughed from her vantage point in the crooked doorframe. "When there are kids around, I'm not sure anything is ever relaxed. Fun, yes. Relaxed, no."

"Was I wrong to yell at him?" I asked as I leaned against the closed door, anxious to hear her reaction.

Grandma made a little humming sound and tapped her fingers against the hollow at her throat. "I'm not sure you're asking the right question. I don't think it was wrong to yell at Simon, but I'm not sure how right it was."

I narrowed my eyes at her. "You talk in riddles sometimes."

"How effective do you think it was to shout at him like that?"

Though I didn't want to picture Simon's face, I could instantly see the way his features hardened with every word I threw at him. It was as if his defeated expression was imprinted on the back of my eyelids. A reminder of the damage I'd done. I groaned. "What was I supposed to do?"

Grandma smiled a cheerless little smile and turned away from me. As she disappeared into the kitchen, she tossed over her shoulder, "I have no idea."

"You have no idea?" I raced after her, feeling something akin to terror that my sagacious mother figure didn't know how to mother in this situation. Grandma was supposed to be all-wise, all-knowing. Full of answers and advice.

"Parenting is hard, Julia. If you read ten different books, you'll get ten different approaches to discipline. Some say be firm; some say be gentle. Some say spank your kids; others say it's abuse. I don't know what you should have done."

"But you were a mother. You raised Dad. You raised me."

"More or less," she agreed. "But I made a lot of mistakes."

"And I made a mistake with Simon this morning." I pushed a hard breath through my nose and went to the counter to pour myself a second cup of coffee for the day. It was going to be a caffeine-rich weekend, I could tell.

Grandma came to stand next to me and put her hand over the top of my cup, preventing me from adding the thin stream of half-and-half that I liked swirled into my French roast. It wasn't like her to interfere, and I raised my eyes to hers in concern. She looked sad, like she was about to say something that she didn't relish voicing.

"What?"

"You did make a mistake with Simon this morning," Grandma admitted. "But it's not what you think."

"What?" I demanded again.

"You forgot something." She paused, gathered herself as if she knew that her words would hurt. "Honey, you forgot that you're not Simon's mother."

I very rarely got angry with my grandmother, but her one small observation made me instantly combative. "Excuse me?" I whispered, too stunned and defensive to raise my voice. "I know I'm not Simon's mother. Janice is. But in case you haven't noticed, she abdicated that role over five years ago. What would you have me do?"

"We've done the best we can with Simon," Grandma said quickly. "You have. And I think you're a better mother to him than Janice ever was. But he's changing, Julia, and I think he's finally starting to grieve her loss. Haven't you noticed?"

"Of course I've noticed!"

"Then you'll understand why he was so upset when you shouted at him this morning. It was on the tip of his tongue."

"What was?"

"*'You're not my mom.'*"

She was right and I knew it instantly. I could almost hear my wounded brother spitting those ugly words at me. The realization flattened me. I was the woman who took the place of his mom, even if I hadn't asked for the job. I was the physical representation of what could have been and what would never be. When had I become the wicked stepmother?

I sank into a chair, cupping my coffee mug in my palms as if it were a life preserver. As if it could save me. "We are such a mess."

"I don't think so." Grandma shook her head as she sank into the chair opposite me. "More like a work-in-progress. A painting half-done."

"We don't even know who we are," I continued to complain. "We're people living together, trying to make it all fit."

Grandma looked hurt. "We're family, Julia. Don't ever forget that."

I had said it a hundred times, a thousand, and I thought that I believed it. *We are a family.* And yet with Simon's miscalculated resentment still weighting the air with the almost-tangible scent of regret, I couldn't help wondering if I had spent the past five years spinning a web of lies for the sake of my own blissful ignorance. What if I didn't want to face the fact that we were falling apart? that our motherless, fatherless quartet of orphans and widows was slowly unraveling at the seams?

Such words were on the tip of my tongue, such harsh, ugly truths, but before I could give my fears voice, Grandma broke the spell of my self-pity.

"I think we're in good company," she mused, more to herself than me. "Jesus Himself said, 'Whoever does God's will is my brother and sister and mother.' And in Ephesians it tells us that God predestined us to be adopted as His sons and daughters. Sounds like a happy, ever-growing work-in-progress to me." She laughed. "And the family of God includes its share of misfits, outcasts, and sinners."

"You mean there's room for Janice?" I said wryly.

Grandma gave me a stern look, but I saw her bite the inside of her lip to stop a smile.

I sighed. "That's all well and good, but it doesn't help me much with Simon right now. What am I supposed to do?"

"I don't know," Grandma said for the second time that morning. "But we'll figure it out. We'll work through it. How many times have we charted our own path?"

She was right. We were old pros at navigating uncertain territory. But I couldn't help fearing that whatever road we were currently on was doomed to end in disaster—a bridge out, an unexpected cliff, a fall from a staggering, dizzying height.

I could almost feel the impact of the earth.

The house was a hopeless mess. No matter how hard Grandma and I tried to keep up with the boys and their proclivity for clutter, we were always a step behind. I had more than my work cut out for me in vacuuming alone—never mind the dust bunnies lurking on the shelves, the stack of papers and mail that was slowly taking over the counter, and the piles of wash in the laundry room—but I abandoned my domestic duties for an hour so that I could get some fresh air. I didn't even tell Grandma I was going. I just left.

It was a cool day, so still and clear it felt almost surreal. Flocks of birds cut a V-shaped incision in the blue-white flesh of an endless sky, their honks and calls distant but distinct. The leaves underfoot were dry and vibrant, still patterned in hues of ripe wheat and apricot and the color of a geranium in the moment before it spilled petals like drops of blood. Trees stood in various stages of undress, their limbs lithe and ready, waiting for the cold baptism of autumn rain or the quiet consummation of an early winter. A modest blanket of snow to hide their nakedness.

I breathed deeply, took it all in. Sometimes we were already housebound by mid-October, hemmed in by ice or biting winds that howled down from the northwest. But this was my kind of fall, the sort of interim that took me by the hand and led me unsuspecting into the cold. It was a peaceful descent, a slow demise, until one day I woke up and felt trapped. Caged. Claustrophobic.

The eighty acres of our property were divided into two parcels of forty. Though the land wasn't quite separated into perfect squares, the end result was close enough. I had figured out long ago that the front parcel, from the barn to the first of two creeks, was approximately a quarter mile on each side. Most girls—women—my age ran on treadmills in their basements or joined gyms with snappy names and high membership fees. Not me. I walked our land. Twice around the front section was a solid two miles of undulating farmland. I liked the view. I liked reaching the point where the soft rise of our property hid the rest of the farm, and I was alone in the middle of nowhere. Alone in all the world.

I felt like a new person by the time I had two miles beneath my feet, and I returned to the farmhouse with my cheeks stained pink and my fingers numb. But I didn't mind the cold. It was as if I had been scrubbed clean, doused in a tub of ice water that left me sharp and purified. Everything seemed much clearer. If the road we were on was about to hit a dead end, we'd simply turn around. Or start laying new blacktop. It was what we did.

Grandma looked up when I joined her in the laundry room, and I saw the satisfied smile that she tried to hide. She was pulling a load of whites from our ancient dryer.

"I feel like a new person," I told her, bending to take over the task so she wouldn't have to stoop. "It's amazing what a little fresh air will do."

"It's amazing what a little prayer will do."

"I wasn't praying," I admitted, facing her.

She smiled. "I was."

Grandma's prayers or my walk, or a combination of the two, buoyed me as I hustled through the rest of my day. As I dragged our canister vacuum up the stairs, I rehearsed my speech for Simon. I would start off by apologizing for yelling at him, then acknowledge that our situation was something I never imagined I'd have to face. No, that wasn't quite right. I didn't want him to think that his presence in my life was an intrusion, a nightmare. Instead I'd say that I had made some mistakes, and together we could figure it out. I'd mention Janice . . . No, I wouldn't. But maybe I should. Did he want to talk about Janice?

I wound myself in circles trying to piece together exactly the right tone and tenor, but in the end I felt confident that we would be okay. Just like Grandma had said, we'd work through it. But all of that would have to wait. When I saw the boys, I'd give Simon a hug and tell him we'd talk later because Michael was scheduled to arrive shortly after Daniel and Simon got off the bus. The very thought of seeing him made my heart take flight, for even though he had been a part of my life for five years, I still couldn't believe he was mine.

Late in the afternoon I took a quick shower and got ready for my date with Michael. The house was immaculate, and I wanted to look as good as my polished floors. Better. I had hoped to be waiting at the table with a cup of tea when the boys came in, but as I was sweeping mascara on my lashes, I heard Daniel burst through the door.

There was chatter in the kitchen and the sound of chairs being pulled back as Grandma laid out an after-school snack for the perpetually ravenous young men in my life. When I had disappeared to clean up, she had started a batch of her melt-in-your-mouth peanut butter chocolate chip cookies, and I could tell by the way Daniel's voice was an octave higher than usual that he was ecstatic about her special surprise.

Smoothing a little gloss over my toffee-pink lipstick, I straightened up the bathroom counter and made my way into the kitchen. Daniel and Simon were both at the table, devouring what could have easily been their fourth cookie each.

"Hey, you two!" I called, greeting them both with a quick squeeze. Daniel leaned into my one-armed embrace. Simon pulled away.

I had hoped the day would soften his hard edges, but my brother didn't seem as eager to forgive and forget as I was. That wasn't enough to deter me. Sinking into the chair beside him, I laid a hand on his arm.

"Simon." I tilted my head to try to catch his gaze. "I'm sorry. I didn't mean to yell at you this morning."

He shrugged. Resolutely avoided making eye contact.

"Come on, I'm apologizing here!" I said, my voice high, singsong. "I'm sorry; I'm sorry; I'm sorry!"

Simon pulled his arm out from under my grip and pushed back from the table.

"You can't be mad!" I pressed on. "Not when Michael is coming. We're going to have such a fun weekend!"

My brother's eyes flashed to mine and I was startled to see fear in them. Fear? What was he afraid of? me? I had never raised a hand against him and rarely raised my voice. Had this morning's altercation upset him enough to leave traces of panic in his dark eyes?

"Honey," I murmured, "what's wrong?"

But Simon didn't answer. Instead, he spun on his heel and ran toward his room. The slam of his door almost perfectly matched the sound of someone knocking.

"Michael's here," I breathed, torn between elation and devastation. Where should I go first? Simon's door? or Michael's?

Another flurry of knocks rattled against our doorframe, and although I was kind of surprised that Michael wasn't just walking in, I rushed through the mudroom and wrenched open the door. I planned to throw myself into his arms, kiss him, and then tell him that although all I wanted was to bask in the glow of his presence for hours, I had to take care of something. Michael would understand.

But just as I was about to launch myself at the man on my porch, I stopped dead.

"What are you doing here?" I demanded.

The smile that had lit up Parker's face when I first swung open the door faded a little. "I'm here to pick up the boys," he said, a look of uncertainty darting across his features.

"What are you talking about? I told you this morning that it didn't work for us today."

"But . . ." He sidestepped a little and looked over my shoulder into the kitchen. His eyes lit up and he waved at Daniel.

"But what?" I nearly shouted. "I told you no!"

"But Simon called me," Parker said, keeping his voice down as if he hardly dared to disclose his source. "Around lunchtime. He said that you had changed your mind and that you wanted me to pick them up and get them out of your hair for a while."

"I never said that." The words tasted bitter on my tongue. "I would never say that."

Parker lifted his hands. "I'm sorry. I thought—"

"He's a kid, Parker. Didn't you stop to wonder why Simon was the one calling you instead of me?"

"No, it never crossed my mind."

I moaned. "You know nothing about children."

"I never said I did."

"You didn't have to. It's pretty obvious." I glared at Parker, but he looked contrite, confused. "It's not your fault," I muttered begrudgingly. "But you have to go. You need to leave. Now."

Suddenly a soft whine pierced the late afternoon. It came from somewhere on the porch, somewhere nearby, hidden in the depths of the lengthening shadows. "What was that?" I spat out.

"My surprise for the boys." Parker rubbed the back of his neck with his hand and studied the slats of our porch floor.

"Excuse me?"

"I brought something to—"

"Obviously, Parker. What did you bring?"

The man before me crouched to grab a cardboard box nestled against the house. The top flaps were folded in over each other, but Parker pried them apart effortlessly and reached into the dark recess. His hands emerged with a puppy. A tiny, black and tan and white bundle with floppy ears and big brown eyes that regarded me with a newborn sorrow. The little thing mewed like a kitten and tried to bury her head in Parker's large hands.

"You brought my boys a puppy?"

Parker shrugged and nuzzled the crying bundle against his chest.

"A puppy? And you didn't ask me?" I was furious, ready to explode, to send Parker and his miniature mess-making machine packing. But before I could utter another word, two things happened at the same time.

First, Daniel finally broke free from Grandma's attempts to restrain him. He slid underneath my arm to stand between Parker and me and immediately caught sight of his inapt present. The squeal that issued from his open mouth was earsplitting.

And in the distance, a car turned off the highway onto

our long driveway, heralding its sudden appearance with the crunch and pop of gravel beneath tires. For a fleeting instant I prayed that it would be a UPS truck, a wrong turn, a neighbor coming by to say hi. But it wasn't.

It was Michael.

surprises

FOR A FRANTIC MOMENT I battled a crazy desire to push
Parker into a closet and tell Michael that the man he saw
standing on my porch was nothing more than a figment
of his imagination. Grandma and I had watched a cheesy
chick flick a couple of weeks ago, and that was exactly what
the heroine did. But something told me the hide-him-in-a-
wardrobe ploy would only work in Hollywood. As for little
old unfamous me, I was frozen in my open doorway, about
to introduce the love of my life to the man who got me
pregnant.

I wanted to throw up.

But I couldn't. Not here. Not now. "Daniel," I said in a voice so no-nonsense, he looked at me instantly. "Go in the house. Now."

He didn't argue, though when I stepped out onto the porch to make room for him, he slammed the door behind me a little too aggressively. I didn't even care. I wanted to slam doors too.

"Parker," I whispered between gritted teeth, "I'm going to have to deal with you later."

"Deal with me?" he sputtered before I could go on. "What do you mean, deal with me?"

My gaze was locked on Michael as he pulled onto our cement pad and turned off his car, but Parker's words caused me to spin on him. In the weeks since he had reentered my life, any semblance of the old Parker—the grad school student who knocked me up and left me—had been buried beneath the newer, contrite guise of a changed man. But when I faced him, the old spark was in his eyes, that still-familiar smirk pulling at one corner of his carved lips.

"I'm not a child," he told me, "and there's nothing to deal with."

"You had no right to—"

"Simon called; I came. End of story. I won't make the same mistake next time."

I bit off a curt "Whatever," but what I wanted to do was curse.

"I'm gone," Parker muttered under his breath.

"Take your mutt with you!"

"I will, Julia," he said, leaning in toward me and offering up the puppy as evidence. "I'll take the dog because she's mine. I didn't buy your boys a puppy; you just assumed that. I brought her along so I could teach the boys about caring for an animal."

"You mean you didn't . . . ?"

"Of course not. I may not be great with kids, but I'm not stupid. I rescued Holly from a neighbor who was going to drown her."

"How very *Charlotte's Web* of you," I scoffed, crossing my arms over my chest. "I'll have to start calling you Fern."

Parker's glare was downright chilling. "You know, you can be a real—"

"What, Parker? What can I be? What am I?" I wanted him to say it, to admit what he was thinking so I could vilify him and ban him from our lives. But as I stepped closer, Parker backed away. He backed down. I watched as the angry lines in his face faded and then disappeared altogether.

"You're confused," he said.

I harrumphed. "I'm confused? You're the one who's confused, Patrick Holt." But my attempt at witty retaliation was utterly meaningless, and I felt like a fool as he bent to retrieve Holly's box.

"Don't worry," Parker said, tucking the tiny puppy between the strips of old towels he had nestled inside. "I won't call again. If the boys ever want to talk to me, you have my number."

He didn't look at me once as he left, pressing the cardboard box against his chest as if it contained a priceless treasure and taking the steps two at a time. I cringed as he almost bumped into Michael at the edge of our sidewalk, but the two men merely nodded at each other and went their separate ways. Michael coming into my life, Parker leaving it. Again.

But I didn't have time to think about that. Suddenly Michael was before me, sweeping me into his arms and spinning me around like I was a little girl instead of a grown woman. He held me so tight, I couldn't breathe, and when he finally pulled away, he cradled my face in his hands and kissed me like he would die for want of love. I was gasping when his mouth finally left mine, faint and tingling, and only half-aware of the sound of Parker's engine as he drove away.

"I missed you," Michael whispered, his lips pressed against my forehead and his hands wrapped around the curve of my waist. "I can't believe how much I missed you."

"Welcome home," I said hoarsely. I dipped my head and laid a kiss against the warmth of his neck. Beneath my lips I could feel the unsteady pulse of his heartbeat.

"You better stop that," he warned, "or I'm not going to want to be polite. I'll whisk you away and forget all about saying hi to Daniel and Simon and Grandma."

"That wouldn't do," I murmured, but I thought it would do just fine. *Take me away,* I thought. *Just make me disappear so I can forget about Parker's unwanted appearance, Simon's disobedience, Grandma's graying skin . . .*

But Michael didn't whisk me away. He took a deep breath, gave me one last suffocating squeeze, and held me at arm's length. "It's so good to see you," he said. Then, "Who was that guy with the box? some deliveryman?"

I nodded, unable to lie to his face but equally incapable of explaining everything when Parker's presence still lingered like a faint but untraceable odor around us. I started to say, *I'll tell you later,* but Michael had already dismissed the anonymous man on the porch and was reaching for a department store bag that he had set on the ground when he lifted me off it.

"I have some presents for the boys," he said, and I caught a glimpse of exactly what Daniel had predicted we'd see: two new packages of shiny Matchbox cars and an oversize bag of sour apple jelly beans.

"What's the book?" I asked, creeping my hand into the sack to extract the one unexpected item.

"A little something for Simon." Michael batted my hand away. "And I have something for Grandma, too. Buried in the bottom."

"What about me?" I pretended to pout, but Michael winked away my plea and took me by the hand.

"Let's get this over with so we can spend some time alone."

"Get this over with?" I coughed.

"You know what I mean. . . ."

Michael's ministrations had nearly transformed my attitude, but I forgot to account for the rest of my family. Simon
was still locked away in his room, and Grandma and Daniel
were sitting at the table in a hunched-over tableau of worry
and alarm. Grandma's forehead was visibly creased, her eyes
a study in concern. And Daniel fixed me with a vicious stare,
a look that told me in no uncertain terms that I was in the
doghouse. How ironic.

"Hey!" Michael greeted them, apparently oblivious to the
tension in the room. He bowed to give Daniel an awkward
hug and fished his gifts from the depths of the bag as if he
were digging for gold. My son's reaction didn't match the
flourish with which his gifts were presented.

"Thanks," Daniel mumbled, turning the bag of jelly beans
over in his hands. They tumbled in an avalanche of green and
made a sound like water over stones.

"You're welcome, buddy." Michael ruffled Daniel's hair
and turned to Grandma. "I've got something for you, too,
Mrs. DeSmit."

She smiled a little, but the expression didn't come close to
reaching her eyes. "You didn't have to bring me anything,"
she said, standing so that she could offer Michael a hug. My
boyfriend embraced my grandmother quickly, then pulled
away and extracted a scarf from the bag he still held.

It was soft, cashmere if I knew anything about fabric—
which, admittedly, I didn't. But it looked luxurious all the

same—knit with a fine, tight weave that could have been plaited by fairies, the pattern was so small. The fabric had been dyed a gentle pink, the sort of mild, glowing hue that came to mind when someone spoke fondly of a peaches-and-cream complexion.

"It's beautiful," I said before Grandma could react. Taking the scarf from Michael's hands, I wound it around my grandmother's neck. It made her skin look flushed, alive.

"It is beautiful," she agreed. The braided fringe dangled against her chest and she lifted it with shaking fingers. I wished I could steady her hand. "Thank you," she said. "You really shouldn't have."

For some reason, it sounded like she meant what she said.

"Oh, it was nothing." Michael dismissed her gratitude with a flick of his wrist. "Where's Simon?"

"He's not feeling well," Grandma declared.

I gave her a sharp look, but when I considered Simon's recent emotional turmoil, I realized her words were hardly a lie.

"Well, I brought him a book, but maybe it'll have to wait."

"Just leave it here," I told Michael. "He might enjoy reading it while we're gone."

Michael shrugged and lifted the last item from his bag, a colorful book with a picture of four children and a train car on the front. I sighed inwardly. Simon had read *The Boxcar*

Children years ago. It was a nice effort on Michael's part, but it reminded me that he didn't really bother to keep up with the boys. Simon had moved on long ago to the classic Hardy Boys series, the Chronicles of Narnia, and autobiographies of his favorite historical figures. Since he often had his nose buried in a book, it didn't take much more than a glance to stay current with his reading preferences. Maybe I could carefully point out some things to Michael later.

"You two better get going," Grandma said as she settled back into her chair. "After all, your time is limited."

"Too true," Michael laughed at the same instant I was about to say, *We can stick around for a while.* I swallowed my words, and he took me by the elbow. "Have a lovely evening, Mrs. DeSmit." He smiled, ever the gentleman.

"Nellie," she reminded him with a smirk.

"We won't be late," I called over my shoulder as Michael ushered me to the door. "We're going to the children's museum at the Pavilion tomorrow, remember? The boys are going to love it."

"The IMAX is playing a movie called *Wild Ocean*," Daniel piped up. Besides his halfhearted "Thanks," it was the first thing I'd heard him say since Michael came inside bearing gifts.

"We're excited to see it, aren't we?" I pulled out of Michael's grip and crossed the space between us to lean over and give my son a good-bye kiss on the cheek. Daniel chose that precise moment to hop off his chair and head into the living room. I was stung. "Be good for Grandma," I called after him, battling a desire to dash across the kitchen floor and scoop him up into my arms.

"He'll be fine," Grandma assured me. "We'll have a wonderful night."

"Thanks," I mouthed. Michael was already tugging me toward the door, but for some reason I didn't feel ready to leave. "The pizza coupons are in the—"

"Organizer by the phone. I know."

"Don't order too late or it'll take an hour for delivery."

"I know that, too." Grandma nodded. "Now get going. Have fun."

"We will." Michael grinned. He waved good-bye and pulled me out the door; I had only a second to yank my coat off the hook before the screen slammed. "Let's get out of here," he whispered against my temple.

I took his hand and let him lead me away.

Although we didn't have to do anything special to enjoy being together, Michael surprised me with reservations at an upscale restaurant in a town that was nearly an hour away. It was one of those limited-seating places with a single dining room and a specialty cook who personally prepared every plate.

I felt a bit underdressed, but Michael didn't seem to mind, and after he talked me into a glass of the house red, the evening began to loosen around the edges. I had no idea that I was wound so tight until Michael began the slow process of unraveling me.

"Eight weeks is too long," he commented, reaching over his decimated plate of something French and unpronounce-able to smooth my cheek with his thumb.

"You have no idea," I moaned. "Are you sure you want to be a doctor? Didn't we have a good thing going at Value Foods?"

"What? You want me to come back and work under you? I don't think so, boss girl."

"Boss girl?"

"Yeah, that's what I call you behind your back."

I laughed. "I can think of nicer nicknames. More appro-priate ones."

"Me too."

"You do know I'm kidding, right? I want you to be a doctor."

"You'd better. Because it's too late now. I'm not quitting."

"But eight weeks without seeing each other is too long," I said, giving his earlier comment a more serious undertone. "And you told me that you had an idea. A plan?"

He shrugged and sat back in his seat with a mischievous gleam in his eye. "Something like that. But I think we should order dessert first. I've heard the crepes are great, but appar-ently the chocolate mousse is the cook's specialty."

"The mousse au chocolat? With candied orange peel and

madeleines?" I questioned, reading from the small dessert menu adorned with patterns of fleurs-de-lis and exotic-sounding delights.

"That's the one."

"Sounds perfect."

I watched as Michael signaled the waiter and pointed to our choice of dessert on the menu. A wordless understanding passed between them, and then the gentleman cleared our plates and disappeared like a mist. Michael turned his attention back to me. "Do you even know what madeleines are?" he teased.

"Of course I do!" I exclaimed, indignant. "What do you take me for, a hick?"

"More like a small town girl."

"Hey, you're a small town boy, remember."

Michael just smiled. Though he loved to poke fun at the fact that most of my life had been lived between the boundary of my grandmother's farm and teeny-tiny Mason, Iowa, there was a certain edge to his taunting that made me bristle. He would say it was all in fun, but I knew that he considered himself more sophisticated than me. More experienced. A year and some odd months in the so-called bustling metropolis of Iowa City had contributed much to his worldly wisdom. Or so he thought.

Normally, I would have fought back or at least let him know in no uncertain terms that his mild attempt at superiority didn't amuse me. But I didn't feel like participating in that sort of go-round tonight. I didn't have the energy. Instead, I slanted across the table and kissed the smile off his face. Gave him something else to think about.

"Mmmm . . . ," he murmured. "Nobody does that like a small town girl."

I sat back, aghast at his subtle insinuation. "Are you telling me that you've compared?"

Michael's eyes slid past mine and regarded something, or someone, over my shoulder. My fingertips turned to ice at the look that crossed his face. I had been teasing, but he didn't look like he was joking around anymore. Was he trying to tell me something? to admit to a fling with some stylish tart who had a more desirable, urban flair?

I tried to pull my hand away when he reached for it, but Michael caught my fingers and wove them through his own as if our hands belonged like that. Tangled. Together. He squeezed, leaned closer to me over the dim flame of the single candle that lit our table.

He was so beautiful. So familiar and foreign, so safe and wild all at once. I trusted him and feared him in the same breath; he held the key to make my dreams come true and yet had the power to destroy me. It was like being suspended above the world where I could soar. Or fall. Whether it was foolishness or true love, I didn't know. But I let myself go. I held on to him, too.

"No," Michael said, a certain gravity in his low voice. "I haven't compared. And I have no desire to measure you against anyone else. You'd win, hands down, every time."

"Who, me?" I demurred, trying to deflect the solemnity of the moment. Michael wasn't the sort to wax poetic on his feelings. He told me that he loved me, but it seemed almost factual. As if he was stating the truth instead of giving expression to something that knotted him up inside. I wasn't used to such flowery professions.

But Michael wasn't done. "I don't tell you enough," he continued, almost whispering. "I don't take the time to tell you that you're amazing. You're absolutely . . . perfect. Gorgeous and funny and strong. You take my breath away every time I see you."

The lights were so low in the restaurant that I was sure he couldn't see the fierce blush that rose in my cheeks. "Michael, don't be silly. It's just me. You've known me for five years. Surely I don't leave you breathless anymore."

"You do." He grinned. And then he sat back to make room for our dessert.

The uniformed waiter was carrying a shallow bowl with two polished silver spoons. He placed it carefully at the very center of our table, where it glimmered in the candlelight like a piece of art. Coils of sugared orange peel decorated the soft rise of a dark, dense hill of chocolate. There were two crisp madeleines pressed into the shape of leaves and an impossibly delicate filigree of dark chocolate in the very center of it all. I was grateful for the distraction and ready to grab a spoon and dig in when I realized that I hadn't quite accounted for everything. On the highest tip of the chocolate latticework dangled something that glowed, that sparkled and danced with a hot, white light.

I would have gasped if I could breathe, but as it was, the only thing I could do was whirl to face Michael. He had slid off his seat and was kneeling beside me.

"You said I've known you for five years," he whispered. "But I want to know you for fifty more. And Lord willing, another fifty after that. I want to spend the rest of my life with you, Julia. Will you marry me?"

I was speechless. Completely beyond any sort of reasonable reaction because this was the last thing I expected when Michael told me that he had a plan. I couldn't even open my mouth.

But Michael took my silence as a yes. He reached for the engagement ring, the graceful white gold band that cradled a diamond like the fragment of a promise. Singling out the ring finger of my left hand, he slipped it past my knuckle to the place where it would fit for all my days to come.

Forever.

decisions

I WAS ENGAGED.

Beloved. A wanted woman. A wife-to-be.

Ever since I was a little girl, I had longed to hear those four incomparable words—*Will you marry me?* I believed they would validate my existence, affirm my worth, make me feel cherished and special and deserving of love. Marriage was a thing of beauty, a promise of "till death do us part" underpinned with declarations of commitment, devotion, and happily ever after.

But after only five minutes of wearing the ring, I knew that engagement was a different thing altogether.

As Michael drove me home, we talked about the particulars. Or at least, we tried to.

"I was thinking a June wedding," he told me as he turned out of the restaurant parking lot. "Early in the month."

"June?" He might as well have said next week, June felt so close.

"Yeah. It'll be perfect timing. I'll finish up classes in the middle of May, and then we can get married, move, and have a week or so to settle in before I start my summer program."

"You're doing a summer program?"

"Well, I'm applying. I just heard about it a few days ago. It's eight weeks long, but it'll give me a big head start if I'm accepted. I'll be shadowing a physician, working in an emergency room, doing a clinical care-based case study . . ."

I managed to utter, "Sounds exciting," but the only thing I could think about was how Daniel, Simon, and I would spend those long hours in a new city while Michael slaved away at the university hospital.

"Don't worry," he said as if reading my mind. "There will be lots for you to do. Iowa City is a great place to live. We have tons of parks and trails, a couple of nice lakes nearby, and a really cool summer rec league. I've already checked into it."

"Daniel's in kindergarten," I said softly.

"He'll be eligible this summer. He could play soccer, tennis, or T-ball . . . or you can sign him up for swimming lessons. He'll love it!"

"And Simon?"

Michael glanced at me out of the corner of his eye. It was too dark for me to read his expression, but I bristled a little when he asked, "Is Simon coming with us?"

The realization that I didn't know the answer to that question made me deflate like a slashed tire. "I don't know," I admitted. "What else would he do?"

"Stay with Nellie? What about Janice? Have you heard from Janice lately?"

Of course I hadn't heard from Janice. What was he thinking? But I bit back my prickly retort and said, "I don't know what Simon wants. I guess we've got some things to work out."

Michael laughed. "That's marriage! Compromise, fighting over the blankets, and sacrificing for the one you love."

But I couldn't help feeling like I was the only one who had to sacrifice anything.

We drove in silence for a few minutes, Michael's hand over mine on the gearshift of his car. When he had to switch gears, he pressed my hand against the smooth ball of the shaft and slid the car from first to second or third to fourth. It was how I had learned to drive a standard. I had ground the gears and popped the clutch on more occasions than I could count, but Michael's patience with me knew no bounds. And while I had mastered the art of the manual transmission years ago, he still guided my hands through the motions so that I never forgot.

It was one of our small, unspoken connections—a way to

remind ourselves that the time and distance between us didn't matter in the grand scheme of things—and I was startled when Michael tapped the brakes for an upcoming stop sign and nudged my hand off the gearshift. He downshifted quickly, and I folded my hands in my lap as if nothing had happened. But it was hard to pretend. Michael had never before removed my hand.

"You don't seem as excited as I hoped you'd be," Michael finally said when we were stopped at the intersection. His words in the stillness of the warm car seemed hard, polished. "I thought you wanted this. I thought you wanted to get married."

"I do! Of course I do!" I couldn't stand the sudden tension between us, but if I was honest with myself, I could hardly blame him for jumping to the wrong conclusion. I hadn't exactly been the sort of fawning fiancée new husbands-to-be expected to parade around. And I'd been engaged only an hour. The sparkly patina of white gowns, layer cakes, and marital bliss should have been far from faded.

I was botching my marriage already.

Rotating in my seat to face him full-on, I took an unsteady breath and said, "You just took me by surprise. When you said two months ago that you had a plan, it never crossed my mind that this might be it. I'm still wrapping my head around the idea. I guess I'm shell-shocked."

"*Shell-shocked*? That term hardly has positive connotations."

"Stunned," I amended. "Amazed, blown away, astonished."

"Better," Michael conceded.

"Mystified, thrilled, ecstatic . . . ," I continued.

There was no one on the highway but us, and when Michael turned to kiss me, I gave in and let myself forget every doubt. Every worry.

At least for a moment.

I was grateful that the boys were already in bed when Michael and I got home. He wanted to wake them up with the good news, but I balked at his enthusiastic suggestion, convincing him that Simon and Daniel were likely fast asleep and would resent the interruption of their dreams. In reality, I was quite sure they were both wide-awake and indulging in a few stolen minutes—Simon reading a book under the covers and Daniel driving new Matchbox cars along the stripes of his comforter. But I wasn't about to admit my suspicions to Michael. I simply wasn't ready to tell my boys. Not yet.

Grandma was a different story. We didn't even bother to shrug off our jackets before we hunted her down in the living room to announce our plans. I couldn't fathom how she had guessed Michael's intentions, but she seemed to anticipate our news long before I took my hand out of my coat pocket and showed her the shining ring. There was a thin smile on her face, but it was paired with a look of phony surprise that made it impossible for me to tell if her joy at our upcoming wedding was sincere or not. As she turned my hand this way and that, admiring the cut of the square diamond and the slender rope of the delicate band, I decided that she was happy for us. She was just preoccupied by the same questions that rattled around in my head.

How in the world were we going to make this work?

"June?" Grandma asked. She gave my fingers one last squeeze before letting go. "A June wedding will be lovely. That gives us . . . How many months to plan?"

"A little less than eight," Michael said without pause. "I've already called the church and booked three different dates. I figured Julia would like to have a few options."

I wasn't able to suppress the stunned look that swept across my features. My mouth was a little O of disbelief, and I had to make a conscious effort to close it. To smile. "You've reserved the church?"

"Fellowship Community." Michael nodded. "I thought you'd want to get married in your own church."

"I do," I whispered. "Of course I do."

Michael grinned, obviously thrilled that he had gotten it right. "And since you can't take pictures of yourself, I booked a lady in Glendale who is supposed to be the best around. But she'll only hold all three dates until Monday. We'll have to make some decisions fast."

"The best around?" I parroted lamely.

"Well, you're the best around," Michael assured me. He wrapped an arm around my shoulders for a quick, placating hug. "But like I said, you can't take pictures of yourself."

"Sounds like you've done a lot of work already," Grandma said.

"I don't want Julia to have to stress about every little detail. Between work and school and the kids . . . she's got a lot on her plate."

Though it wasn't in my nature to be suspicious, it seemed to me like Michael's tone held the smallest twinge of accusation. But before I could speculate about the origins of his resentment, it hit me that Daniel and Simon weren't the only things I would have to sort out against the backdrop of a new life, a new home. There was also my schooling, my job, and my fledgling photography business. And I hadn't even begun to consider what my marriage plans would mean for my grandmother.

"Actually," Michael began, holding me a little tighter, "my mom has taken care of a few more things. . . ."

"Your mom?"

"I didn't think you'd mind. It's no big deal, really. I just asked her to take a peek at some flower arrangements and put together a few cake ideas."

"Flowers? Cakes?"

"Yeah." Michael grinned. "Remember the bouquet I sent you a couple months ago? the one that you got right before I told you I had a plan?"

My mind flashed to the delphiniums, chrysanthemums, and freesia. The roses that were painted to match a morning sun. It was a bouquet that had been handpicked by someone who knew me. Who loved me.

"Your mom picked out those flowers?"

"No, she has someone to take care of everything for her: decorating, hair, arrangements . . . you name it. The lady at the Flower Cart put together that bouquet. Did you like it?"

"It was perfect," I whispered.

"It was you." Michael dropped a kiss on my forehead. "I described you to the florist, and that's what she came up with."

"Did your mom find someone to do the cake, too?" Grandma asked.

I couldn't tell if there was a catch in her voice or if I was only imagining it. Years ago, when I was still naive enough to dream about a fairy-tale wedding replete with bridesmaids, birdseed, and a sumptuous buffet, we had delighted in the idea of making our own cakes, a gift of sorts for the people who came to celebrate in our joy. Little ones for every table, Grandma had decided. A different flavor each, with white fondant and flowers from our own garden.

But Michael didn't know about our distant daydreams. "Lily's makes amazing cakes," he said. Like we didn't already know that. "She'll do a three-tiered vanilla cake for a very reasonable price. It's not big, but we can do the rest as sheet cakes."

"You sure know a lot about wedding planning," Grandma said kindly.

I pulled out of Michael's half embrace and spun to face him. "Hang on. How do you know so much about wedding planning? I can't believe you're taking an interest in this. I can't believe you know anything about three-tiered cakes and wedding bouquets."

"It's the only thing my mom and I have talked about for weeks," Michael groaned, flopping down on the couch as if it was exhausting just to discuss the planning process. "I am so glad that it's finally official and I can turn it all over to you. My mother has been driving me crazy."

I almost said, *Maybe your mom can just plan our wedding.* But even though my heart was a twisted knot of emotions, I knew that my sourness would be misunderstood. It wasn't that I didn't love Michael. I did. And the last thing I wanted to do on the night of our betrothal was ruin his excitement with my whininess.

Everything was just happening so fast.

"Crazy." I said the word quietly, grounding myself. "I can do crazy."

"Good, because I've had more than my fair share." Michael reached up and pulled me to sit beside him on the couch.

I was concerned that he would want to engage in more wedding talk, but instead of continuing on about the plans he had made with his mom, he reached for the remote and clicked on the TV. It was as if the room exhaled, as if everyone breathed a sigh of relief that the topic of our nuptials could be shelved for at least the length of the late show. We settled into a somewhat-comfortable silence, until Grandma got up and announced she was going to bed. I could hardly believe she had stayed up as long as she did.

"Congratulations again," she whispered, giving me one last tender look. Michael's attention was fixed on the television and she didn't have to manufacture any emotions for his sake. I felt like I was finally able to gauge her real reaction to my new fiancé's proposal.

There was a gentle delight in her eyes, a soft contentment that told me in no uncertain terms that she still longed for my happiness. But there was more. In her deep, cream-and-coffee eyes, I read uncertainty, disquiet, even melancholy. And I knew exactly why. Michael's proposal marked the end of an era. The beginning of a new life that neither of us could quite call into focus no matter how hard we tried to squint at the future.

I was sure that my face mirrored her own.

When Grandma was gone, Michael pulled my head down onto his shoulder and relaxed into the couch. I was sure that he would have gladly fallen asleep there, nestled in the warm embrace of his future bride. But when the late show eventually went off air and an old rerun of a corny sitcom filled the living room with canned laughter, I gave him a little nudge.

"I should get to bed," I whispered. "And so should you. We have a big day tomorrow."

"A big day?" Michael asked, blinking at me as if I had indeed woken him.

"The children's museum?" I reminded him. "Daniel and Simon have been looking forward to it."

"Oh yeah. It'll be fun," Michael said.

"Not if we're both cranky and groggy."

"I'm a med student," he reminded me. "I sometimes get to see the sun rise."

"Me too, but it's at the end of a good night's sleep. That's something you're going to have to learn about me: I need a good night's sleep."

Michael left reluctantly, drawing me into long kisses that I had to extract myself from with patience and poise. He was so blinded by the promise of never having to say good night again that he seemed to forget we had to say, "I do" before that particular marital perk kicked in.

By the time I finally had him out the door, I was exhausted, and my head felt like it had taken one too many spins on a Tilt-A-Whirl. It was a sick, hungover feeling, though I could hardly blame the few sips of wine I had with dinner for leaving me so nauseous and dizzy.

What, then?

More importantly: What was wrong with me?

This was exactly what I had wanted. What I'd yearned for since almost the first day I laid eyes on the painfully handsome Michael Vermeer. He was an amazing man. A future doctor. The catch of the century with cornflower blue eyes, hair the color of jet, and a heart so kind, so generous, I would be a fool to do anything but dance at the prospect of being his wife.

So why wasn't I sashaying across the kitchen floor?

Because I hadn't expected Michael to propose.

Because I was tired.

Because it meant I would have to make a lot of tough decisions.

Because my future husband hadn't picked out the flowers I loved or asked me if I would like to get my wedding cake from the local bakery or consulted me about who I wanted to be our photographer.

Because his mother planned our wedding while mine was incommunicado.

I had a hundred reasons marshaled like soldiers ready to take the fall. If one was shot down, another rose to stand in the line of fire. I could massacre an army of excuses and still find recruits among the ruins of my secreted thoughts.

The sigh that escaped me was a long, low deflation. I felt emptied in the hush of Michael's absence, alternately grateful that I was alone and struck by the depth of my loneliness. It seemed strange that I could feel isolated in a house that was bursting at the seams with life, but with everyone in bed and the night so dark around our farmhouse we could have existed in the hidden recesses of a black hole, I might as well have been the only person on the face of the earth.

Instead of going to my room, I slouched in a kitchen chair

and loathed myself. And just like it was easy to come up with explanations for why I wasn't tap-dancing in the wake of Michael's proposal, it was a cinch to divine a dozen reasons to hate the girl in the mirror. For fighting with Simon. For not giving Michael the reaction he deserved. For nitpicking when I had been handed my dreams on a silver platter. For sending Parker away.

Shoot. I had almost forgotten about him.

My purse was on the table next to me, abandoned there when Michael and I came home hours before. I reached for it and extracted the stack of postcards, minus one. Paging through them with an inordinate amount of care, I chose the giant corncob. It seemed appropriate, a big picture for big news.

But I didn't know what to write.

So I started with her address, another stab in the dark.

>Janice DeSmit
>c/o Ben (Benret? Benmet?)
>Minneapolis area, Minnesota
>USA

And then I traced three simple words: *I'm getting married.*

It wasn't until they were on the paper that I realized I had never said yes.

normal

THANKFULLY, I CONVINCED MICHAEL to postpone the news of our happy union until Sunday, after our outing with the boys. Simon and Daniel had been looking forward to the science museum and a trip to the IMAX for weeks, and I wasn't about to overshadow their excitement with the considerable implications of my engagement to Michael. I wanted them to enjoy one day that was dedicated entirely to them. One day that would allow me to see how we could function as a family.

After tucking the diamond ring in the dark recesses of my

underwear drawer, I woke the boys, made a quick breakfast, and waited for Michael to arrive.

He was late.

I could hardly blame him. After all, we weren't the only people in his life that he hadn't seen in two months. His family was large and boisterous, filled with sisters-in-law to balance out all the Vermeer brother testosterone and small nieces and nephews that made mealtime feel like a feeding frenzy at the zoo. I didn't mind it so much, but Daniel and Simon seemed to find the chaos intimidating. And since no one seemed to notice when we were absent, Michael spent most of his time in Mason over at our house. But I shouldn't have expected him to slip out so early on his first morning back. It wasn't fair of me.

"He's probably catching up with his mom and dad," I told the boys. "We can't be mad at him for that. He'll be here soon."

When Michael showed up over an hour after our scheduled meeting time, Simon was cross, Daniel antsy. Even I felt slighted—the least he could have done was call to let me know that he was running late. But Michael seemed oblivious to our gravelly moods. As we piled into the car for the long drive to the museum, he gave me a surreptitious wink and a kiss, whispering a quick apology but no explanation.

The rest of the day was not quite the sort of familial bliss I had imagined. Simon acted like he was too old for the interactive displays at the museum, even though I had been convinced the science experiments would be right up his alley. And Daniel was unusually clingy, all but glued to my side as we walked from exhibit to exhibit. He was so out of sorts that he refused to participate in the hands-on activities unless I half forced him.

Since the museum was designed for kids, it was full of opportunities to get messy. I had entertained visions of laughter and bonding as we made discoveries together, but no one seemed willing to participate. After nearly two hours of wandering around, we stumbled upon an entire wing of the museum dedicated to erosion and its effects on the rich farmland of the Midwest. I attacked the display with as much enthusiasm as I could muster, but I was the only person in our little party of four who would dig in the enormous sand basin with my fingers.

It was cathartic somehow, all that dense, wet sand in my palms. I spread it with my fingertips and coaxed it into soft hills and hollows with an almost-childlike abandon. I could have made sand castles or sculptures; I could have climbed up into the display and spread out on the cool, simulated beach. Pretended I was somewhere, anywhere, else. Alone.

But I wasn't alone. I was orchestrating a reluctant union.

"Make it rain!" I called after I had created a series of creeks and rivers that were supposed to channel the water as a slow spigot dribbled simulated spring melt.

Simon sighed and turned on the pipes full blast. He acted as if it were an enormous chore to rotate his wrist a couple of degrees.

But I ignored the sulky plunge of his lips and watched with

fascination as the trickle of water soon turned my carefully constructed canals to soup. I cheered the process on, still flicking wet sand from dirty hands, but when I turned to see how everyone else was responding to the intriguing presentation, they had all slunk away. Simon was scuffing his foot against the concrete floor, making high-pitched squeaks with the rubber soles of his tennis shoes like little cries of protest. Daniel was leaning against a wall sign that read "Area Water and Its Effect on Plants," head hung as if he was sleepy. And Michael, several steps away, muttered into his cell phone.

I gave up after that. We ate a quiet lunch in the museum cafeteria, then headed back to Mason hours before I thought we'd make the homebound trek.

They know something's up, I reasoned as I watched the watercolor landscape fly past my window. It was raining softly, and water streaked the car and blurred the scenery with mellow strokes of ash and gray as if the world had burned and was melting before my eyes.

"Michael and I are getting married," I said to my reflection.

The car was quiet; there was no way they could have missed my sudden declaration, but for a moment no one said a word.

"Isn't that great?" Michael chimed in after a heartbeat. He reached for my hand and held it fast.

I swiveled to face him and found that his eyes were balanced between delight and surprise. We had planned on spilling the beans after church tomorrow.

"A June wedding," Michael continued. "So you boys are

going to have to be fitted for tuxes. Monkey suits. I bet you've never worn a monkey suit before."

Pulling out of my fiancé's grip, I stuck my head between the bucket seats and regarded the boys. Simon was looking out his window, jaw set in a firm, resolute line, but Daniel's gaze was trained on me.

"What do you think?" I asked him softly.

He just stared.

"Michael and I are getting married," I repeated. "Do you know what that means?"

It took Daniel a second, but he nodded.

"Exciting news, isn't it?"

"Congratulations," Simon muttered from his corner of the car.

"Congratulations," Daniel echoed.

I watched my boys for a flicker of understanding, for the smallest glimmer of excitement at my life-changing announcement. But they seemed as bewildered as I had been when Michael first slipped the ring on my finger.

Time, I decided, settling back into my seat. I watched the hazy roadside signs tick past, marking the path home, and thought, *They just need a little time.*

I wish I could say that life went back to normal when Michael went back to school. But I've learned that *normal* is a relative term. Loosely applied and often overused.

It's true that we settled into our daily routine—school, work, family time, sleep—but the whole pattern seemed off, as if someone had nudged the axis of our quiet world and we were left to spin just the tiniest bit crooked. I felt the shudder of each lopsided orbit at the core of my very bones.

There were things we didn't say. Words that were just below the surface, that echoed through the house like private whispers. Just a smidge too soft. Just out of reach. Murmurs of weddings and husbands and stepdaddies. Soft moans of discontent. Sighs of Parker. The heavy syllables settled in the corners, weighted the walls with unspoken burdens so that each rotation of our unbalanced life allowed new cracks to form in the foundation. I wanted to skimcoat everything. Pretend it was fine.

Near the end of October, Grandma announced that it was time to go wedding dress shopping.

"Now?" I asked, surprising myself. Of course I was thrilled to participate in such an exciting rite of womanhood, but somehow it seemed too rushed. Too soon.

"Actually, we should have gone the day after Michael proposed," Grandma said. "I've heard that you need to order wedding dresses six to nine months in advance."

"Six to nine months?" I did the math. "We have almost eight."

"Exactly. How's Saturday for you? I've already called the Walkers, and Jonathan can watch the boys for the afternoon."

"Mr. Walker? What about Mrs. Walker?"

"She'd like to come with us." Grandma looked a little sheepish, but there was no need for her to feel awkward. The moment the words were out of her mouth I remembered a long-ago promise I'd made to my friend and mentor. Though Mrs. Walker had two daughters of her own, she claimed that wedding dress shopping with me would be one of the highlights of her motherhood experience. Even after Francesca gave her two beautiful granddaughters, Mrs. Walker still considered me family.

"Sounds like fun," I managed. "The three of us will have a wonderful time together, I'm sure."

Grandma pursed her lips like she had more to say.

"We won't have a wonderful time together?" I amended, confused.

"No, of course we will. I just think that it should be the four of us."

"Four? Who else would come?"

"Mrs. Vermeer."

"Michael's mom?"

"That's pretty standard procedure, Julia. She's going to be your mother-in-law. We need to at least invite her."

It wasn't that I had a bad relationship with Michael's parents. It was more that I didn't *have* a relationship with them. Holidays and Sunday dinners with his family were deafening affairs, filled with chaos and void of any meaningful conversation. We were lucky to get out a "Please pass the potatoes" over the raucous din. Michael's mother felt like a stranger to me. But I made the requisite call anyway, and she seemed pleased to be invited along.

On Saturday afternoon, we met at our farm for brief introductions, then piled into Mrs. Walker's Suburban. Grandma and Mrs. Walker sat in the front while my future mother-in-law and I climbed into the back. The radio was turned up a touch too loud, so Mrs. Vermeer and I couldn't hear what the ladies were discussing in the front seat. We were left to fend for ourselves.

Mrs. Vermeer was a petite woman, well over fifty but a stunning beauty in her own right, with dark hair and bright eyes that left no doubt as to where Michael got his good looks. Fortunately, Michael favored his father in stature. But tiny or not, Mrs. Vermeer was an intimidating woman, the sort of refined lady who never had a hair out of place or a perfectly manicured nail tip smudged. I couldn't keep my fingernails clean with two boys in the house, much less manicured. I wondered how she did it with five grown sons and nine grandchildren.

Alone in her presence for the first time in my life, I felt utterly tongue-tied and desperate; I couldn't think of a single thing to say to this woman who would soon be a part of my family. More accurately, I would be a part of hers. What if she didn't want me?

"I—I love my engagement ring," I finally ventured after we had traveled a few miles in utter silence. "Did you help Michael pick it out?"

"No," Mrs. Vermeer said, not unkindly. "He wanted to do it himself."

"Well, he did a good job."

"I saved my mother's ring for Michael's bride, but he wanted to buy you something new."

The statement stunned me. Michael had turned down a family heirloom in favor of purchasing a chain store engagement ring that had likely been mass-produced? Why? All of a sudden I feared that Mrs. Vermeer assumed it was my fault—that I had wanted something expensive and new. Had insisted on it.

"I would have loved to have your mother's ring," I said quickly. "I'm sure it's beautiful."

"Oh, it is. But it probably wouldn't have fit you anyway."

Mrs. Vermeer reached to touch the curled ends of her hair, and I saw the tiny bones in her slender wrist when the hem of her coat fell back. If her mother was anything like her, Mrs. Vermeer was right: the ring would never fit me. I wasn't a large girl, but I was easily double the size of Michael's diminutive mom.

"Well, then, maybe it worked out for the best," I muttered, feeling like an idiot.

We drove the rest of the way pretending to listen to the conversation that was going on in the front seat. Mrs. Walker and Grandma had been friends for decades, and they settled into an easy pattern of talk and laughter that we mimicked from the backseat. When they laughed, we chuckled along. When they spoke, we listened intently—or at least attempted to.

The first and only dress shop that we stopped at was in Glendale. Since it was a college town, the boutique stayed busy pretty much year-round, and Grandma had needed to book an appointment for me with the sales consultant. We were right on time, and as we neared the glass doors, they swung open for us as if by magic.

"Welcome to the French Door!" a plastic-looking young woman oozed at us. "I'm assuming you're with the DeSmit/Vermeer bridal party?"

I stared at the high plane of her marble forehead and the mass of butter-colored curls she had swept into an updo that towered six inches above her head. She was going to help me pick out a wedding dress?

"Yes," Grandma said, stepping into the brocade interior of the potpourri-scented shop, "that's us."

I followed my grandmother dumbly into the store and was struck with a sense of claustrophobia so acute that I almost turned around and left. We were standing beneath a chandelier as big as our kitchen table and surrounded by gaudy silk arrangements in gold urns that were nearly as tall as I was. Wedding dresses lined the walls in a blinding tapestry of pearl on ivory on white, and music that made me think of cherubs and bare-bottomed cupids floated around us. It was stifling. But Mrs. Walker and Mrs. Vermeer were behind me, and my only route of escape was effectively cut off. I couldn't go anywhere without barreling through them.

"Well, let me take your coats," the saleslady purred. "My

name is Liv and I'll be helping you today. Can I get you
something to drink?"

"Water," I managed.

"Not for you, silly!" Liv grinned at me. "You have to try
on dresses, and we wouldn't want to spill anything on the
gowns, now would we? That is, unless you're the bride." The
clerk tweaked Grandma's arm conspiratorially.

"No," Grandma assured her, "the pretty one is the bride."

My little entourage was brought flavored coffee and spiced
green tea while I was whisked away by my Barbie-doll atten-
dant. She marched me up and down the aisles of gowns,
pressing me for information about my likes and dislikes, my
childhood dreams of marital ecstasy. To her, it all came down
to the dress.

"You have to have some idea," Liv finally said, exasperated.
She had grilled me about length, sleeve design, necklines,
waistlines, and trains, and when I stared at her blankly, she
started in with specific cuts and styles. "Ball gown? Empire
waist? A-line? Sheath?"

I shrugged.

Liv moaned. But just as quickly as she showed defeat, she
perked up. "So we're starting with a blank slate. A tabula rasa.
And I get to write on you!"

She sounded just a little too excited about the idea.

A half hour later I was standing on a pedestal in front of
more reflective surfaces than a house of mirrors. I stared at my
hair and wished that I would've done something special with

it because my limp, mousy brown waves looked downright ridiculous paired with the frothy confection Liv had squeezed me into. I looked like a grubby little girl playing dress-up.

"This is a very special dress," Liv was saying as she focused her attention on the three women seated beneath me in tawny leather armchairs. I could tell she hoped they would prove more invested in this fashion show than I was. "It's a classic ball gown with a sequined bodice and a full tulle skirt."

I ran my hands down my prickly, glittery waist and pulled self-consciously at the stiff material of the scratchy skirt. It felt like fishnet. "It's not very . . . me," I said, surprising myself by voicing the words aloud.

"Of course it's you!" Liv chided. "Every girl gets to be a princess for one day in her life. Your wedding day is that day. If you look like a princess, you'll feel like one."

"I don't feel like a princess," I admitted. "I feel like the Sugar Plum Fairy."

Grandma and Mrs. Walker laughed. I couldn't tell if Mrs. Vermeer joined in, and by the time I caught her eye in the mirror, her mouth was arranged in a thin, neutral line.

"Try something else," Grandma called. "I don't think this is the one."

Liv had me try on an A-line next, a smooth wave of fabric that clung from chest to hip, then swelled in a curve of satin that fell to the floor in the shape of a dinner bell. With the wired crinoline I was wearing, I could tip one way and then the other without disrupting the perfect circle of the beribboned hemline.

"Better," Grandma said with a smile, but Liv did not seem impressed with the ticktock of my bell-like sway.

"I don't like the flowers," I said, indicating the champagne-colored roses that trailed in a meandering line from one spaghetti strap around my waist and all the way to the very hem of the skirt. "Too froufrou."

"Froufrou?" Mrs. Walker chortled. "Yeah, you're not exactly the fancy-Nancy type, are you?"

"Less sparkle," I instructed Liv. "And no flowers or ribbons."

"Now she develops an opinion," Liv teased. But I could sense her irritation.

I paraded out in three more gowns, adding a new imperative with each: no sequins, no ruffles, and nothing strapless. Even after wearing the strapless dress for five minutes I was irritated by the constant need to pull it up. Liv guaranteed that it wasn't going to fall down, but I wasn't about to chance it.

My sixth and final dress was something I had pulled off the rack at the last minute. Liv tried to talk me out of it, and I wondered why until I caught a glimpse of the tag and realized it was about half the price of the other gowns I'd been trying on. Grandma had assured me years ago that my wedding would never be a problem—she had been saving up since I was sixteen years old. But I still wanted to try to be frugal, and the simple empire waist of the dress appealed to me. Best of all, the fabric was actually touchable, soft. It reminded me a bit of the dress that Janice wore when she married my father. Of course, their marriage hadn't lasted, so maybe it was macabre for me to be drawn to the unpretentious throwback. But the skirt was like water in my hands, and I knew that the square neckline and straps would flatter my figure. Other than the hint of hand-stitched lace on the straps and at the waistline, the dress was unadorned.

"What is this fabric?" I asked Liv, reveling in the flowing shimmer.

"Crepe over a layer of sparkle organza," she said. "You shouldn't touch it so much. The oils in your hands will discolor the fabric."

I folded my hands in front of me and walked out of the dressing room ahead of Liv so she could carry the chapel-length train.

"Ooh!" Grandma cried the moment she saw me. "I love this one, Julia. It's so you."

Mrs. Walker agreed, and for the first time since we arrived at the French Door, I actually started enjoying myself. The gown was gorgeous, and just wearing it made me seem pretty too. No, not just pretty. Beautiful. Liv had been wrong. I didn't want to be a princess; I wanted to be me. Normal Julia, but amplified somehow, as if for once I could be seen as I was meant to be.

"What do you think, Mrs. Vermeer?" I asked, twirling so she could get the full effect of the classic, elegant dress.

"You don't have to call me Mrs. Vermeer," she protested,

shaking her head so that the pearls of her drop earrings gleamed in the bright lights. "I'm going to be your mother-in-law. Call me Diane."

"Okay." I smiled. "Diane. Do you like the dress?"

She tilted her head and studied me with a shrewd eye. I had hoped she'd be as enthusiastic as Grandma and Mrs. Walker, but Diane wasn't about to give me an easy thumbs-up. Running her fingernail against the curve of her lower lip, she finally nodded a little and said, "It's pretty, but I don't think that it would be Michael's choice."

My heart sank. I hadn't even given Michael a second thought. Wouldn't he be pleased with whatever I chose? When we had talked the night before, he assured me that I could show up in a flour sack and he'd still happily say, "I do." Maybe I had misread him. Maybe he was only pretending not to care.

"Which one do you think Michael would like?"

"Oh, I don't *think*—I *know* which one he'd like." Diane laughed. "He's been a groomsman in all four of his brothers' weddings, and when you're immersed in all the planning and hoopla, you learn pretty quickly what works for you and what doesn't."

I had been to two of those weddings with Michael, and he had never commented on any of the nuptial details, much less the bride's gown. I just assumed he felt the same way I did about it all: mildly indifferent. But if he secretly harbored some wedding dream, I needed to know. After all, I was the only person who could make that dream come true.

"The strapless one?" I guessed, remembering one of Michael's sisters-in-law's gowns.

"No." Diane smiled. "The first one. The princess one."

The Sugar Plum Fairy one, I thought. But it didn't matter if I felt like a marshmallow in the dress. I gave Diane a slight nod of thanks, then turned back to the mirror. Taking a long look at the gown I was wearing, I forced a smile and balled the supple cloth in my hands. I crinkled the folds of crepe and organza, loving the feel of the fabric one last time and intentionally ignoring Liv's muted gasp.

"The first one," I mimicked, repeating Diane's proclamation. "I'll take the first one. When do I need to come back for a fitting?"

second chance

"IT'S NOT TOO LATE," Grandma said.

I peeked up from my paperwork and caught a glimpse of her frown before she snapped the newspaper to attention and disappeared once again behind the Home and Garden section.

"Not too late for what?" I pretended I had no idea what she was talking about. Maybe she'd get the hint and go back to her recipes. Of course I knew she was referring to the dress—it featured as the main course in most of our conversations these days—but I was hoping she'd realize sooner or later that I wasn't going to budge and drop that hot-button topic once and for all.

I scribbled my signature on the bottom of our utility check and sat back to wait for Grandma's response. Tried to prep the perfect comeback: *"The dress is a gift to Michael. It's just one small way I get to say, 'I love you.' . . ."*

But instead of starting in on the glittery cupcake that was to be my wedding gown, Grandma merely kept reading her paper.

The wise thing to do was just to let it go and focus on the stack of bills and mail at my fingertips. But it hurt me that Grandma thought I was making a mistake by buying the dress Michael wanted instead of the one that was so obviously meant for me. It was just a dress, after all. Yards of material and thread and beadwork. I almost groaned at the thought of all those sequins and beads, but I swallowed my disappointment instead and said, "It's only a dress, Grandma."

She laid the newspaper down carefully. "I know it's just a dress. I wouldn't care if you wore jeans and a T-shirt to your wedding. I just think it's indicative of . . ."

We were finally getting somewhere. "What? It's indicative of what?"

Grandma shook her head as if to clear it. "Nothing, honey. Besides, when I said, 'It's not too late,' I wasn't talking about your wedding gown."

"You weren't?"

"No." She turned the page of her newspaper and lifted

it, creating a wall of words between us. "I was talking about Daniel's painting."

Naturally. Why deal with one problem when there were a host of issues to confront?

I reached across the table for the rolled-up picture that Daniel had brought home in his backpack that afternoon. It was crinkled from drops of spilled water and smudged in places, but it was a clever rendering all the same. Of course, it was too early to tell if Daniel would have a gift for art, but if his kindergarten creations held any clue of what was to come, we had a little Picasso on our hands.

Carefully spreading open the construction paper with my palms, I surveyed Daniel's bright scene for the hundredth time. In the center of the page was a pool of ultramarine poster paint, a glob so thick I could have peeled off the entire chunk with my fingernails. At first glance, I had thought the round centerpiece was a trampoline, but upon closer inspection it hit me that the sea of blue was a body of water. A pond, to be exact. And there were five people scattered around it. A stocky, yellow-haired Daniel; Simon, who was a skinny, frowning figure that stood taller than Daniel's rather plain-Jane interpretation of me; a gray-haired, skirted lady who was obviously Grandma; and a final, grinning man with sunburst hair to match my son's.

I didn't have to ask who the fifth person was.

When I first saw Parker smiling from the middle of Daniel's painting, I wanted to scream. He was still a stranger to us, a relative unknown when we were surrounded by friends and family who had been our help and support for years. Why did Parker have to round out the painting? What did Daniel see in him?

His daddy, I thought involuntarily. *He sees his daddy.*

But that was impossible. It was ridiculous to imagine that something deep inside of Daniel resonated with the man who gave him nothing more than a set of chromosomes. Sperm donation does not a father make, I decided with a sense of finality. Besides, hadn't Parker proved his instability? One little fight on the porch and he was gone. No phone call. No e-mail. No apology. And best of all, no Parker. We hadn't seen him or heard from him in weeks.

"It's just a painting," I told Grandma with a sigh. "Daniel drew it because of that day at the pond. Remember? He found a water bear. The painting is really about his water bear."

"If that's true, why didn't he paint a microscope? or a tardigrade?"

I covered my eyes with my hands and let Daniel's painting swish back into a loose roll. "Fine," I groaned. "It's about Parker. What would you have me do?"

"It's not too late," Grandma said again. "You can still call him."

"Why in the world would I do that?"

"For Daniel."

There was nothing I could say to that. I was being selfish, but I didn't want to hear it.

Grandma continued softly, "Everyone deserves a second chance, Julia."

"He just blew his second chance."

"Then you give him a third and a fourth . . ."

"I doubt he'd even talk to me," I argued, hoping that if I turned the tables, she'd realize I'd already done all I could. Hoping she'd let me off the hook.

"You could apologize."

"Apologize? For what?"

My eyes were still pressed closed, my head cupped in my hands, but I heard the distinctive rustle as Grandma folded her newspaper and dropped it on the table. "Nothing, I guess."

The legs of her chair squeaked against the laminate; then her slippered feet padded past. She touched my back, but before I could raise my hand to cover hers, she was gone.

"Good night," I called.

The only reply was the soft click of her bedroom door as it closed.

"Call Parker," I muttered to myself. "As if I don't have enough on my mind. I'm planning a wedding, for goodness' sake."

Rather than picking up the phone, I gathered my stack of mail and deposited it in the drawer where I kept items needing my attention. It'd still be around tomorrow, I decided, and now that Grandma had brought up Parker, I certainly wasn't in the right frame of mind for balancing our budget and sorting through paperwork. It was times like these that I could be convinced an online shopping spree was infinitely more important than groceries.

I would have gone for a walk, but the first snow of the season had begun to fall around noon, and though it was still technically autumn, winter was asserting its might. School had been let out early due to blizzardlike conditions, and I doubted if the boys would make it in tomorrow. At the very least they'd have a late start. I smiled. Just the thought of a snow day brought me back to my own childhood, to cold winter mornings huddled around the radio with my fingers crossed. There was nothing quite so sweet as hearing the words *Mason Elementary* and *canceled* in the same sentence.

When I was little and had a snow day, Grandma always made doughnuts for a treat. All at once I wished I were a more conscientious mother. I should have watched the forecast and stocked up on snowed-in necessities like hot chocolate and mini marshmallows. I threw open the cupboards and refrigerator and scanned our shelves for the necessary ingredients. Maybe hot doughnuts sprinkled with sugar and cinnamon would soften the boys toward me. And if we didn't have dough for biscuits, I could try chocolate chip cookies, cinnamon rolls, snickerdoodles, anything.

In less than a minute I was able to account for enough ingredients to make all my imagined treats and more. Though the truth was, none of it would do me any good if the boys were stuck at home. I'd still have to make my way in to Value

Foods. If school was canceled, Grandma would have to carry on the snow day traditions, not me.

She was a better mother than me. A better grandmother than I someday would be. A better person all around.

A string of unexpected thoughts wound themselves around my heart, binding my chest until it ached to breathe. I loved my grandmother more than my own life, but since Daniel was born, there had been times when I throbbed with an impossible jealousy toward her. Tonight, that envy felt like it would choke me.

I didn't want to think of my many shortcomings as a mother. Of Parker and second chances. Or even third chances. But Grandma had planted a seed in my mind with just a couple of words and the brush of her hand. And now that she was gone, her gentle reminders filled the room with an air of anticipation.

Maybe she was right. She usually was. Maybe it wasn't too late.

There was homework waiting for me in my messenger bag, but I couldn't bring myself to concentrate on the psychological particulars of childhood dysfunction. Nor could I stomach the thought of mindless TV. I hadn't been to the library in months, and the only magazine we had at the farm was *Better Homes and Gardens*, an old issue I had paged through twice already. The only thing left for me to do was the one thing that Grandma probably hoped I'd do even more than she prayed I'd call Parker. I got out my Bible.

With a storm raging both outside the windows and inside my heart, it hardly seemed like the opportune time to get my devotional life on track. But the house was quiet, and my mind was anything but. I needed something to distract me from the unsettling truth of Grandma's words.

In the half decade since Grandma had given me her precious Bible, it had only become more dog-eared and over-stuffed. I picked up her habit of collecting things, and the yellowing pages of Scripture were fat with letters, poems, church bulletins, and love notes—mostly from Daniel and Simon. It was hard to even find the chapter I was looking for, but more often than not I still stumbled across a treasure when I cracked the binding of that aging NIV.

It was on my way to Jeremiah that the little slip of paper fell from the pages and fluttered to the kitchen floor. I bent to pick it up and turned the bookmark-size scrap over and over in my hands in the hope of recognizing it. But although I thought I had been through every fragment contained in Grandma's Bible, this was new to me. It was a couple of penciled lines written in a strong, willowy hand that leaned slightly to the left as if blown by a breeze: Grandma's beautiful script in the years before the palsy made her fingers tremble.

I don't want Julia to be happy.
I don't expect her life to be easy.
I don't insist that it be painless.

But I do want her to be content.

I want her to love and be loved.

I want her to be holy.

The first line was like the quick stab of a knife, a wound I hadn't expected. *I don't want Julia to be happy.* Why not? Didn't I deserve happiness? Don't we all?

But even as I bristled in self-defense, my eyes scanned the rest of the words and I knew with a certain unflinching acceptance that my grandma's hope for my life was saturated with love and truth—the sort of honesty that couldn't be found in modern parenting tomes, where ease and happiness reigned paramount.

Happiness is fleeting. My dad had said those words to me a hundred times in our years together. A thousand? I didn't get it at the time; in fact, I thought my dad was a closet sadist for the enthusiasm with which he echoed ridiculous sayings like *No pain, no gain. Adversity builds character. We acquire the strength of what we have overcome.* Life was never about chasing butterflies for my dad. It was about swatting flies with a smile on his face.

I smoothed open Grandma's little proverb for my life and studied her wishes again. When had she written it? after Dad died? before? I could almost imagine her bent over the table where I now sat, weeping silent tears for her son and trying to arrange a life for the granddaughter she never planned to parent. Most mothers made lists of rules: No talking back.

No rudeness, put-downs, or insults. No skipping school, blowing curfew, or going out without permission. But my grandma made a life list. A scribbled prayer for more than just my behavior.

A hope for my life.

It was hard not to compare myself against her expectations, to wonder how I measured up. Grandma's words almost rang prophetic, for my life had been neither easy nor painless. But was I the woman she wanted me to be? Was I content? Did I know how to love and be loved? Was I holy?

Weighed down with wedding woes, brother battles, and the unresolved pain of Parker, I felt like a complete and utter failure. I had survived five years on my own. Five years as a single mother to two young boys who, for better or worse, were fiercely loved by a bruised and broken me. It didn't feel like enough.

I wish I could say that when I picked up the phone, my intentions were pure and my heart was ready for all that was to come. But mostly I did it out of duty, a sense of obligation to Daniel, and a desire to be the woman my grandmother wanted me to be. Calling Parker wouldn't make me happy, and it probably wasn't the holy thing to do, but for some reason it felt like the right thing to do.

His number was saved on my cell phone, and I selected it and hit Send before I had the chance to change my mind. It wasn't terribly late, but I wished for a fleeting moment that he had already silenced his cell for the night. I could hang up.

Or maybe leave a message, something short and meaningless. At least I could ease my conscience by knowing that I had tried.

He answered on the very first ring.

"Parker here."

I gulped. "Hi. It's Julia."

"I know. Your name came up on caller ID."

Resisting the urge to roll my eyes and hang up, I blurted out the first thing that came to mind. "How's your puppy?"

Parker laughed, but it was short and hollow-sounding. "She's fine."

We were silent for what felt like ages, the only sound between us the faint buzz and hum of a poor connection. I couldn't think of anything to say to him; I wondered why I had called at all, why I let myself be guilted into doing the one thing I dreaded most.

"How are the boys?" Parker finally asked. His voice was quiet, strained, as if it was difficult for him to form the words.

"They're fine." I glanced at the long spool of my son's painting and offered, "Daniel is proving himself to be quite the artist."

"Really? I thought he was going to be a scientist."

"He's a true Renaissance man."

"Like Leonardo da Vinci—an artist and a scientist. Or maybe his fascination with biology will fade. He could be the next Grant Wood."

"Who's Grant Wood?" I asked, the question tumbling out.

"He painted *American Gothic*. You know, the Depression-era farmer and his daughter? the pitchfork?"

I'd seen parodies of that painting on everything from *Green Acres* to *The Simpsons*. As usual, I felt like an idiot for asking such a stupid question. To cover up for my cultural gaffe, I said, "Daniel is five, Parker. I don't think he needs you to plot out the rest of his life."

"I'm not plotting. I'm dreaming."

I fought the urge to tell Parker he had no right to dream on Daniel's behalf, to fantasize about his future. But I hadn't called to pick a fight, and I reminded myself that I was doing this for my son, no matter the cost to myself. Instead of baiting Parker further, I put a steadying hand against my collarbone and forced myself to say, "I'm sorry about . . . what happened on the porch."

"Me too."

"Me too"? I hadn't expected that. I opened my mouth to tell Parker that I shouldn't have jumped to conclusions, but he beat me to the punch.

"I should have never just showed up like that. I know I put you in a really awkward spot."

"You did," I admitted, "but it wasn't entirely your fault. Simon can be pretty convincing."

I could almost hear the smile in Parker's voice when he agreed: "He's a charmer."

My own faint smile bloomed in response. "Are we . . . talking?"

"I think that's what they call this."

"I mean, civilly."

"We're trying."

"Good for us."

"Julia?"

"Yeah?"

"Why did you call?"

"I think we need to work this out," I said carefully, measuring out each syllable as if it mattered much. "For Daniel's sake, I think we need to find a way to . . . coexist."

"Me too," Parker whispered.

"But we need to set up some boundaries. Some guidelines for interaction."

"Guidelines for interaction? You make it sound like I'm being admitted on a trial basis."

"You are."

Parker sighed. "Okay. Fair enough."

"And . . ." I paused, wondering if I should tell him the rest of it or if my big news could wait. But there were enough secrets and lies between us; if I truly wanted to give this a shot for Daniel's sake, I had to come clean with everything. "And I need you to know that I'm getting married. In June. To the man you ran into at the farm that day."

"Congratulations." Parker cleared his throat and said it again. "Congratulations."

"Thank you."

"Will . . . will your fiancé want to . . ."

"Adopt Daniel?" I finished. "We've talked about it, but Michael doesn't have any definite plans. At least, not yet. I guess that's something we'll have to work out."

"Okay."

"Okay," I repeated. For the first time all night I felt confident, sure. "I think we could make this work."

"Me too," Parker agreed. But when he hung up, he didn't say good-bye. In fact, he didn't say anything at all. A moment later the line went dead, and I was left to wonder if the call was dropped or if Parker had severed our connection.

Just when I was trying to repair it.

a matter of the heart

WHEN I TOLD DANIEL that Parker was coming to visit, he nearly jumped out of his skin. I had waited to tell him until I knew for sure that Parker would keep his word, because after our phone conversation was cut short, I was left to wonder once again if Daniel's father would simply fade back out of our lives. But he called a couple days later and timidly asked if he could come up on Saturday to spend some time with the boys.

I agreed.

"He's coming?" Daniel squealed. "Parker's going to visit us?"

"On Saturday," I confirmed. "He'll come up around noon and we'll all have lunch together here; then he'd like to take you sledding."

"Sledding? Are you kidding me?"

I laughed. It was like I had just told him he was going to Disney World. "Honey, it's just to the golf course hill. Nothing fancy."

But Daniel was already gone. And although I wanted to resent his infatuation with Parker, I couldn't stop myself from chuckling as my son ran through the house, screaming for Simon.

Remarkably, Daniel wasn't the only person excited about Parker's impending visit. In the days leading up to the weekend, Simon seemed to relax, to loosen around the edges. I even caught him smiling once or twice and laughing at Daniel's ridiculous five-year-old jokes instead of barely concealing his annoyance.

"Are you looking forward to Saturday?" I asked him one evening as he got ready for bed.

Simon flashed me a quick, wary look. "Yeah," he said slowly. It was almost as if he was afraid to admit it.

Since things were calm between us, I didn't want to pry. But his answer took me by surprise, and I just had to ask. "Is it because of Parker? or because you're going sledding?"

"Sledding," he coughed out and disappeared down the hallway to his room.

"I'm sure it'll be lots of fun!" I called after him, trying to muster up some enthusiasm. His response left me unsettled. It felt like there was a family secret I wasn't privy to, and I existed in my own home like a stranger, an outsider who was left to wonder why everyone was smiling.

Even Grandma seemed in on it. She was quick to notice my hesitation when it came to Parker, and though she seemed almost amused at the duplicity of my on-again-off-again reaction to his reinstatement in our lives, she appeared eager to support our fumbling endeavors. Almost too eager.

"Maybe you should go with them this afternoon," she suggested on Saturday morning. We were buttering buns for a quick lunch of barbecued beef sandwiches and potato chips. "Parker might need an extra hand with the boys."

"They're not babies," I argued. "They practically take care of themselves. I think Parker can handle it."

"But he's not used to kids," Grandma reminded me. "He might not know what Daniel is capable of or overestimate Simon's ability to—"

"Fine," I cut in. "You're right." It was hard to discount the evidence of Parker's lack of parental expertise. There was his unannounced visit, his categorical acceptance of Simon's invitation, the fact that he brought along a puppy—even if it was his own—without questioning the appropriateness of the gesture . . . Grandma was right. Leaving the boys in his hands for an entire afternoon was just asking for trouble. Especially on the steep hills of the golf course. Especially armed with inner tubes and toboggans.

"I'll go along," I conceded, noting the air of satisfaction that settled around my grandmother like a soft fragrance. "Why don't you come too? You could sit in the clubhouse with a cup of coffee and enjoy the festivities."

Grandma patted my arm. "No, you kids just go. Since the house is going to be quiet, I might take a nap."

"You feeling okay?"

"A little bug." Grandma brushed off my concern, wiping it away with long, easy strokes as she smeared butter on both sides of the last bun. She tucked the roll back into the bag and secured it with a twisty tie. "You want to peel some carrots?"

"Sure," I said, "but while I'm doing it, I want to hear more about this bug. Do you need to go in?"

"To my doctor? It's just the flu."

"You have the flu?"

"No." Grandma shook her head quickly. "I'm just feeling a little under the weather. Achy, tired, chilled . . . You know."

"How long has this been going on?" I paused as I bent over the vegetable drawer of our refrigerator and studied her face. Grandma was no liar, but I could tell when she was stretching the truth.

"A couple days."

Her eyes slid away from mine when she said it. I knew her so-called flu had been going on for longer than that. "How long?" I asked again.

"A week or so."

"Two?"

"Maybe."

I yanked the bag of carrots out of the fridge and heaved the door closed. "Grandma," I chided, "you need to see your doctor."

"For a little virus?"

"You don't know that you have a virus."

"My dear, when you've been around for as long as I have, you get to know your body. I have a winter bug. I'll be fine."

She sounded so sure of herself, but I couldn't quiet the voice inside my head that distrusted her easy explanation. *Press her,* I thought. *Make her listen.* But as wise and wonderful as my grandmother was, she was also stubborn. I didn't have to speculate about where my greatest strength and weakness came from, nor did I have to continue questioning her to learn that as far as her health was concerned, her lips were sealed.

Parker arrived right on time. In fact, he knocked on the door exactly one minute before noon, our agreed-upon hour of rendezvous. I glanced at the clock on the wall and wondered if he had intentionally sped up and slowed down on the two-hour drive or if he had stood on the porch for a couple of minutes so that his entrance would be punctual, precise.

I was grateful that Daniel and Simon were waiting at the door so I didn't have to be the one to welcome Parker back into our house. It had been three weeks since we had last seen him. Since he had shown up out of the blue, bearing a puppy and nearly ruining everything by running into Michael.

Michael. Just the thought of my future husband made me fold my lower lip between my teeth. I was startled by the faint taste of metal on my tongue, a reminder that I needed to break the nasty nervous habit of lip biting. But it was subconscious, and as long as Michael didn't know about Parker, I knew I was destined to keep doing it. Grandma had warned me that it was past time to fill in my fiancé about the reintroduction of Patrick Holt into my life, but I couldn't quite bring myself to do it. At least, not over the phone. That sort of serious conversation deserved face-to-face contact, at the very least.

But I didn't have time to think about that now. Parker was in my mudroom, unlacing his snowy boots and laughing with my kids.

In less than a minute they had all spilled into the kitchen, a trio of shoving, laughing boys who seemed far too at ease with each other to betray the infancy of their untried relationships. All the same, there was something endearing about the easy way they delighted in each other's company, the almost-coltish play as they pushed and pulled, half-wrestling, half-embracing.

"Hi, Parker," I said as I put the last plate on the table.

He had Simon and Daniel in matching headlocks and looked up at me with a sheepish grin. "Hi, Julia. It's nice to see you again."

I should have said, *You too,* but I couldn't do it. I didn't want to. Though I appreciated what he did for my boys, how he made them feel, it was hard for me to separate our history from this more recent, happier plotline. I simply wasn't there yet, and I didn't know if I would ever be.

"You're just in time," I told him stiffly. "Lunch is ready."

"Smells delicious." Parker sniffed the air and released his hold on the boys. "You'd better go wash your hands," he told them. "Something tells me your paws are far from clean."

"You too!" Daniel shouted, taking him by the hand.

I was grateful that my son questioned Parker's cleanliness. I wasn't comfortable with the thought of being alone with him in the kitchen, even if it was for only a few minutes.

Our shared meal was uneventful but far from peaceful. Hearing Daniel and Simon giggle and talk over each other and make crazy plans for their afternoon of outdoor fun was enough to make me forget all about my discomfort in Parker's presence. I think even Grandma regretted her decision to stay home as the boys continued to strategize more and more elaborate feats of daring.

"Be careful," she warned, the wrinkles in her forehead deepening in worry. But the boys weren't paying attention, so she gave me a hard look filled with meaning. A look I took to mean, *It's on your shoulders.* Wasn't everything?

When we got to the sledding hill, it had just started to snow, a soft, light curtain of flurries that made filigree patterns in the sky like a sheet of gauzy crochet. The parking lot was nearly empty, and the hill all but abandoned, I assumed because parents were worried about another storm. It was perfect. We had the place to ourselves and a fast-accumulating layer of fresh snow to gentle every fall.

I stood at a distance as Parker unloaded a cache of sledding equipment from the trunk of his car, a stockpile of sleds and disks so new, they still had the price tags on.

"Did you buy these just for today?" I whispered as he handed Simon a molded piece of plastic that looked like a cross between a snowboard and a spaceship.

"Does it matter?" he muttered back.

"Well, you didn't have to do that. The boys have sleds. . . ." But I doubted that he heard a word I said. The three of them were each armed with their weapon of choice, and before I could issue my favorite "Don't do anything stupid" speech, Simon let out a whoop and made a mad dash for the top of the hill. Daniel giggled and followed, with Parker only steps behind.

I watched as they launched, one by one, over a barely visible edge of white on white. There were three puffs of snow like subtle explosions of flour and three rowdy, boyish cries of elation. Then they were gone.

Alone in the golf course parking lot, I raised my palms to the sky and watched snowflakes collect on my mittens.

The crystals fell in arabesque patterns, gathering in concert to rise like fairy-tale castles from the dark contours of my palms. They were all the same, I decided. Castles made of sand and snow. They were pretty, but they didn't last. They never did.

I knew it was a matter of the heart. That this careful construction of imaginary landscapes was a wild, secret thing. Days like today were a sanctuary, a magical world where anything seemed possible but nothing truly was. As I watched the turrets slowly take shape in my hands, I realized that we did this to ourselves. Our searching souls pursued happy endings. And the heart was capable of great and deceiving beauty.

I sighed and brushed my palms together, loosening the snow, ruining the fantasy. Suddenly I was exhausted and sad, concerned that the daydream my boys were experiencing was destined to be short-lived. It would end in heartbreak. How could it not?

The worst part was, I was encouraging it.

By the time they trekked back up the hill, I was morose. I had convinced myself that reaching out to Parker was a huge mistake, a colossal blunder that I might spend the rest of my life trying to overcome. But the boys were immune to my mood, and when Daniel saw me still leaning against Parker's car, he came screeching across the snow.

"You have to come down with us!" he yelled even though he was standing right in front of me.

"I don't know, honey. I don't want to make you miss a single turn."

"You won't have to," Parker said, coming up behind Daniel and putting a gloved hand on his shoulder. "I bought four sleds."

"Four? But you were supposed to take the boys alone. I only decided to come along this morning."

Parker lifted his shoulder as if to shrug off the implications of my words. "Always be prepared."

"Here, Mom." Daniel handed over his sled and raced around me to the gaping trunk of the car. He lifted out a final, flat disk and jumped to close the latch. But he couldn't quite reach it.

"I got it, buddy," Parker said. And without warning he leaned in and brushed past me to shut the trunk.

I don't think he realized how close we would be when he slanted toward me to slam the latch home. How we would, for the briefest of seconds, be connected. Blessedly, it was all over in a flash, a mere instant of contact, but when Parker backed away, I was dizzy with the warm memory of his breath on my cheek, the weight of his chest against mine. Michael was all that I knew, all that I remembered, and I was shaken by my own reaction to Parker's proximity.

"Uh, sorry about that," he mumbled, as red-cheeked as I must have been.

But my son was oblivious to the tension between his mother and his beloved friend. "Let's go sledding!" Daniel bellowed. He poked us both with his sled, prodding us in turn until we left the car behind and led the way to where Simon was waiting, legs spread wide and arms crossed against his chest. King of the hill. King of the snow castle we insisted on building.

I blinked snowflakes from my eyelashes and determined to wipe my mind clean, at least for the afternoon. No more worries about Michael and Parker, about impossible dreams or awkward moments. Today was not about the heart. It was about having fun.

At least, that's what I told myself.

"Grandma, we're home!" The moment we stepped in the door, Daniel announced our arrival with such gusto, it was as if we had been gone for weeks instead of hours. "It was awesome!"

"Stop shouting," I scolded him. "Hang up your gear and go find her if you want to talk about your adventure."

"I can't get my snow pants off," he complained.

Of course he couldn't. They were bunched around his ankles, tangled on the Velcro straps of his drenched boots.

"You have to take your boots off first," I told him. "Like Simon. Watch how Simon does it."

My brother was already stripped down to his street clothes, coat and snow pants hung on his hook and mittens and hat positioned over the heat register for efficient drying. It had been a while since he had taken the time to be so conscientious, and I wanted to give him a hug for not abandoning everything in a pile on the floor. Instead, I winked when he caught my eye. Though he didn't exactly smile in return, I believed he stood just a little straighter.

"I'm going to go find Grandma," Simon said, stepping around the rest of us as we continued to struggle with damp coats and ice-caked mittens.

"And I'm going to get those boots off." Parker crouched down to help Daniel. "On the count of one, two, three!" The boot popped off and Parker went flying backward. An affected show if ever I saw one, but it made Daniel giggle, so I figured it was worth it.

"Hot cocoa, anyone?" I asked. "And maybe doughnuts? Would you like to make some homemade doughnuts?"

Daniel's squeal was answer enough, and I turned from the mudroom with a grin on my face. I nearly ran into Simon.

"Julia!" he wheezed, grabbing at my arms, my shoulders, even the fabric of my worn sweatshirt. His fingers were like claws, hooked with a frantic desperation that seeped into my bones with every touch. "Julia, help!"

My chest tightened and the blood in my veins seemed to freeze over. "What's wrong?" I cupped his face with cold hands. "Tell me what's wrong."

"It's Grandma. She's . . . she . . ."

Parker had come to stand in the mudroom door, and I

thrust Simon into his arms. "Hold him!" I commanded. "Keep them both here!"

The boys were whining, fighting Parker as they tried to follow me, but I could hear the soothing tenor of his voice as he attempted to calm them down. I couldn't worry about the boys now. I had to find Grandma.

She was in the living room, slumped in her favorite knitting chair. The footrest was up, but one of her legs dangled off the side. A ball of robin's-egg blue yarn had tumbled to the floor and unraveled halfway across the room, a winding trail of reflected sky that looked like the map of a river against the wood-grained laminate. I took in the details in a single pulse: the crooked blanket across her lap, the way her hand fell over the arm of the chair, palm opened heavenward as if she were waiting for someone to hold it.

Before my heart could beat again, I knew.

Suddenly I was on my knees at her side, her brittle hand tucked in both of mine, my lips on her lined forehead.

"Grandma." My voice broke on the word—shattered, really—around a sob that tore from my throat.

But she responded. "Julia . . ."

I threw myself back and studied her face. Blue lips, pale skin, eyes that registered pain and confusion, but also understanding. She saw me. She knew me.

"Parker!" I screamed. "Parker! Get in here! I need you!"

He was at my side before I could become completely hysterical. I felt him put his arms around me and pull me away from her, out of the way so he could slide his hands beneath her and hold her close. He lifted her out of the chair like she weighed nothing at all. She was a child in his arms, a delicate little girl as breakable and fine as porcelain.

"I'll call 911," I whispered.

"No. We'll take her. By the time they dispatch an ambulance, we'll already be at the hospital. You can call from my cell phone when we're in the car."

"The boys . . ."

"We have to take them. We can't leave them here alone."

I melted into Parker's confident authority, so grateful for his presence, for his arms around her, that I could hardly breathe. There was nothing I could do but trace his footsteps and trust that he'd lead me in the right direction. I couldn't think. I couldn't pray.

But as I tucked the boys against me and settled them, weeping and shaking, in the backseat of the car, every fiber of my being groaned and whimpered and cried.

Save her.

Part 3

different world

GRANDMA'S HEART ATTACK was acute.

The doctors in the ER started thrombolytic therapy almost immediately because they were more concerned about saving her life than the elevated risk of stroke complications. And as a social worker helped me wade through the necessary medical waivers and documents, the cardiac surgeon at the heart hospital two hours from Mason prepped for a lengthy operation.

She was whisked away before I could say good-bye.

I didn't know if I'd ever see her again.

In spite of Grandma's critical condition, the doctors assured me that she was stabilized and ready for airlift transport. But when I heard the muted thrum of helicopter blades fading away into an unknown sky, I went weak in the knees.

"Let's sit down," Parker murmured, catching me around the waist. He escorted me down the hallway to the nearest bench, bearing most of my weight so that the soles of my feet barely kissed the floor. "She's in the best hands."

"She is," one of the ER doctors assured me. He didn't look much older than Michael, and I was disgusted by the almost self-satisfied smile he wore. Though it was likely he was only trying to reassure me, his easy platitudes and unruffled demeanor just made me more agitated. Shouldn't his stethoscope be crooked? his perfectly coiffed hair out of place? his white coat missing a button? Where was the blood? the macabre signs of trauma that would testify to the horror of this night?

But Grandma hadn't bled. She hadn't cried or struggled or fought. Instead, she withered quietly, barely moving when they hooked her up to an EKG machine, tried time and again to draw blood from flaccid veins, and started an IV for infusions of nitroglycerin, aspirin, and what the nurse called "clotbusters."

Remembering the roller coaster of our hospital nightmare, I suddenly felt faint. The ER doctor must have noticed that any remaining color drained from my cheeks because one moment he was standing in front of me, and the next he was kneeling at my side with his hand on the back of my neck.

"Put your head down," he instructed. "Between your knees . . . that's the way. Now breathe; just breathe." He patted my back awkwardly, and I longed to wiggle out from under his patronizing touch. But my vision was dotted with a million points of light, bright stars that danced behind my eyelids and made me too nauseous to move a muscle.

I took shallow gulps of air between my lips, each inhalation hissing over the sharp lines of my teeth as if I were having a heart attack too. And it felt like I was. My chest was bound so tightly that I realized I couldn't get enough oxygen no matter how hard I tried. I gasped and coughed and wheezed. I panted. I choked. And I was so focused on my own implosion that it took me a very long time to realize there was a sound like fear in the room, a low moan of agony so acute, I finally lifted my throbbing head to see where it was coming from and why.

It was coming from me.

Parker materialized in front of me out of nowhere. I felt him more than I saw him, felt his hands on my shoulders as he pulled me to him and then his arms around me when my head fell to his chest. I sobbed against him, soaked the fabric of his T-shirt with my tears, and he only drew me in tighter. It felt like he was trying to press the ache out of me with the strength of his embrace. He didn't say anything, just shushed quietly as if I were a child, and somehow the sound was soothing.

I don't know how long we crouched like that, Parker on

his knees on the hard, tile floor, and me on the edge of a molded plastic bench with the burden of my agony like a deadweight between us. But my tears subsided gradually, and my lungs began to function again. I wasn't having a heart attack, and I didn't know if that was a blessing or a curse.

"I'll be okay," I whispered. I ducked my head and pushed away from Parker, yanking the cuffs of my sweatshirt down over my hands so I could wipe my face with the soft, gray material. If I could have, I probably would have hidden there forever, tucked behind the refuge of my cotton sleeves, where I could pretend everything was okay. But nothing was okay. The boys were terrified, blind and ignorant of all that had happened as they waited with a secretary in the prayer room. And Grandma was on her way to surgery. At best, she would end up in the intensive care unit of a hospital 120 miles away. At worst . . . But I couldn't think about that.

"Take your time, Julia," Parker said.

"She's been through a lot tonight," the doctor began as though I weren't sitting right next to him. "You might want to give her a sedative when you get home so she can sleep."

"We're not going home. We're going to the heart hospital," I sniffed, emerging from behind my tearstained sweatshirt. "At least, I am. You can go home, Parker, and the boys can—"

"I'm not going anywhere," Parker insisted. "And we'll take the boys along. I can stay with them while you . . ."

What? While I did what? paced the halls? held her hand? A fresh wave of helplessness made me whimper.

Parker didn't even try to tell me it would be okay.

We sat in silence for a few more moments; then I took a deep, shaky breath and heaved myself up. Unbelievably, my legs supported me. My head felt foggy but capable of forming a coherent thought. I even nodded as the doctor handed me a few brochures on emergency coronary artery bypass grafts and heart disease in women. Only minutes ago I had been a blubbering mess, but I had more or less completed the transformation to a normal, functioning human being. Although nothing about the evening seemed anywhere near normal.

After a round of handshakes and a well-rehearsed wish for my grandmother's full and complete recovery, the doctor disappeared down the hallway and Parker and I were left alone. It was a vacant feeling. A solitary, almost-desolate feeling, for where was I to turn from here? Grandma was in a helicopter speeding toward an operating room. Michael was six hours away in Iowa City. And the only person I had to lean on was a virtual stranger. A man who had cradled my grandma as if she were his own and held me when I cried, but an outsider all the same. Who was Parker to me but a complication?

It struck me that for the first time in my life, it was just me and God. Everything else, everyone else, had been stripped away. And Simon and Daniel would look to me the way I had looked to the woman who now lingered in precarious condition in the belly of a helicopter.

"Julia?" Parker asked, severing the thin strand of my concentration.

"Let's go get the boys," I said.

"What are we going to tell them?"

"The truth," I sighed, feeling my voice splinter on the word. I swallowed, tried again. "They deserve the truth."

He nodded and turned to lead the way. For just an instant, we were side-by-side, almost leaning against each other as we began the short journey to the prayer room and the distraught boys who waited for us there. We matched our steps, and Parker's hand brushed my arm from elbow to wrist like he was going to lace his fingers through mine. As if that was the only way we could face this: together. It almost felt natural, and I turned my palm out to receive his touch, but before I could grasp the implications of such an action, Parker veered away a little and put empty space between us. It felt gaping.

Simon and Daniel must have heard our approach down the empty hospital hallway because they came flying out of the prayer room before the disgruntled secretary could stop them.

"Hi, guys," I whispered as they crashed into me. Simon tucked his head against the hollow beneath my collarbone, and Daniel pressed his face into my side. I curled my arms around them and dropped my cheek to Simon's dark hair. When he didn't protest, I kissed his head. Once. Twice. Three times for good measure.

"Is she going to be okay?" Simon murmured against my shirt.

"We don't know that yet."

He flung himself away from me. "What are we supposed to do?"

I didn't know if his question was rhetorical or if he actually wanted an answer, but I couldn't stand the way grief and confusion mingled in his eyes. There were paths of dry tears that left narrow tributaries down the smooth plane of his cheeks, and his lips trembled with barely contained emotion. It nearly ripped me in two to see him so upset. "There's not much we can do," I told him gently. "We'll go to the heart hospital and wait for her surgery to be over."

"She's in surgery? For what?"

"Her heart. She had a heart attack."

"Grandma has a perfect heart," Daniel said, looking at me. His expression was so earnest, so innocent, I bent to drop a kiss on his smooth forehead.

"Her heart is perfect," I agreed. "It's just . . . old."

"What else?" Simon demanded.

"What do you mean?"

"What else can we *do*?"

I looked over his head and caught Parker's troubled gaze. The man across from me appeared appropriately worn by the events of our afternoon. His shirt was half-tucked in and half-hanging out of the waistband of his creased jeans. His hair was disheveled and his skin looked ashen. As I watched, he tugged his lips into the semblance of a smile, but it was crooked and sad, and I was grateful when he abandoned his optimistic endeavor and simply mouthed the words, *I'm so sorry.*

"Julia," Simon demanded yet again, "what do we do?"

Turning my attention back to my brother, I brushed the line of his perfect cheekbone with my knuckles.

"We pray."

Instead of taking the boys along to the heart hospital, I called Mrs. Walker and filled her in on the situation. At first, Simon was irate at the thought of being left behind, but by the time we stopped at home to pack an overnight bag, close up the house, and make a few necessary phone calls, both of the boys were glassy-eyed and numb. There was little for them to do but curl up on the Walkers' couch and accept the cup of hot cocoa that Maggie had prepared for each of them. I watched as the young woman whom I loved like a little sister covered my boys with plush blankets and turned on a DVD that drew their gazes like moths to a flame.

"Thank you," I said, my throat so full of gratitude I could hardly speak.

Maggie gave me a grim smile and a tight hug, then released me to the shepherding arms of her mother. "We'll take good care of them," Maggie promised as I left the room.

Mrs. Walker ushered Parker and me into the kitchen and eased the pocket door closed behind us. She wore a confident expression in front of the boys, but when we were alone in the kitchen, her features crumbled. "Oh, Julia, I'm so sorry!"

I wrapped my arms around her and said with more conviction than I felt, "She's going to be okay. But I want to be there when she gets out of surgery."

Mrs. Walker swept her fingers beneath her eyes and backed away. "Of course you do. Don't worry about us; we'll be just fine." She threw Parker an uncertain look, and I realized that I hadn't even bothered to make introductions.

"I'm not thinking clearly," I muttered, shaking my head. "Mrs. Walker, this is Patrick Holt. A . . . a family friend."

I could tell that her confusion was mounting, but the evening had already proven to be astonishing and she didn't pry further.

"Parker is on his way home," I began, but before I could explain, he cut in.

"Actually, I'm going to drive you to the hospital."

My attention snapped to him. "No, you need to get home."

"I don't think you should make the trip alone."

"She shouldn't," Mrs. Walker agreed, siding with Parker though she had known him less than five minutes. "Let him take you, Julia. I'd go myself, but someone needs to watch the boys."

I wanted to argue, but my fingers were tingling and my

head felt swathed in cotton. Maybe I wasn't in the best condition to drive. "Fine," I mumbled.

"We'd better take off," Parker said with an air of irrefutable authority.

I wasn't entirely thrilled with the way he was telling me what to do, but I felt powerless to protest. Rather than arguing or trying to assert control over the situation, I let him lead me out of the kitchen to the spacious entryway.

"Call me anytime day or night," Mrs. Walker told me, following closely in my footsteps. "I'll keep the phone by my bed."

"The boys only grabbed enough clothes for tomorrow, but as always, the door is unlocked in case you need anything. If we decide to stay . . ."

"Stay as long as you need to. I mothered five children; I think I can handle two more for a couple of days."

As Parker was lacing up his boots, I crept into the living room and gave Daniel and Simon one last hug and kiss. They were both clutching their mugs of cocoa and staring blankly at the television. I breathed a prayer over their heads, pleading with God to hold their hearts, to give them hope. To give us all a reason to hope.

The car was still running and Parker had left the heat on full blast. I was gripped by a desire to turn on the air-conditioning or at least throw open the windows, but I shrugged off my coat instead.

"Hot?" Parker looked at me out of the corner of his eye as he backed down the Walkers' long driveway.

"I'm okay."

"Don't say that," he complained. "You've said that a dozen times already tonight. You're not okay. And you don't have to be."

He was right. I wanted to fall apart at the seams. But hearing him prescribe my emotions as if he knew me and knew how I should and should not feel irritated me to no end. "Excuse me? If I say I'm fine, I'm fine."

"You said okay."

"Whatever."

Parker backed off and consulted the map that a nurse had drawn for him.

"Do you want me to drive?" I ventured.

"No."

"It's just that you don't know the area very well . . ."

"I can read a map. Besides, you should sleep. Lay your seat back or something. It's going to be a long night."

"As if I could sleep."

"You could try."

I exhaled sharply. "I don't appreciate being bossed around."

"I'm not trying to tell you what to do," Parker sighed. His eyes caught mine for a second, and I read sympathy there. Pity? Compassion? Whatever it was, it was rich and heady and dark. He said quietly, "I'm trying to help."

My blood was pounding in my temples, so I looked away and didn't bother to answer. We drove in silence, and I stared out the dark windshield at the straight stretch of deserted highway, mesmerized by the way the wind whipped the inch or so of new snow across the road. What had fallen so softly was now lashed in shallow drifts with severe peaks and chasms. It seemed that I could drag my fingertip along the edge and split my skin like the flesh of a ripe peach. Everything felt violent. Harsh.

The world was a very different place than it had been only hours before.

I can't do this alone, I prayed without saying a word. *You have to be with me. You have to show me that You're here.*

God didn't answer, but as soon as my heart said *amen,* Parker broke the stillness with a tentative ahem. "So . . . tell me about your grandmother."

I squinted at him in the dim interior of the car, uncertain about his motivations. It was a strange thing to ask. But even as I contemplated ignoring him, I found that I wanted to talk about Grandma. Memories bloomed over me, a rush of sudden remembrances that stirred my soul in spite of everything. She was so beautiful. So good and kind and loving. What would she do to bridge the space between? How had she comforted me when Dad was diagnosed with cancer?

Grandma prayed. She smiled. She filled my life with story.

"My grandma raised me," I said.

Parker seemed to relax a bit. "Go on," he prompted.

"Really, she's more like the mother I never had. . . ."

autobiographies

GRANDMA PULLED THROUGH SURGERY with flying colors. At least, that's what the doctors said. To me, *flying colors* was a bit of an exaggeration, for in the days following her double-bypass operation, my usually vibrant grandmother seemed as insubstantial as mist. Her hair, which had been the color of silvered granite for as long as I could recall, had turned white overnight. It was as fine and weightless as duckling down, and it feathered across her bleached hospital pillow like a translucent vapor. I smoothed the gauzy strands from her forehead with the barest of touches, my fingertips tracing wrinkles in skin the color of bone and eggshells.

Everything about her seemed white and light and tenuous. Her breathing was so shallow that sometimes I would put my cheek next to her lips just so I could feel the slight puff when she exhaled. It shocked me that even her breath was cool and wispy, weightless—like the frosty air that emanated from the frames of our ancient windows.

Grandma was a winter queen, a sleeping angel, a sweet and fleeting dream.

"She's going to make it," the doctors told me.

But I couldn't help feeling like the woman I had known for nearly twenty-five years was already gone.

The Saturday after Grandma's heart attack, Michael drove up from Iowa City and surprised me with a quick visit. I was sitting by Grandma's bedside as she slept, and when I felt the burden of his hand on my shoulder, I knew who he was without turning around. The sob that swelled inside of me was a savage, uncontainable thing, and I flew to my feet and yanked him into the hall, where I could hold him and weep without waking her.

It was so good to feel his arms around me, to inhale the familiarity of his scent and savor the sound of my name on his lips. I never wanted to let go. I could have climbed inside of Michael in that moment. I wanted to peel back his skin and step in, to become a part of something other than myself so that I didn't have to carry the weight of all my worries alone.

But Michael extracted himself from my desperate grip after a few gulping, gasping moments and led me to the cafeteria. He sat me down at a tiny round table and gave me a handful of napkins to clean myself up. Then he disappeared, mumbling about how I was becoming downright scrawny, and returned with a tray filled with food.

"Chicken soup," he said, pointing to a bowl of unappetizing yellow liquid. "And a hamburger and fries if that sounds better. Or pie and ice cream."

"What kind of pie?" I muttered thickly. My tongue felt too big for my mouth, my throat lined with sandpaper.

"Cherry."

"I'll take the coffee." I reached for one of the mugs of oily coffee, but Michael batted my hand away.

"You have to eat something first."

When I didn't respond, he lifted the bowl of soup off the tray and placed it in front of me. "Start with this," he instructed. "We'll see where we go from there."

Michael ate the hamburger and fries while I spooned watery chicken broth into my mouth with methodical concentration. Every time he took a bite, I tried to follow suit. But the soup tasted funny to me, metallic and fake, like I was eating reconstituted noodles and imitation chicken. I gave up after a while and soothed my stomach with the mug of lukewarm coffee that he had denied me earlier. It was terrible, but I had grown used to it in a week of eating and drinking little else.

Our conversation was sporadic at best, for what was there to say with my grandmother languishing in a hospital room? We could hardly gab about wedding plans. Or discuss what we wanted to get the boys for Christmas. Thanksgiving was just over a week away, but that seemed completely irrelevant to me. Nothing mattered but the woman in white, my matchless, ailing grandmother.

"How's she doing?" Michael asked when it became obvious that I had eaten all I could stomach.

"Good, they say."

"What do you mean, they say?"

I bit my lower lip and traced the rim of my coffee cup with my finger. "She's recovering as well as can be expected. She walks to therapy every day, and her appetite is starting to pick up."

"Those are all good things."

"I know."

"And she's out of the ICU," Michael reminded me.

"Yeah. I don't have to scrub up to visit her."

"So why so glum?" Michael reached over and stopped my hand from tracing its squeaky path along the cheap hospital porcelain. He laced his fingers through mine and pulled my hand to the table between us, where he held it fast.

"She's . . ." I gulped, suddenly afraid I would cry. Not again. I didn't want to break down again. "She's just not herself," I managed in a whisper. Offering Michael a little smile, I sniffed and tried to pull my hand away. He wouldn't let go.

"What do you mean, she's not herself?"

I didn't feel like talking about it, so I used my free hand to lift the dessert plate that contained the uneaten piece of cherry pie. "Want to split this with me?" I asked.

Michael gave me a knowing look, but he seemed willing enough to let me keep my secrets until I was ready to share. Rather than forcing the issue, he abandoned his attempt to get me to talk and gathered two forks from the messy tray. He happily ate more than his portion of the mediocre pie. I swallowed because I had to.

Michael spent the rest of the day by my side. He held my hand, chatted with Grandma when she woke, and even talked shop with the doctor who made rounds in the late afternoon. My fiancé seemed perfectly at ease, and it struck me that he would be an excellent doctor someday. Calm and confident. His very presence a quiet comfort. Pride rose in me like bread baking, but there was a certain maternal quality to my delight that made me realize we hadn't spent nearly enough time alone lately. Where was the passion? the ache at my center when Michael was nearby? But obviously the hospital was hardly the place for romance. It was nothing but a fleeting thought.

I was grateful that he came and sorry when he went.

Toward the end of Grandma's second week in the heart

hospital, her surgeon informed me that she was almost ready to be discharged.

Although her stay had been a nightmare of uncertainty, of driving back and forth, passing off Daniel and Simon for days at a time, and relying on the goodness of the Walkers, the boys' teachers, and even Parker to help pick up the slack, I was shocked to think of taking her home.

"Already?"

"There's nothing we can do for her here that you can't do for her at home. She'll have to continue cardiac rehabilitation, of course, and you'll be in charge of her medications. The nutritionist has drawn up a loose meal plan for the first few weeks, and one of our nurses will be in contact about follow-up visits."

My mind whirled with the implications of everything he said. Therapy, medications, special meals, more appointments . . . Of course, I would gladly follow each instruction to the letter and do everything in my power to aid in my grandmother's recovery. But standing in the hallway outside her room, I couldn't help feeling overwhelmed.

And scared.

When he walked away, I whispered, "Lord, help me."

I hadn't heard Grandma's favorite nurse come up behind me, and I jumped when she wrapped an arm around my shoulders. She smiled a little and gave me a quick, tight hug. "He will," she told me, her eyes holding mine in a gaze that was both serious and soothing. Then she breezed into the room and left me to wonder how she knew just what to say.

With discharge only days away, I was forced to focus on my home life. Grandma assured me that she would be fine in the heart hospital alone, and I used the opportunity to throw myself at the responsibilities I had neglected since her heart attack.

My desk at Value Foods was an uncharacteristic clutter of mail and documents and Post-it notes with scribbled pleas from my coworkers. I took the boys along with me one evening and worked until nearly ten o'clock, allowing them to play Uno online while I tried to make sense of my rat's nest of responsibilities. By the time I left, I only felt more tangled.

But work wasn't the only thing clamoring for my attention. Though I had e-mailed my professor at the tech school and explained my grandmother's situation, I still had to complete the coursework. He had gladly granted me an extension, but I knew that if I didn't get caught up before Grandma came home, it might never happen. The biggest obstacle I faced was my fifth activity: an autobiography.

I was supposed to disclose important family interactions and relationships, as well as analyze my most memorable grade school year and other major life events. It was an easy enough task, but complicated by the fact that nothing about my life seemed simple. What could I say about my early family interactions? Through the lens of my adulthood I could clearly see that my mom was a drifter, a deadbeat. When I was really honest with myself, I was able to admit that she was what the older ladies at our church would call a floozy. And as much as I worshiped my dad, he was an enabler. He loved her, for better or worse, and he put up with things that should have never gone unchecked.

So what was I to write? that I grew up in a family fraught with dysfunction? that I was abandoned and ignored by the woman who was supposed to love me best? that all of my major life events seemed to revolve around the loss of something or someone?

It was too depressing to consider. Instead of examining both sides of the coin that was my youth, I took out the polished side—the surface that played back the shiny memories, the ones I cherished. I spent two evenings admiring the pretty things, the times my dad took me fishing or when my grandma taught me how to bake her secret-recipe peanut butter chocolate chip cookies. I smiled as I wrote the paper because I pretended that the flip side didn't exist. It was all I could do when the best part of my past and present was two hours away in a hospital gown.

What did my future hold?

Simon seemed to be pondering the same question because Grandma's hospitalization ratcheted him to a new level of angst. It felt more like there was a temperamental teenager in our midst than a fifth grader. He was sullen and petulant, quiet but angry. I hated it. But I didn't know what to do about it.

"Do you miss her?" I asked Simon one night as we sat watching TV. Daniel was long in bed, and my brother and I were supposed to be enjoying a little time alone. Unfortunately, he didn't seem to be enjoying anything. His arms were crossed over his chest, his features frozen in a grimace that would ensure he had crow's-feet by twenty. He didn't even glance up at me when I spoke.

"Who?"

I rolled my eyes. "Grandma."

He shrugged, but I suspected he felt her absence even more acutely than I did. Ever since he came to live with us nearly six years ago, he'd adored her with a devotion that betrayed his need for a mother figure—for someone to love him unconditionally. When Janice abandoned me, I at least still had my dad.

Simon didn't bother to respond to my question, so I filled in the silence for him. "She'll be home in two days. It'll be nice to have her around again, won't it?"

Still no answer.

"It's okay to miss her, Si. It's okay to be sad. And confused." At least, I hoped it was okay to be sad and confused. I sure was.

"I'm fine," Simon muttered.

I watched him for a moment, torn between stomping out of the room and rushing over so I could wrap him in a bear hug. Neither option seemed quite right. Finally I rose from the rocking chair I had been sitting in and joined him on the couch. I kept my distance, but he seemed to shrink away from me as if he feared my touch.

"Hey," I said softly. "Look at me."

Simon didn't turn his head, but he peered at me out of the corners of his eyes. His hair was getting long, and it flopped over his forehead so far, it brushed the line of his dark brows. I had to resist the urge to smooth it away from his skin, to press my lips to the curve of his temple.

"Simon, I know you're hurting," I said, trying to choose my words carefully. "You don't have to pretend that everything is okay. It's not. But it's going to be. You'll see. Grandma will be home soon and everything will go back to the way it was."

"Until June," Simon grunted.

I squeezed my eyes shut and took a deep breath. With two words, my brother had conjured up every fear and uncertainty I faced. What would happen now? With Grandma diminished by her illness and my wedding on the horizon, what would become of our family? Simon's options had been taken away from him. He had to come with us whether he wanted to or not—Grandma couldn't care for him on her own. And what would she do? join an assisted-living community? go into a nursing home? The thought made me ill.

"It's going to be okay," I said again, realizing how lame and deceitful the words sounded even in my own ears.

Simon acted as if my assurances were meaningless. He

pushed himself up from the couch and disappeared into the refuge of his messy room. As I watched him vanish from sight, I wondered what his autobiography would look like someday. If he found himself faced with an assignment to recount his childhood, would there be a shiny side? memories he could treasure in spite of it all?

I found myself dialing the number for the triage station on Grandma's floor before I even realized what I was doing. It was a daily ritual for me to check in with her nurses, but I had already made my customary call for the day. Besides, it was nine o'clock, past the time she usually fell asleep for the night, and I doubted that they would have any news to relay. All the same, I was desperate for some connection with her. For some indication that I wasn't in this completely alone.

"Nurses' station. Lindy speaking."

"Hi, Lindy," I said, clutching the phone tighter as I appreciated how silly it was for me to be bothering her again. But she had already picked up. I couldn't just sever the connection. "It's me, Julia DeSmit."

"Oh, hi! I didn't expect to hear from you again today."

"I know; I'm sorry to bother you. I just had this strange urge to . . ." I faltered, not entirely sure what I wanted from her.

"Would you like me to put you through to Nellie's room?" Lindy asked, her voice cheerful and accommodating. She probably got calls from concerned family members all day long.

"No, I don't want to wake her up."

"She's not asleep. In fact, she has a visitor."

"A visitor?" Mrs. Walker hadn't told me that she planned to make the trek to the heart hospital. Normally she called if she was going to go so I could send along something for Grandma. "It's kind of late for that, don't you think?"

"Your grandma is doing very well, but you're right. Visiting hours are over at nine. I'll go tell him it's time to wrap things up."

"Him?" I repeated, dazed. In a flash, all of my worries about Simon, our shared lives, and the broken stories of our youth evaporated. They were replaced by a new, more urgent concern. "Who's there?"

"A nice young gentleman," Lindy said, sounding pleased. "Very handsome, if you ask me."

"Could you put me through?" I asked thickly.

"Sure thing."

There was a click and then the phone rang twice in Grandma's room. I could picture her there, propped up in the bed, but it disturbed me that I didn't know who occupied the chair beside her.

"Hello?"

"Grandma?"

"Hi, Julia. It's so good to hear your voice."

"You too," I told her. And she did sound good. Tired but content. Happy even. I knew her hair was still white, her frame still slight, but she sounded more like herself than the last time I had seen her a couple of days ago. "I just called to see how you were doing tonight, and the nurse told me that you were awake."

Grandma gave a quiet little laugh. "Shocking, isn't it? I'm up past my bedtime. Do you think I'll get in trouble?"

In the background I could hear a man chuckle. His voice was deep and rich, resonant, even over the phone line.

"Who's that?" I tried to make the query light, even disinterested. But the suspense was killing me.

"It's Patrick, honey. He came to visit me."

Parker? I nearly choked. Why in the world was Parker visiting my grandmother? And why did she sound so pleased about it? "Excuse me?"

"Just a minute, Julia," Grandma said. "Patrick is leaving, and I'm going to say good-bye. Would you like me to call you back in a minute?"

I stared at the living room wall, mute and numb.

"Julia?"

"No." I gave my head a clearing shake. "No, Grandma, don't worry about it. I didn't really have anything. Just wanted to say hi and see how you're doing."

"I'm doing just fine," she assured me.

"I'm glad to hear that." I paused for a moment, hoping she'd say something more. When she didn't, I murmured, "I love you."

"I love you, too, Julia. I'll see you in two days."

"Two days," I affirmed.

"Bye, honey." And then the line went dead.

I was left staring at the blank LCD screen, wondering how this unexpected scene fit into the winding narrative of our complicated lives.

the night tree

GRANDMA WAS DISCHARGED from the hospital the day before Thanksgiving. I had hoped that Michael would be able to help me with the transition, but since he was coming home for an extended Christmas break, he was stuck in Iowa City. And I would have asked the Walkers for a hand, but I felt guilty enough for dropping my boys in their laps every time I decided to make the drive to the heart hospital. Besides, though the Walkers celebrated Thanksgiving with their family before the official holiday, in recent years they had begun holding a second feast on the actual day—a gathering of sorts for the castoffs and lonely souls of Fellowship Community. I knew that my longtime friend and adopted auntie would have her hands full with preparing the stuffing, pumpkin pies, and a monumental, seventeen-pound bird. In the end, the task fell to the boys and me, and while I was still nervous about bringing her home, it felt right that my grandmother's homecoming would be a family event.

I cleaned Grandma's room from top to bottom in preparation for the move, wiping the walls, cleaning cobwebs out of the corners, and even changing dusty lightbulbs for new, low-wattage lights that glowed soft and golden. Simon helped me rotate her mattress, and the three of us took all of her bedding to the Laundromat in town, where we washed her plush comforter and fluffed her pillows and shams. Then we vacuumed and scrubbed and polished and shined until we could see our reflection in the wood of her heirloom armoire and the glass on her window was as clear as glacier ice.

"Spring cleaning in November," Simon commented. His voice seemed tremulous to me, uncertain, as if he didn't understand this new world we lived in. This place where we cleaned as if it were May instead of the beginning of a long, hard winter.

"Just Grandma's room," I told him. "We want it to be perfect for her."

Daniel sniffed the air. "Smells like lemon."

"Is that perfect?" I asked.

He nodded. "Smells like Grandma."

I smiled because he was right. I had forgotten in the weeks that we spent in the hospital. Grandma's signature, and inadvertent, fragrance of cinnamon and lemon dish soap had been replaced by the odor of antiseptic, of sterile rubber gloves and industrial cleaners and sickness. But that would change. She was coming home. It would be only a matter of time before she was up and around, smiling as she baked cinnamon rolls in the kitchen or humming while she helped Simon with his homework.

When everything was exactly the way we wanted it, I made sure every light in the house was off and hung a fresh towel over the handle of the oven. Then I ushered the boys to the mudroom. As we donned our coats and boots, I felt a rush of gratitude that they didn't have school and I wouldn't have to bring Grandma home alone.

I knew nothing important had changed—she was still the woman I had always known—but in the aftermath of her heart attack I found myself timid in her company, as if the landscape of our lives had undergone a natural disaster because her heart had stopped working the way it was supposed to. It was ridiculous, I knew, a mixture of panic and worry and helplessness, but I couldn't seem to talk myself out of it. And it didn't help that Grandma herself was subdued, tired. Our conversations were brief and graceless, punctuated by long stretches of silence and often cut short when she fell asleep midsentence.

The repercussions of her illness were ripples that hadn't

yet reached the banks of our present reality. It was going to take time to sort out, and I was glad to have my boys at my side. I gave them each a hug as they finished zipping up their plush coats.

We stepped out onto the porch under the cold, mid-morning sun and were greeted by a bashful-looking Parker. He was carrying a laundry basket overflowing with incongruous items. Among a half-dozen or so indiscernible objects, I saw a Crock-Pot, a bag of McIntosh apples, a jar of popcorn kernels, and a large package wrapped in white paper like the kind we used at the Value Foods meat counter.

"Hi," he said. If I wasn't mistaken, there was a hint of timidity in his careful greeting.

The boys rocketed across the porch and assaulted Parker with hugs and playful punches. Simon poked at the bag of apples, unable to contain his grin.

"What are you doing here?" I was more surprised than upset, intrigued by the odd assortment of things in his basket.

"I know Nellie is being discharged today, and I wanted to make her homecoming special. Tomorrow is Thanksgiving, you know."

"Yeah," I whispered, stunned that Parker would be so considerate. How did he know we didn't have any plans for Thanksgiving? And how did he know that Grandma was coming home? All at once I wondered if Parker had taken an even greater interest in my grandmother than I had realized.

Maybe his mysterious visit to her hospital room was just the tip of the iceberg.

"I don't mean to barge in," he continued, "or to impose. I actually thought you'd be gone by now."

I glanced at my wristwatch. "They told me to pick her up at noon. We've got plenty of time."

He nodded. "Do you care if I use your kitchen for a little while? I'll just prep your meal and be gone by the time you get back."

My jaw felt slack and I realized I was staring at him gape-mouthed. I pursed my lips with a little pop and forced a dazed smile. "I forgot that you cook."

"Spaghetti and anything I can throw in a Crock-Pot. I'm a bachelor, you know. It's either that or ramen noodles every day of my life."

"What are ramen noodles?" Daniel asked, trying to peer over the edge of the basket.

"Nutritionless cardboard," Parker said. "That's why I'm making you roast chicken instead. It's not turkey, but—"

"I like chicken!" Daniel yelped.

"Me too." Simon fixed me with a pleading look. "Can he stay? Can Parker cook for us?"

"I'll be gone before you get home," he promised again.

But the thought of bringing Grandma home to an empty house made a current of dread race through my chest. I shivered. "No," I said, and Parker's face fell. I rushed to explain. "No, I don't mean you have to go; I mean stay. Go ahead and cook your meal, but don't hurry back to Minnesota. We'll be back sometime this afternoon, and the boys would love it if you'd eat with us."

Simon's eyes went round and even Parker seemed surprised by my invitation. I still felt awkward around him—even more so after the blizzard of emotions that surrounded the night of Grandma's heart attack and so unexpectedly finding him at her bedside—but I felt like he deserved this much. If he was going to stay and cook for us, the least we could do was share our meal.

Parker regarded me with open curiosity. "What about you, Julia? Do you want me to stay?"

His question felt probing, intimate, though it would have been simple enough to make a joke and laugh it off. But I couldn't. I brushed past him before he could see the color that had risen in my cheeks and said, "We'll be back soon."

The boys assaulted him with a chorus of *please*s as I made my way to the car. Parker's answer was a foregone conclusion, and by the time we were buckled in and pulling out of the driveway, I was sure that he would be around when we came back.

While Parker turned our immaculate kitchen into his personal culinary playground, Simon, Daniel, and I chauffeured Grandma home. She was still pale and delicate, a frail woman who seemed half the size she had been only weeks before. But she was smiling, and her eyes shone with something that could only be labeled pure joy. She stared at the boys, clutching their hands, their faces, their arms, as if she longed to crush them to her but didn't have the strength. And she pressed my hand to her lips, murmuring hopes and prayers against my fingers as the nurse pushed her out of the hospital in a wheelchair.

"I'm so ready to go home," she whispered, just for my ears.

"We're so ready to have you home," I said. Gazing at the top of her snowy head, I added, "Don't ever do that again."

She laughed. "I'll try not to."

The boys were a little ahead of us, taking turns setting off the automatic doors at the hospital exit. I reached down and secured the quilt I had brought along around Grandma's legs. "I should warn you," I began, "Parker is going to be at the house when we get home. Are you okay with that? Because I have his cell phone number and I can call him and tell him that—"

"Julia," Grandma interrupted, "I'm happy that Patrick will be there."

"You are?" I looked at her quizzically, desperate to ask her about Parker's visit and why she seemed so open to his presence in our lives. But I didn't dare.

"He's a nice boy," she murmured, patting my hand.

"He's hardly a boy. He's thirty-one."

"You're right. He's not a boy. He's a baby."

I laughed. "What does that make me?"

"Just starting out, my girl."

I didn't tell her that I felt old. Closer to an end than a beginning.

The drive home was peaceful. Grandma dozed a little, and that was fine with me. The boys played travel Yahtzee in the backseat and I snuck peeks at my grandmother's sleeping profile. She seemed so serene with her head tilted back and her hair like a halo against the crepe of her pale skin. I wished I had my camera with me. I would have loved to capture the way the light fell on her face, the tranquil half smile that graced her lips.

In some ways, she was the grandmother I had always known and loved. In others, she was a stranger to me. Uncertainties aside, I looked forward to getting to know her. To exploring the boundaries of our new relationship.

By the time we got home, I was actually anticipating the noise and chaos that seemed to follow Parker like a whiff of cologne. It was impossible for him to enter our house and not elicit giggles and shouts, and I was anxious for the rowdy games that would undoubtedly take my mind off Grandma's mortality.

Not to mention the home-cooked meal. Even if it was a paltry Crock-Pot offering, it was better than serving my grandmother frozen pizza on her first day back. Suddenly I remembered the meal plan her nutritionist had drawn up, and I grasped the fact that frozen pizzas were a thing of the past in the DeSmit house. Maybe it was time to dust off our own Crock-Pot and start putting it to better use.

I pulled the car as close to the porch as I could, packing the thin layer of snow into the dead grass of our lawn without pausing to wonder if my off-roading would do permanent damage. I hoped that Grandma felt strong enough to do the steps with a little assistance, but my worries were put to rest when Parker materialized on the porch. He jogged down the wide staircase and opened the passenger door, then offered Grandma his hand like a true gentleman and welcomed her home.

"Thank you, Patrick," Grandma said, and though I couldn't see her face, I could hear the smile in her voice.

"It's a bit slippery," he told her. "May I do the honors?"

"Absolutely not. But you may help me."

"Good enough," he agreed.

I watched as he half lifted her out of the car and wrapped a thick arm around her waist. Grandma didn't want to be carried over the threshold, but I could see that Parker supported much of her weight as they made their way up the steps. Her doctor had told me to continue slowly increasing her level of activity but that at her age it was unlikely she would ever regain all she had lost. In short, my grandmother had aged ten years in two weeks. The change was evident in the way she leaned into Parker and painstakingly made her way up the same steps she had all but raced up only a month or so before.

By the time I parked the car and took off my snow gear in the mudroom, Grandma was seated at the kitchen table with a cup of tea between her hands. I noticed that Parker had settled her on the seat with the new cushion, a red gingham-patterned pillow that didn't even seem to compress beneath her petite frame. And through the archway I could see that Parker had turned on the TV for the boys. Not my first choice of activity, but considering the gravity of the day, I could hardly complain that he had given them the chance to unwind.

"You're so domestic," I told Parker in greeting. I sank into the nearest chair and marveled at the realization that for once there was absolutely nothing for me to do. The house was clean, the kids were quiet, and supper was made. In fact, the kitchen was thick with the tantalizing aroma of spices and roast chicken, and I could see a chocolate cake on the counter by the refrigerator. "You'd make an excellent housewife."

"Not really. I tossed a chicken and some onions and carrots into a Crock-Pot. The potatoes are from a box." He looked at Grandma and mouthed, *Sorry*. "And I bought the cake from the bakery."

"Smells delicious," Grandma told him, and I had to agree. It was three o'clock in the afternoon and my mouth was watering as if I hadn't eaten in days.

"If all you did was throw a chicken in a Crock-Pot, what did you do with all those hours?" I asked.

"I cleaned the garage," Parker admitted, pouring me a cup of hot water and passing the tin that contained our tea bags.

"You did what?"

"I didn't know what else to do. Besides, it was messy."

It was more than messy. It was a disaster. Since I knew nothing about hardware, tools, or organizing a traditional "man's space," I had let the garage go for years. There were coffee cans of rusty nails, haphazard piles of the boys' outdoor toys, and even old equipment from the days when my grandpa still ran the farm. I had found a rusted scythe in the far corner once and shoved it up in the rafters so that the boys couldn't get ahold of it.

"It took a while," Parker said. "I hope you don't mind."

"We don't mind," Grandma assured him. "We're grateful. Thank you."

"Thank you," I echoed numbly.

We chatted for a bit and Grandma took tiny sips of her tea. I could tell within minutes that sitting up in the kitchen chair was draining her, and when I had counted one too many long blinks, I gently suggested that she take a nap.

It felt good to tuck her into her own bed and pull the crisp sheets all the way up to her chin. I perched on the edge of the mattress for a few moments, holding her hand and watching as she slowly gave in to sleep.

To my surprise, a hot tear slipped down my cheek when her breathing became slow and even. My ribs felt ready to crack at all the emotion I couldn't contain. It was a building pressure, a geyser of love and hope and grief. But I couldn't cry over her. Not now. Not when she was sleeping so soundly. So I drew a shaky breath and swallowed my tears, bending for just a second to lay a whisper of a kiss on her cheek.

As I stood up, I wondered how many times she had hovered over me like this. How many nights had she cried at my bedside? spun wishes around me? prayed?

More importantly, when had we switched roles?

Parker was waiting for me in the kitchen with his own unspoken question. I could see it in his face the moment I laid eyes on him, and though I was dying to grill him about his visit to the heart hospital, I simply wasn't in the mood to talk. I tried to give off an aura of detachment. Maybe if I acted aloof, he'd leave me alone.

He caught on quickly. "Why don't you go take a nap? I have a little project to do with the boys."

A nap sounded like heaven, but Parker's project piqued my curiosity. "What are you going to do?"

"We're going to decorate a night tree."

"Excuse me?"

Parker pushed back from the table and grabbed a pair of cookie sheets that had been resting on top of the fridge. He set them on the table before me, and I marveled at the layers of narrow apple rings that he had painstakingly sliced and laid out to dry. They were crimson at the edges, but curled and browning where the soft ivory flesh had once been. Even wasting away, they were pretty—earthy and honest.

I picked up an apple ring and studied the way Parker's sharp knife had split the black seeds in two. "What are they for?"

"Garlands." He retrieved a giant bowl of popped popcorn

and the last shopping bag that had been hiding in his laundry basket. Upending the paper sack, he poured out fishing line, a bag of sunflower seeds, pinecones, glue, and dried cranberries. "Haven't you heard of a night tree?"

"Never."

Parker shrugged. "It's a family tradition. My sister and her husband have been doing it with their daughters for the past several years."

"You have a sister?" I asked, suddenly becoming conscious of the fact that I knew absolutely nothing about Parker's personal life, history, or family.

"Just one. She's five years older than me and has two girls."

"I bet you're a great uncle," I murmured.

"I try." Parker began to gather everything into neat piles. From his back pocket he extracted a small, cardboard folder that contained a few thick needles with blunt tips. "Do you trust Daniel to use one of these?"

I put my finger to the point and pressed. "I think so."

"I'll watch him carefully, I promise."

"I will too."

"I thought you were going to take a nap."

"Nah," I said. "I think I'd rather learn more about this night tree."

Although I had worried that the boys wouldn't respond well to Parker's little art project, their excitement mounted as he explained the particulars of a night tree. While we threaded popcorn, apple slices, and cranberries on the fishing line and glued sunflower seeds to the pinecones, Parker relayed stories of his nieces' night trees and the Christmas evenings they had spent beneath the boughs of their chosen evergreen.

"So you wrap these garlands all around the tree and hang the pinecones just like you're decorating a Christmas tree."

"But it's for the animals?" Simon asked.

"And the birds. It's a winter offering. A gift to everything that lives in your grove."

"And what are we supposed to do?" Daniel wondered as he put a sunflower seed at the very tip of a large pinecone.

"Watch," Parker said with an air of mystery. "Sit and watch and wait. Listen. There is nothing quite so beautiful as when a bird sings her winter song. And in the morning you can take stock and see what's missing."

"You said it's called a night tree," Simon said.

"That's because it's most beautiful at night. When it's dark, you can enjoy a still world. You can talk or just look at the stars. Or pray."

"Pray?" The word slipped out before I could stop it. "I didn't realize you were religious."

"I'm not," Parker confessed. "I've never been a big fan of religion."

"But you said *pray*," Simon reminded him. "Who do you pray to?"

Parker's lips curled in a secret smile. "The same God you do, Si."

"So you're a Christian?"

He shrugged. "I've never been a big fan of labels, either."

I just stared at him. He had spent the last several months trying to convince me in word and deed that he was a different man, but I had no idea that this was part of his transformation. I thought back to our fledgling relationship all those years ago and realized that religion was something we had never really discussed. He knew that I went to church, but his own faith—or lack thereof—had never come up.

Parker caught my eye and seemed on the verge of saying more. Then he clamped his mouth shut and handed Daniel a new pinecone. "Let's just say I'm asking a lot of questions these days. Embracing the faith of my youth. Trying to figure some things out." He bumped Simon with his elbow. "Life's hard, kid. Even grown-ups don't have it all together."

Simon looked confused for a moment, but something in Parker's words must have made sense to him because he began to nod slowly. "Yeah," he affirmed as if Parker were the arbiter of true wisdom.

Though Parker's allegedly nonreligious beliefs plagued me like a nagging itch, I didn't have the energy or inclination to engage him in front of the boys. So instead of trying to learn more, I set his enigmatic confessions aside and focused on the project in front of us.

There was something undeniably appealing about Parker's vision of a night tree. I loved the thought of standing beneath one of the saplings in our grove and watching the night sky fade from blue-black to onyx as the galaxies spun above me. It sounded peaceful. Like a place where I could indeed pray. Or cry. Or shout.

When the kitchen table was teeming with our homemade swags, Parker began to gather everything and place it in his empty laundry basket.

"You going with us?" he asked when I didn't move to stand with the rest of them.

I cast a glance over my shoulder in the direction of Grandma's room. "I'll walk you to the porch."

"She's sleeping," Parker said gently. "Let her sleep."

"But . . ."

"We'll be back in fifteen minutes. She'd be furious if she knew you stayed back."

Unconvinced, I bit my bottom lip and tried to come up with a better reason to stick close to my grandmother. But as I watched, Simon lifted a finger and quietly, secretly summoned me to him. How could I not go?

There was a wordless excitement in the air as we all stepped into our boots and searched for our mittens in the box of winter gear. The sun was already setting, but I knew the perfect tree, a young fir that had sprung up amid a ring of tall-standing oaks. Years ago, I had believed that it would not survive, but now the lovely little tree arched a couple of feet above my head and spread out thick branches of beryl-colored needles that seemed extended in welcome.

Grandma will love it, I thought. And then I remembered

the way she shook, the tiny steps she took, and I knew that there was no way she would be tromping through the snow this winter. The realization almost made me sick.

But as the four of us stepped single file off the porch, I saw Parker in the lead with the basket cradled in his arms. He turned his head a little to say something to the boys, and in that instant I could see her nestled in his embrace. I knew that she wouldn't have to walk alone. Parker would carry her there.

"Thank you," I whispered as my feet traced the path his boots had made in the snow. He couldn't hear me, but I hoped he knew.

winter solstice

DECEMBER PASSED with all the indirection of a blown leaf. I felt tossed by the wind, whisked this way and that as if I had no moorings, no constant whatsoever to cling to. And I didn't. Michael was gone, Grandma was healing, and the boys were left looking to me for direction. The problem was, I felt lost.

"I want Grandma to play checkers with me," Daniel said one night.

It was his first day of Christmas vacation and I could already tell that the two-week break was going to be long and tiresome.

"I think she's napping," I told him. "I'll play with you when I'm done paying these bills."

"But you were going to make caramel corn."

I sighed. "Okay. Why don't we make caramel corn together? I can play checkers with you when we're done."

"I don't feel like making caramel corn."

"Neither do I," I muttered.

Daniel puffed an angry breath through his nose and slouched into the living room, where Simon was supposed to be finishing up a social studies project. Grandma's hospitalization must have affected the boys in ways I still didn't fully understand because the report Simon was working on was one that had been due before the Christmas break. His teacher had graced me with a courtesy call and a grouchy warning: if Simon didn't turn in his report the first day back from break, he would be in danger of failing social studies for the semester.

I had yelled; he had sulked. It was depressing to see Simon's interest continue to deteriorate even as my own mothering skills seemed to revert to the Dark Ages. I felt like a failure. But he was doing his project: a state report on Iowa. It was a homemade book that was to be filled with pictures and information about state flowers and birds, industry, and natural resources. How hard could it be?

Unfortunately Daniel wasn't in the living room for more than a couple minutes when the yelling started. It had been months since the boys engaged in the sort of name-calling, fist-throwing fights that marked Daniel's younger years, and I tried not to roll my eyes as I pushed back from the table to break up their noisy scuffle.

"What in the world is going on in here?" I demanded, hands on hips like a proper, no-nonsense mother.

Simon was working on the floor, pages spread out around him in a mosaic of colorful construction paper. But one of his sheets was clutched in Daniel's hand, and Simon had his fingers wrapped in a death grip around his nephew's small wrist.

"I told him to let go!" Simon seethed, squeezing tighter.

"Ow!" Daniel howled. "I just want to look at it!"

"Let go," I warned him. "Simon is working on a project."

"But I just want to see the picture of the bird!"

"It's a goldfinch," Simon spat out. "You see those every day in the summer."

"But—"

"But nothing," I interrupted, my voice steel. "Let go of the paper, Daniel."

He looked at me with big, hurt eyes and let the blue piece of construction paper fall to the floor. Simon snatched it up in his other hand and thrust Daniel away, knocking the younger boy off-balance so that he sprawled on the floor.

My irritation with Daniel evaporated in an instant. "Honey," I said, sinking to my knees. "It's okay. Simon's just very busy right now." I put out my arms, suddenly anxious for the feeling of his small body against my chest, his head on my shoulder.

But instead of running into my arms, my son brushed past me and pounded up the stairs to his room. Just before he disappeared around the corner, I saw the silent tears that rolled down his cheeks.

I exhaled a long, low breath and cradled my head in my hands. "Simon," I whispered, drawing out his name into a petition, a plea, "couldn't you have just let him look at the paper?"

"I thought you wanted me to finish this project."

"I do. But I don't see why it would be such a big deal to let Daniel look at the stupid bird."

"Don't let Daniel hear you use that word."

I slapped my hands on my thighs and gave Simon a stony look. "What is with you these days? We are all trying so hard to keep it together, and I would appreciate it if you'd drop the attitude."

"You're the one who said *stupid.*"

It took great effort not to crawl across the floor and grab my brother by the shoulders so I could shake some sense into him. He was so antagonizing these days, so angry and yet seemingly indifferent to our pain. I didn't understand how in less than half a year the sweet boy I had known could morph into such an exasperating young man. *He's hurting too,* I tried to remind myself. But it didn't feel that way. It felt like he was giving in to selfishness and apathy.

I almost threw my arms up. I almost said, *I give up on you.* But as my lips formed the words, God placed His hand over my mouth in an act of profound grace. I swallowed. Grasped what my rejection would have meant to Simon and shuddered.

"Just get it done," I murmured.

In the kitchen I shoved the bills aside and pulled out another postcard. This one featured a startling prairie sunset, a peaceful farm outlined in charcoal against a red-orange sky that shimmered with warm, autumn tones. Even though the silhouette of the farm featured a giant corncrib and the comical shapes of at least thirty fat cows, it was idyllic. Nothing at all like our farm.

Grandma had a heart attack, I scribbled. *Come back.*

After that, the point of my pen stuck to the paper and I watched as a pool of black ink collected beneath the silver tip. I wanted to write more. To say, *Your son needs you.* But that wasn't true. The truth was much harder to write.

Impossible to accept.

We need you.

When the boys were in bed and the house was dark, I spent many cold evenings shivering beneath our night tree. I had walked the route so many times that there was a path worn down in the snow, a narrow trail that marked my nightly passage so well, I no longer needed to bring a flashlight to illuminate the way. Habit told me how to weave between the trees, and when I finally stepped to the base of our decorated fir, I felt like I was entering a sanctuary. Like I was coming home.

Birds and animals had indeed found our meager offering, and the boys enjoyed racing around the tree to see how many apple rings were missing and which pinecones had been knocked to the ground and stripped of seeds. They straightened things out, replenished garlands, and kicked the spent pinecones beneath the sweeping boughs. But for me, the night tree wasn't nearly so complicated an enterprise. It was nothing more than a place to be still. A place where the air was crisp and sweet, like the first bite of an apple or a sip of cold peppermint tea. A place where my shoulders could fall back and shrug off the extra weight of everyone who depended on me. At least for a while.

The night tree was a haven.

Sometimes I prayed. But only sometimes. Mostly I just stood there and watched the sky spill moon silver on dark, graceful limbs as if the stars saw fit to anoint our little tree with light. It was a holy experience, wordless and beyond explanation, but I felt as if God was indeed there with me. Making the tree sparkle. Interceding for me when my heart couldn't speak. And every once in a while, I felt like He whispered to me.

The night after I penned my third postcard to Janice, I

huddled beneath the tree and felt God touch me not once, but twice. The first invitation was nothing more than a breath of wind, a sigh so slight that it barely ruffled the popcorn swags. But though it seemed innocent, the hushed entreaty hit me with the blast of a full-force gale.

At first my heart rebelled at the suggestion. It was too shocking, too fraught with potential disaster. But as I struggled to reject what had been so easily placed in my mind, a small part of me had to admit that it made sense. For the first time in a long time, I was given a reason to hope for Simon—for all of us. A reason to believe that everything could work out better than I had dared to imagine.

But it was risky. Filled with vague implications that could put our family through even more heartache than we had already experienced.

I banished the thought from my mind.

It was old habit to close myself off after that. I wrapped my arms around my middle and made my mind as blank as the snowy ground at my feet. I thought if I was distant and unreceptive, He would ignore me. But when I finally turned to go, God decided to give me one last instruction. It was as clear and bold as if He had bent down and whispered it in my ear: *Tell Michael.*

I froze. Tell him what? But of course, I knew. Tell him about Parker. About Simon and our struggles. About Grandma and my fears. Since his proposal more than two months before, my conversations with Michael had been reduced to hollow shopping lists, little more than the passing of pertinent but rather meaningless information back and forth. My fiancé knew the particulars of my life, but he didn't know how I felt.

Michael didn't know that I loved my child psych class but that I often had to stay up into the early morning hours to finish my homework. He didn't know that my job at Value Foods was tying me up in knots. Or that things with Simon had only gotten worse. He never guessed that Grandma's heart attack had shaken me to the core—that everything I thought to be true became suspect the moment I found her slumped in her knitting chair. He didn't know that I was exhausted and sad and frightened.

Somewhere along the way we had lost each other. And though I didn't like to admit it, I knew that the soft nudge I felt at the foot of the night tree was wholly justified. It was time to tell Michael everything.

Thankfully, he came home the very next night.

"I'll be back for winter solstice," he had told me the week before. "That's fitting, don't you think? The days will only get longer from there. . . ."

It was a buoyant thought. Like the rest of our lives could begin to unfold from just one day. If only we could leave everything else behind and walk into that spring unencumbered. But I knew that although the nights might get shorter, there was a lot of winter left to live.

Michael didn't pull into Mason until eight that night. He

called me from his cell as I was helping Daniel get into his pajamas.

"Go ahead and put him to bed," Michael told me. "I'll be home for ten days—we'll have plenty of time to hang out."

I buttoned the last button on Daniel's pajama top and pulled back the covers of his bed for him. *Do you want to stay up?* I mouthed. Normally, he'd hop at the chance to postpone his bedtime, but rather than jumping up and down, Daniel crawled into bed. He shook his head no and reached for the book I had placed on his nightstand.

"Okay," I told Michael, angling the phone under my chin again. "He's sleepy. You can see him tomorrow."

"Perfect. I'm looking forward to spending some time alone with you tonight."

"Me too. I have something I want to show you."

"Sounds mysterious."

"Not so much. But I think you'll like it."

Michael promised to come by soon, and I hung up after my customary "Love you."

"Are we going to Michael's house for Christmas?" Daniel asked when he heard the phone click off.

"Not this year. Grandma would like to stay close to home, so we're going to have Christmas here."

Daniel grinned.

"I thought you liked going to the Vermeers'."

"It's okay. Home is better."

It was the perfect thing to say. Honest and unexpected.

It comforted me to know that even in the midst of our uncertainty, we could make our home a place that Daniel loved to be. I covered his face in kisses until he giggled and pushed me away.

By the time Michael arrived an hour later, our house was a picture of serenity. Daniel was asleep, Simon had retreated to his room, and Grandma was curled up in bed listening to the Bible on the iPod I bought her for an early Christmas present. She wasn't much of a TV watcher, and while she was perfectly capable of knitting and doing small things around the house, I didn't want her to get bored and overexert herself in the first few months after her bypass. The iPod seemed like the perfect solution. She was already halfway through the Old Testament, and I was wondering what to download after she finished the seventy-seven-hour production.

Michael slipped into the house without knocking, but I met him at the door. He was in a navy tweed peacoat with a cable-knit scarf wound twice around his neck. The creamy softness of the pale yarn contrasted sharply with the midnight of his hair, making him look exotic and strange, startlingly handsome.

I exhaled a little, but the rest of my breath caught on my raw joy at seeing him. It flattened me that he could still elicit that sort of reaction, that I was still just an infatuated girl in his presence. Maybe I should have worried about my worn jeans and my dad's ugly, old Mack jacket that I had thoughtlessly layered over a lined fleece. Maybe it should have hit me that Michael was too good for me—too beautiful, too brilliant, too perfect in every way—but it didn't. I dashed across the space between us and threw myself into his arms.

He seemed equally excited to see me. Instead of backing out of my fervent embrace or even pausing to say hello, Michael took my face in his hands and touched his lips to mine. It was as if we hadn't seen each other in months. And in many ways, we hadn't. For those moments in the mudroom, I kissed him with the pent-up passion of all the things we had left unsaid. With all the unexpressed delight of the adoration I still harbored for him. I wound my fingers through the long hair at the nape of his neck, the place where his dark ringlets just began to curl, and moaned.

"Julia," he murmured after a while, his lips still nipping at the corner of my mouth. "We have to stop."

I traced the line of his jaw with my mouth and nuzzled into the soft spot just below his ear. "I know," I whispered. And just like that an errant thought dispelled the magic of our reunion: What would Simon do if he caught us like this? The passionate kisses I shared with my husband-to-be could be interpreted as just another reminder of Simon's uncertain future.

Michael felt the shift in me and put his arms around my shoulders to pull me into a less fiery embrace.

I rested my head on his chest. "Welcome home."

"I think that's the best welcome I've ever received."

I would have laughed, but I didn't think that my need for him was very funny.

"Why are you wearing a jacket?"

"Oh." I pulled away from him a little and surveyed my ensemble all the way down to my feet. The snow boots I had donned were ratty and frayed, but they kept the cold out better than the new pair I had bought only a month ago. "I wanted to show you something."

"Of course. The mysterious something. It's outside?"

"Yeah," I said reluctantly. With Michael at my side, my news seemed less urgent. Was this really the right time to tell him? Did I really have to take him out to the night tree and try to explain everything? But even as I questioned myself, I knew the answer. *Tell him* still rang in my ears like a chorus I couldn't get out of my head.

Michael seemed hesitant to leave the warmth of the house behind, but he didn't complain as I took him by the hand and started toward the grove. I had forgotten to bring along a flashlight, so I led the way and Michael followed close behind, moving his hands to rest securely on my hips so he could mirror my every step.

We were at the tree in minutes, and though I had expected an aura to surround the place or the moon to shine brighter, in the dim nighttime light the ornamented fir was less than inspiring. I pursed my lips in disappointment and willed it to be enchanting. I willed it to glow for Michael the way it seemed to shimmer for me. But it was just a tree hung with dried apple rings and cranberries as small and hard as pebbles.

"What is it?" Michael asked, for in spite of its shabby appearance, it was obvious that we had tried to do something special with the tree.

"It's a night tree," I told him weakly. "The idea came from a children's book by Eve Bunting. . . ." But I trailed off because I didn't really know what else to say.

After a minute or so, Michael rubbed my back as if I were a child and said, "It's nice. I'm sure the boys had fun doing it."

"They did," I agreed. "It's for the birds. And the animals that live in the grove during the winter. It's a place to come and be still."

"Sounds like a good idea."

I loved Michael for trying, and because he was making an effort, I decided that I had to do what I set out to do. He deserved that much from me.

"It's been a neat project for the boys," I forced myself to continue. "It gives them something to look forward to. The last few weeks have been really hard."

Michael wrapped an arm around my waist and pulled me close. "I know."

"But the tree has been helpful. And so has . . ." I swallowed. "So has Parker."

"Parker?" Michael asked, obviously nonplussed.

I squeezed my eyes shut and grounded myself, pressing

my weight into my heels so that when Michael removed his arm from me, I would be able to stand on my own. "Actually—" I cleared my throat—"his name is Patrick Holt. He's Daniel's father."

Michael did move away from me, but it was a slow departure. His hand slid off my arm and traced my spine before he came to stand face-to-face. "Daniel's father?"

I could just make out his features in the pale light. He didn't seem angry or even mildly upset. He seemed confused. "Yes," I whispered. "Do you remember that guy you ran into on my porch the day you proposed?"

"The UPS guy?"

"He's not a UPS guy."

"Whatever."

"Do you remember him?"

Michael shrugged. "Sure. Some guy on your porch."

"That's him."

"That's Daniel's biological dad?"

I nodded. "He contacted me several months ago. He wanted to get to know Daniel, to be a part of his life. And it just sort of happened."

"What do you mean, it just sort of happened?"

"I mean, it seemed like a good idea to let Daniel spend some time with his dad. So Parker's been coming by."

"A lot?"

"Twice a month?" I guessed, trying to tally up his visits. "But Daniel doesn't know that Parker is his dad. At least, not yet."

Michael was mute for a long time, and I tried not to fill the silence with explanations and excuses. I shouldn't have kept this from him for so long, and he had every right to be furious with me. His gaze was fixed on me, and though I couldn't see his eyes, I felt the appraisal of his stare with a hot shame. I couldn't stand to even look in his direction, but I didn't budge once as he scrutinized me.

After a while I simply couldn't take it anymore. I was still studying the way my boots disappeared into the darkness, but I ventured to say, "I'm sorry, Michael. I'm so sorry. I should have told you a long time ago. . . ."

"You should have."

"I know. And I'm so, so sorry . . ." I would have gone on, begging his forgiveness and confessing my own short-comings, but Michael stopped my outburst by placing a finger over my lips. I looked up.

"It's okay," he said, shaking his head as if I were being ridiculous. "I wish you would have told me sooner, but I'm not upset. Daniel should have his father in his life."

"He should?"

"Of course. My dad died, Julia. I know what it's like to want a dad. Before my mom married my stepdad, I used to wish for a father of my own. I would never deny Daniel that chance."

"But I thought—"

"I'm fine, Julia. Really. It's not that big of a deal."

I was floored. Completely stunned that Michael was not

only taking it well, he seemed to be almost welcoming the news about Parker. "It's not a big deal?"

"Nah." Michael rubbed his hands briskly up and down my arms. "Can we go in now? I'm freezing."

I nodded meekly and let him lead me back down the well-trod path. I should have been ecstatic that he wasn't angry. I should have jumped up and down. But I felt numb.

We didn't say anything on the walk back to the house. What was there to say? Worst of all, the same thought circled in my mind like an intent vulture, a scavenger that threatened to haunt our relationship until I confronted Michael with what I had always believed to be true. Until now.

I thought you wanted to be Daniel's dad.

tagalong

SINCE MICHAEL SEEMED RELATIVELY UNCONCERNED that Parker had weaseled his way into our lives, as the winter stretched on long and frigid, I permitted Parker greater access to the boys. I might be marrying Michael, but I didn't see any harm in allowing Daniel and Simon the joy of Parker's affection. After all, Michael had encouraged it. Maybe he could be my boys' stepdad and Parker could be their honorary dad.

I was surprised at how little that thought troubled me.

And I wasn't the only one happy with our new arrangement. Michael seemed relieved that I was no longer trying to fill his already-overflowing plate with fatherly duties, while Parker loved the fact that he was welcome to spend nearly every weekend with my boys. As for Daniel and Simon, they reveled in all the masculine attention. Parker took them ice fishing in January, skating in February, and introduced them to the wonderful world of golf when spring arrived in an unseasonable frenzy of snowmelt and sunshine in mid-March.

By the time the tulips were starting to press heavenward, their bowed heads small and soft and sweetly reminiscent of turtles poking glass-green noses through the dark soil of our flower beds, everything bore the faint fragrance of newness. Spring carried with it a certain sense of satisfaction, of finally being able to exhale a deep sigh of relief. As the weather began to gently warm, I couldn't escape the tingling sensation that I was waking up. Everything reverberated with a sense of purpose, of life, and I realized that the winter we had endured was just a season after all.

The earth around me whispered praises, and what could I do but join in? Grandma was doing better, the boys were flourishing beneath the gentle hand of Parker's ministrations, and my wedding was less than two months away.

Two months. The thought was both exciting and terrifying, a confusing tangle of emotions. My pulse quickened with every detail that fell into place like another bolt sliding home, securing our fate. I just couldn't figure out if my heart beat faster out of love or fear.

Surely it was love.

But there was a hesitant quality to our planning too, a place where everything seemed to simply fall off the edge of the earth. The particulars of the wedding were there, as well as the reception and even a quick honeymoon, but the days after that were blurry and indistinct, lost in a fog that seemed thick with uncertainty. Would Simon come to Iowa City with us? Would Grandma?

Michael tried to broach the topic of our long-term plans on several occasions, but I devoutly refused to be drawn into a conversation that I both did and did not want to have. Simply put, I wasn't ready. The days of our old life were precious and fleeting, and with the spring sun warming the world, I wanted to savor every minute. Maybe I should have forced myself to grow up and face the inevitable, but I couldn't do it. I didn't want to.

My selfish interlude lasted until the second week of April.

When Michael called one Friday night as I was finishing up the supper dishes, his voice was thin and pinched, filled with something cool and unexpected that took me several minutes to identify.

"Got plans for the weekend?" he asked after we had chatted about the boys, the above-average weather.

"Yeah, Parker's coming down to take Simon and Daniel fishing."

"Simon and Daniel?"

The question caught me off guard. I wondered if my finger had slipped in front of the mouthpiece of my small phone. Adjusting my grip, I said, "Yup. Simon and Daniel."

"And you?"

"Maybe," I admitted before I could wonder at his reason for asking. Sometimes I accompanied Parker and the boys on their adventures, but sometimes I used the break to catch up on housework or homework or spend time alone with Grandma. She liked to walk out to the night tree—our impromptu gathering place that prevailed long past the holiday season—and sit in the Adirondack chairs that Parker had given us as a Christmas present.

They were a pretty pair of whitewashed loungers that we had set in a little clearing near our decorated tree. Parker spoke of digging a fire pit when the ground thawed, and though it hadn't happened yet, we continued to congregate around the chairs, drawn by the subtle magic of the place.

Afternoons with Grandma were undeniably a treasure, but the truth was, I had been looking forward to fishing with Parker and the boys. Simon and Daniel had begged me to take them fishing for years, but I had demurred because although I could bait a hook no problem, I couldn't bring myself to grasp a poor, writhing fish and tear the curved barb from its gaping mouth. The very thought made me sick to my stomach. But Parker apparently had no issues with the ethics of fishing. This weekend would mark my boys' very first time. A monumental expedition if ever there was one.

I had once hoped that Michael would be the one to walk them through this rite of passage, but it was no secret that he hated fishing.

Michael must have caught the hesitation in my tone. "What do you mean, maybe?"

"I was thinking about it," I admitted.

There was an impatient huff on the other end of the line. As Michael released his obvious frustration, it hit me that his brusque tone resonated with the slap of jealousy. Was he jealous of Parker? of the time Parker got to spend with the boys?

"Michael," I rushed to pacify him, "you don't have to—"

"Don't patronize me," he interrupted.

"But I—"

"Julia, do you realize that we're getting married in eight weeks?"

"Just over," I whispered.

"What's that supposed to mean?"

"Nothing. Just that it's not eight weeks; it's a little more than that. . . ."

"Do you want it to be more?"

"No."

Michael sighed, and the weight of the world seemed conveyed in his tired voice. "You can't have it both ways."

"What do you mean?" I asked, genuinely confused.

"Me and Parker. Parker and me. We're not a packaged pair."

"Excuse me? You were the one who told me that Daniel should have his father in his life. This whole arrangement was practically your idea."

"I thought he was going to be a part of Daniel's life. Not yours."

My life? I was speechless.

"Are you planning on taking Parker to Iowa City with you?" Michael grumbled.

"No. Of course not." I threw down the dish towel I was holding and glanced out the window over the sink to where the boys were playing in the grass near our untamed grove. The sun was setting between the treetops, and the leaves were infused with an outpouring of gold as if the sun had split open and was leaking its iridescent glow in a sudden, bright baptism. Simon and Daniel were bathed in light, their skin burnished bronze and their eyes almost savage with delight. They looked so happy, so at peace with themselves and the world, that Michael's envy seemed small and inconsequential in comparison. Parker was good for them. I was looking at the evidence of his unexpected grace.

I stifled my own sigh. "Don't be like this," I said, more to myself than to him.

"Don't be like what, Julia?"

The anger in Michael's voice was so unfamiliar, I almost didn't know how to respond. "Look," I began after a moment, "I know you love the boys."

"I do."

"Of course you do. But you're so busy with school, and so focused when you're here, that they haven't had much of a chance to bond with you."

"You're blaming me for that?"

"No," I sputtered. "It's not your fault. But Daniel and Simon need a man in their lives on a more . . . consistent basis."

It was the wrong thing to say, and I knew it the moment the words were out of my mouth.

"You're saying I'm inconsistent? that I'm not enough of a man for Daniel and Simon?"

"No," I groaned, gripping the edge of the sink and hanging my head. "That's not it at all. It's just that you're so far away. Things will change after we're married. We won't be separated anymore."

"Is that what you want? Because the last I heard, we didn't even have set plans for after the wedding. What are we doing? Is Simon moving in with us? What about Nellie? The apartment I'm renting has two bedrooms, Julia. *Two*."

"We'll rent a bigger apartment . . . ," I said weakly.

"You're being impossible."

"This isn't easy for me," I shot back, feeling my hackles rise.

"Marrying me isn't easy?"

"There's more to it than that, and you know it. Besides, where is all of this coming from? We've been fine up until now. We're working it out."

There was silence on the other end for a long time. It was

so still, I wondered if Michael had hung up on me. But then he gave a little hiss, a noise that was both furious and sad, and said, "My mom saw the four of you at the park last week."

My mind rewound the days like reels of film. There it was, a day nearly a week ago, when I had hopped into Parker's car at the last minute and joined the boys at the park. Grandma was on her way to tea at a friend's house, and the thought of a couple of hours' playing with Daniel and Simon had sounded like bliss. Innocent. But as I remembered, the image came into sharper focus and I saw the four of us as Mrs. Vermeer must have seen us: a laughing, tight-knit family unit.

There was Parker, teaching the boys the fine art of the wrist flick when it came to throwing a Frisbee. Then Daniel and Simon, laughing as they bumbled their earnest attempts. And me, watching from the sidelines until my son grabbed me by the hand and pulled me into their impromptu game, a spirited round of catch that turned into a sort of truncated ultimate Frisbee. I had gotten grass stains on my jeans.

Parker never touched me. Never even got close. It was about the boys. It was all for them; everything always was. But how could I expect my fiancé's mother to know that? To her, every smile was probably laced with desire.

"We were playing Frisbee," I said quietly.

"I heard."

A retort bubbled inside my chest and popped out before I could stop it. "Does your mother always spy on us?"

"I had to wrench it out of her," he spat back. "She told me

an hour ago because I made her. I knew there was something wrong when we talked on the phone."

I could just imagine how hard Michael had to wrench. He probably said, "What's up?" and Diane spewed the whole story without further provocation. But I was being unfair and I knew it. I pushed myself away from the counter and walked into the mudroom, where I slipped into my worn clogs. The house felt too close for this kind of conversation, too confining.

"I'm sorry," I said when I had descended the porch steps and the expanse of ginger sky was above me. He deserved that at the very least. "I didn't mean to hurt you. But you have to believe me that there is absolutely nothing going on between Parker and me. He wants to be involved in Daniel's life, and Simon is just part of the bargain. I only tag along because I'm bored."

"Don't tag along anymore."

I held my breath, knowing that my answer couldn't be lightly given. Deep down, I understood that Michael's request was wholly justified. If the situation were reversed, I'd loathe any woman who spent time with my fiancé. But I was reluctant to give up my outings, my fun with the boys.

"Okay," I finally agreed, though I worried my promise didn't carry much conviction. "Parker can hang out with the boys. I'll stay out of their way."

"Thank you," Michael said, though he still sounded peeved. "And there's something else you need to do too."

"What's that?"

"By this time next week, I need you to figure out how this is going to work. How *we're* going to work."

I could have played dumb, but I knew exactly what he meant.

It was time to make some very tough decisions.

We said the requisite *I love you*s, but they sounded forced and rote instead of heartfelt. Michael and I rarely, if ever, fought, and as I snapped my phone shut and dropped it into the pocket of my hoodie, I felt a wave of nausea roll through me like a tide. Mrs. Walker had assured me months ago that every bride-to-be went through this. That prewedding jitters were simply a part of the marital equation. She even admitted that on the morning she was supposed to marry Mr. Walker, she had been gripped by the almost-overwhelming urge to get in her car and drive. Just drive away like some girl in a movie instead of the strong woman of God I knew she was. Of course, she hadn't driven away. She had stepped into her gown, sat quietly while the hairdresser swooped her pretty waves into something that resembled a beehive, and walked down the aisle on her father's arm. In nearly thirty years of marriage, she had never looked back.

Differences and spats notwithstanding, I would do the same. Though instead of my dad, Grandma would walk me down the center aisle of Fellowship Community. Or I'd walk her. A smile split my tight-pressed lips at the thought of Grandma and me clinging to each other as we made our way down a petal-strewn path.

"Good talk with Michael?" Grandma asked, coming up behind me. She had been wandering the yard in her slow, dawdling way, pausing to admire the buds on the trees and the evidence of new life as she went. I had watched her when she set out after supper, marveling at the way her strength grew every day but unable to suppress a surge of disappointment at the fact that she was still, and forever, changed. Gone were the days of dropping to her knees so she could give the flower beds a quick weeding.

"Yeah," I managed, though it was apparent from the way her eyes narrowed slightly that my attempt at blithe deception had no effect on her.

"Wedding jitters?"

"No," I told my perceptive grandmother, at once dismayed and comforted that she knew me so well. "No cold feet here."

"I have cold feet," she laughed.

"I didn't realize this was a discussion about circulation."

"It's not." She linked her arm in mine and leaned into me. We were so used to walking like this that it felt only natural to have her hand tucked in the crook of my elbow. Matching our steps was effortless, and when Grandma tugged a little in the direction of the grove, I was already angling my steps that way. "And it's pretty typical that you and Michael aren't seeing eye to eye right now," she continued.

"Our disagreement is less about the wedding and more about . . ." I trailed off, wondering if I wanted to admit that

Parker was the linchpin in our uncharacteristic quarrel. It made me shy somehow to admit it, to say his name out loud and paired with Michael's as if they carried the same weight. They didn't. Michael was going to be my husband. Parker was just the guy who played daddy to my boys.

My heart lurched inside my chest at that thought. Was that really how I felt about Patrick Holt? I didn't think so, but I knew instinctively that he would be devastated to learn that I considered his interactions with my boys merely a game— even if it was only for an instant.

"I don't know," I said finally. "There's just a lot to think about."

"Simon," Grandma said, ticking off his name on her finger.

I nodded.

"Me."

I kissed her forehead to let her know exactly how I felt about her.

"And . . . Parker?"

"Him, too," I agreed. "Michael actually thinks that Parker is spending too much time with us."

"With the boys?"

"With me."

Grandma's sideways glance was multilayered and unfathomable.

"You think I spend too much time with Parker?"

"I didn't say that."

"Then what was the look for?"

She smiled at me and patted my hand where it rested against her own fingers. "You have a lot to think about, Julia."

I threw back my head. Gave a sour, abrupt laugh. "Tell me about it. What are we going to do?"

"It'll come to you," Grandma said, still smiling in an impossible, self-satisfied way. "The answers are just around the corner."

I wanted to bite back, to tell her that her tidy solutions seemed light-years away. But just as I was about to say something caustic, we did indeed round a corner and stumbled upon a sight that wiped any thoughts of Michael and weddings or Parker and fatherhood from my mind.

At the edge of the clearing where our night tree still stood sentinel, Simon and Daniel had found their way into the Adirondack chairs. They were sprawled across the curving wood, long limbs wrapped in torn jeans and arms bare beneath the ragged lines of faded T-shirt sleeves. Simon's dark head was tilted toward Daniel's blond one, and as Grandma and I watched, Simon pointed out something at the top of a nearby tree. Daniel spotted it. His profile reflected the sunset blush of fascination, and his lips parted in an exuberant grin when the woodpecker we couldn't see began his furious rat-a-tat-tat high in one of our oaks.

"They're such a pair," Grandma murmured, tightening her grip on my hand.

"They are," I agreed. "Brothers."

At least that was one decision that no one had to make. Some things just fell on you. Like light. And love.

And apparently, brotherhood.

balance

WHEN PARKER CAME on Saturday, he was cheerfully ignorant of my conversation with Michael and the repercussions
it would have for our evolving relationship. We had lived the
past several months in a comfortable and predictable routine of platonic interaction, and when he walked in the door
just after breakfast without knocking, it struck me that we
had indeed taken liberties with each other. He greeted my
grandmother with a kiss and wordlessly teased me about my
two-inch ponytail by giving it a friendly tug.

"Where're the boys?" he asked, craning his neck so he
could see into the living room. It was empty.

"Outside." I moved around the table in one discreet motion, putting a little distance between us so he wouldn't be tempted to touch me again. Even if it was only the razored edge of my hair.

Grandma had advised me to be honest with Parker, to tell him that our interactions made my fiancé uncomfortable. But I opted for a more hold-your-tongue-and-delicately-disengage approach. All I had to do was convince him that I was busy whenever he was around. Of course, he could still hang out with the boys. At least until we made the move to Iowa City.

And we would *all* be making the move. Somewhere around 2 a.m. I had determined that once and for all. Michael and I would just have to make do in a two-bedroom apartment until we could find something bigger. Maybe we could rent out the farm and use the income to pay for the mortgage on an actual house. I didn't know how Grandma would feel about my master plan, as I hadn't yet informed her. But her inevitable protestations were a moot point. We had switched roles. It was now my job to care for her, right? She couldn't make it here on her own, and there was no way I was sending her off to some old folks' home. No way, nohow. I refused to separate the boys who had become brothers, and I wasn't about to allow my grandmother to spend her twilight years without a family.

All that was left to do was convince everyone in my life— Michael, Grandma, Daniel, and Simon—that my decision

was the right one. Parker's reaction to our imminent departure never even factored into my thinking.

"The boys are outside?" Parker parroted, oblivious to the
inner dialogue that made it hard for me to concentrate.

"It's supposed to be in the low seventies today." I was only
repeating what the meteorologist had predicted on the radio
a half hour before, but Parker grinned at me like I had personally orchestrated the gorgeous weather with a casual flip
of my fingers. It was hard not to smile back. "They weren't
going to miss a moment of sunshine."

"Me, either," he enthused. "I didn't see them when I drove
up, so let's go find them and take off. We can get our fishing in
before lunch, and if the sunshine holds, we could head down
to the state park and walk a few trails when we're done."

"You're feeling ambitious today," Grandma commented,
a sparkle in her eye.

"Maybe I could start a fire," Parker continued. "Show the
boys how to roast the fish we catch."

I couldn't stop the snort that escaped my lips. "You do
that? Seriously, Parker. Who does that?"

"I do." He rapped his chest with his fist proudly. "You
don't even have to fillet them. Just gut 'em, jab 'em on a stick,
and roast 'em over the fire."

"That's gross."

"You're going to love it," he taunted. "I can even teach you
how. Just a little slit from the tail to the—"

"Stop it!" I screeched before he could go into specifics.

"I don't want to hear about your penchant for mutilating fish."

Parker laughed and reached across the table for the cuff of my corduroy jacket. "Let's go. We're going to have to stop at the gas station and pick up a bundle of wood. And maybe some Gatorade or water bottles for the cooler. Snacks? For those of us who have an aversion to food the way God intended it to be eaten . . ."

He jerked on my sleeve, waiting for me to come around the piece of furniture I had so intentionally placed between us, and follow him out the door like I usually did.

Usually. The word stung a little because it was true. I had given Michael the impression that I sometimes went with Parker and the boys on their excursions. But the truth was, I usually went. The evidence was written all over Parker's face. He was waiting for me to fall in step behind him. To pick out bottles of Gatorade and packages of Little Debbie snacks while he gassed up the car and filled his trunk with firewood.

"I'm not coming." Even to my own ears my declaration was laced with disappointment.

"Why not?" Parker looked stricken.

"I have lots to do today." My eyes shot to Grandma, but she turned away when I caught her gaze. No help there. "The boys are really looking forward to some time alone with you."

"Oh." Parker let go of my jacket and brought his hand to

his face. "Is it the fish? Because I promise I won't make you touch them."

"No, it has nothing to do with the fish."

Though I didn't mean for my comment to be rude, Parker seemed taken aback. He rubbed his chin, scratching the stubble that he had neglected to shave off this morning and then running his fingers through his sandy hair. His disappointment was almost palpable.

I was shocked. Since when had I become a part of the equation? Maybe Michael was right—spending time with Parker wasn't such a good idea.

But that didn't negate the fact that a part of me still longed to go. "It'll be good for them," I said to solidify my stance. "Some time away from their boring mom is just what the doctor ordered. You know, guy time. Man-to-man."

"Sounds great," Parker agreed, but his voice told me it sounded anything but. He was a good sport, though, so he conjured up a smile and gave Grandma's shoulder a parting squeeze. "I guess I'm off, then. But you'd better help me track them down, Julia. I have no idea where they could be hiding on this farm."

He had a point; our rambling farm could be a labyrinth if you weren't familiar with the landmarks, so I waved good-bye to Grandma and went into the mudroom to lace up my tennis shoes. Maybe when they left, I would take a nice, long walk around our parcel. The air would undoubtedly clear my head.

Though the forecaster had predicted a warm day, the spring

morning was still brisk when Parker and I stepped outside. I was grateful for my stylish little jacket and turned up the collar against the light breeze. Parker was in a T-shirt, and I nearly said something about his being too cold, but when I glanced at his arm, I could almost see the warmth of his skin. His forearm was thick and corded, muscular in an easy, natural sort of way. This was a man who didn't need a membership at a gym—his everyday life was workout enough. Suddenly the sight of his bare arm—the light smattering of freckles from the sun and the way his wrist bones stood at the arch to his strong hand—made me shy. I veered away from him slightly.

"They're not in the grove?" I asked, clearing my throat.

"I had a pretty good view of the trees as I came down the driveway, and I didn't see them."

"I told them to stick around," I muttered. Then, cupping my mouth with my hands, I shouted, "Simon! Daniel!" Their names echoed over our property, reverberating off the slumping buildings and careening into the trees.

No answer.

"The garage door is closed," I said, taking mental stock of the nearest possible hiding place. There was only one way into the shedlike garage, and that was through the heavy hung door. I wasn't entirely sure that they could even lift it by themselves.

"They're on a grand adventure." Parker chuckled. "Maybe I should have stayed home today."

"No, they're excited to see you. They're just also easily distracted."

This time Parker raised his hands to his mouth and roared, "Daniel! Simon!"

We stood in the dewy grass and waited, but the only response we received was the chirping of a hundred birds in the trees.

I sighed. "Sorry about this."

Parker shrugged to show me how little the boys' disappearance bothered him. He cocked his head in the direction of the stable and raised his eyebrows in question. "Shall we start there?"

"Oh, the boys aren't allowed to play in the outbuildings. They're around here somewhere."

"Aren't allowed to play in the buildings?" Parker gave me a wide-eyed look. "Are you kidding me?"

"It's not safe," I defended.

"But it's what boys do," he protested. "They explore; they hunt and gather; they discover. . . . They're in one of the buildings, Julia."

"No, they're not."

"Yes, they are. I'm sure of it."

"They listen to me." Parker was starting to make me angry. I had banned the boys from the outbuildings and I believed that they obeyed my instructions.

"I'm sure they do," he soothed. "But this is just too good to pass up. Come on, you can hardly blame them for investigating the great unknown."

"You're wrong," I snarled through clenched teeth.

Parker smirked. "I'm right. In fact, I'm so sure I'm right that I'll make you a deal."

"What kind of a deal?"

"If you're right and the boys are innocently strolling around the property, I'll send you and Nellie for manicures while we're fishing. Girls like that, don't they?"

I laughed in spite of myself. "Sure, Parker, girls like that." I studied my hands for a moment, taking stock of the dry knuckles, the dirt beneath my short nails. "I could use a little pampering. You've got yourself a deal."

I stuck out my hand so Parker could shake it, but he batted it away. "You haven't heard the second half of the bet."

"That's because I know you're not going to win."

"Humor me."

Smiling, I put my hands on my hips and regarded Parker with a cool gaze. "Fine."

"If I'm right and Simon and Daniel have been constructing some incredible fort out of old boards they found in one of these buildings, you have to come fishing with us today."

I opened my mouth to object, but the truth was, it felt like a win-win situation for me. "That's it?"

"That's it."

"I don't have to be your indentured servant or wear some T-shirt declaring your eternal superiority?"

"Nope."

"And I don't have to gut fish?"

"You don't even have to touch them."

Tapping my fingers against my lips, I pretended to think long and hard about Parker's deal. "Okay, fine," I groaned after a long pause. "I'll take you up on your ridiculous bet."

"You're so gracious." He rolled his eyes at me, but the next instant he pulled my hand into his own and held it. For a heartbeat we just stood there, hand in hand, and then he gave me an arm-jiggling shake to seal the deal. "I hope you prove handy with a knife. By the way, do you have any lemons? They take the smell of fish guts right off your skin. Well, kind of . . ."

"You promised!" I yanked my hand away and aimed a punch at his shoulder, but he took off at an easy lope toward the stable and I had no choice but to follow.

Like I had hoped, the musty horse building was utterly untouched. The metal-latch door still held the rusty wire that I had twisted through the handle to secure it. And once we pried back the stiff pieces and opened the creaky door, the inch of dust that covered the floor gave evidence enough that no one had stepped foot over the threshold in a very long time.

"Cats!" Parker said in a mock whisper, pointing at a set of delicate footprints that led from a hole in one boarded-up window to the first stall.

"Fiends," I growled. "I told them the outbuildings were dangerous too."

After we shut the door and retied the fine wire, we zig-zagged our way toward the chicken coop. It was in much better shape than the abandoned stable, and I wondered as we walked up the short stone steps if I should go through it with a fine-tooth comb this summer and then let the boys have this one space as their own. It wouldn't take much. A few broken windows had scattered fragments of antique glass across the floor, and there was a handful of loose planks that sported crooked nails. I shivered at the thought of tetanus, but Parker was right: boys would be boys. Maybe I was expecting too much of them. Being too strict.

But as we unlatched the door, I remembered in a wave of sorrow that there would be no more summers on the farm. We were moving to Iowa City. To an apartment. As Parker and I stood for a second in the shadow of the old chicken coop, I was gripped by a sense of loss. Of regret. Why hadn't I let my boys experience all our farm had to offer?

"They're not here, either," Parker told me, though I could see as much with my own two eyes.

"It would make a nice fort," I mused.

Parker gave me a sidelong glance and nudged me gently with his elbow. "It would."

That one moment of understanding, of tenderness, was so unexpected that it all but knocked me off-balance. I almost confided in him. I could feel the words like water on my tongue, liquid and heavy with all the emotion that sprang from the well of my doubt. But the inappropriateness of such an intimate confession was not lost on me. I swallowed all I longed to say and hopped down the steps without acknowledging his small act of kindness.

The barn was the only building left, and though the farm was filled with other nooks and crannies—the dense interior of the grove; the wooded graveyard, where Grandpa had piled rotten sections of old fencing; the unused horse field lush with prairie grass that rose chest-high—I was starting to believe that Parker was right. There was a certain allure to the ancient structures of our farm. They seemed to whisper with the near-forgotten echo of years gone by. If I closed my eyes, I could almost see my grandpa's shadow as he disappeared around a corner, a length of rope slung over his arm and his Norwegian elkhound Lucy at his side.

"I hear something coming from the barn," Parker said as we made our way up the hill.

"Sure you do," I sighed, for our morning banter had lost its luster for me. I was feeling nostalgic and more than a little depressed—downright sick with the knowledge that my chance to bring up farm boys was rapidly coming to an end.

"No, Julia. I mean it." There was something in Parker's tone that made my head snap up.

We both paused for a moment, ears angled toward the barn, straining to hear whatever had given Parker reason to wipe the seemingly ever-present smile off his face.

"Somebody's screaming," he exclaimed.

And he was right. It was faint but unmistakable.

We started to run at the same moment, but Parker was faster than me. I watched helplessly as he rocketed toward the barn, his long legs eating up the distance as if he was used to taking off at a flat-out sprint up a fairly substantial incline. As we neared the barn, I could see that the bottom section of the red-painted door was closed, but the top half was open just a crack.

Daniel and Simon were in the barn. I was sure of it.

Parker entered the long shadows of the tall building several paces ahead of me and wrenched open the door. As he disappeared inside, I sent a prayer after him. A desperate, wordless plea for help, for strength, for whatever he would need to make everything okay within the darkness of a place that I hadn't stepped foot in for almost a decade. It seemed unfamiliar to me, alien and filled with countless hazards. With danger.

Gasping, I finally gained the gaping door and threw myself into the half-light of the barn, blinded by the sudden gloom. But it didn't take long for my eyes to adjust.

Parker was standing next to Simon with his strong arm wrapped tight around my brother's slight shoulders. Had I once believed that Simon was on the path to young adulthood? He looked like a child beside Parker, a scared little boy. I was about to shout their names, to make them tell me what was going on, when I heard a whimper from somewhere above me. I followed Parker's gaze and saw what they were staring at.

Daniel was suspended above us.

He was at the center of the same beam that I had crossed a hundred times. The only difference was, I had never fallen off. Daniel was clinging to the solid girder of thick timber for dear life, his slender legs dangling into an expanse of open space that seemed as deep and cavernous as the Grand Canyon.

"Daniel!" I screamed.

"Mommy!"

I felt rather than saw Parker turn to shush me. "Don't distract him," he warned, his words tense with authority.

"Distract him?" I shrieked.

Parker crossed the space between us in a flash and grabbed my arms. He gave me a little shake and forced me to look him in the eye. Although I was choking on my own fear, I was startled to see that his face was flushed with the same emotions I was feeling: terror and love. A nauseating sense of *This can't be happening.*

"We're going to get him down," Parker hissed, his jaw clenched in determination. "He'll be fine."

But even as he spoke the words, I knew that it was too late.

I floated out of my body when Daniel fell. I saw his fingers slip and heard his scream, but it was as if those things were disconnected. They were merely two elements from the filming of a bad movie, a pair of recordings that would comprise a whole when edited together. But they meant nothing apart. Fingers skidding off a splintered board. A scream that sounded shocked, unearthly.

It was all over in a flicker. A blink. There was nothing more than a flash of red from Daniel's T-shirt and the humming-bird beat of his legs as he bicycled in the nothingness above us. I gasped at the innocent puff of dust and the sudden, high-pitched cry when he landed. It pierced my soul.

And then, everything was quiet.

falling down

I HATE EMERGENCY ROOMS for the obvious reasons. The smell; the cold, clinical feel; the thin atmosphere punctuated by worry and fear. But my dislike for the ER goes much further. I abhor the cutesy nurses' smocks—the ones with ugly cartoon characters or giant pastel daisies like lick n' stick appliqués from some craft project gone wrong. And I loathe the way the doctors' eyes never meet yours, the way they are too occupied to look you in the face for even a second as they scan charts, monitor their patients, and mentally assess the damage. I don't like how my shoes stick to the floor with every step or the little sucking sound that accompanies each footfall. I don't like the unfamiliar noises or the bustle or the sense of macabre excitement. When it comes down to it, there is little I find redeeming in an emergency room.

But I could have kissed the middle-aged doctor who informed me that my son had fractured his talus.

"Talus?" I wheezed. It could have meant imminent death for all I knew.

"His anklebone."

"Daniel broke his ankle?"

"Yes, ma'am. But it's a nice, clean break. No need for screws or surgery. We'll put it in a hard cast and he'll have to stay off it for four to six weeks. Your son will be good as new by summer."

The relief that rose inside me was a flower that grew from seed to brilliant, open-petaled glory in the span of three short words: *good as new*. They were the most beautiful three words in the world. Better even in that moment than *I love you*. I repeated them out loud, loving the soft way they rolled off my tongue: "Good as new."

"Yup. He was lucky. How far did you say that fall was?"

"I don't know . . . fifteen, twenty feet?" It was little more than a guess, for distances to me were measured in quantities like time or steps or the energy it took to achieve my goal. If I were to gauge the distance from the beam of the barn to the dirt-covered floor according to my own personal experience of it, Daniel had fallen from the height of heaven.

The doctor shook his head and made a final notation on the chart he was holding. "That could have been a lot more serious. Just goes to show you that kids really are made of rubber."

I grinned as if nothing could be funnier than that statement. But even as I rejoiced in the very limited scope of my son's injuries, I worried that something had been overlooked. "You're sure it's just his ankle? No internal injuries? When he hit the ground, I thought . . . I thought he was dead."

"He probably had the wind knocked out of him. He was screaming pretty good by the time you got him here."

The doctor was right. Daniel had been beside himself with pain, writhing in the backseat of Parker's car in such a frenzied state of panic that the corners of his mouth were frothed with foamy spittle. More evidence that he was surely on his deathbed.

But just as I was about to drill the ER doctor further, a pair of nurses rolled Daniel's gurney back into the large emergency room bay.

"Honey," I breathed, stepping to his side and taking his small hand in both of my own. "Are you okay?"

They had let me accompany him to X-ray, but when they performed the MRI, I was left to hug myself in the brightly lit room and imagine every worst-case scenario. Now I could see that my Daniel, the boy who held my very soul in the palm of his hand, still existed beneath the patina of pain. They had obviously given him something, and his crooked smile was relaxed and just a bit loopy.

"I got to ride in a spaceship," he told me.

My eyes shot to the nurse, and she mouthed the letters *MRI.*

"Sounds like fun," I said, pressing my lips against his forehead, his temple, his cheeks in turn. "I'm so glad you're okay."

"I broke my ankle."

"I know." It probably wasn't the time or the place for an interrogation, but I was desperate to know why Parker and I had found Daniel clinging to the beam that spanned our barn in the first place. "What were you doing up there?"

"Learning to tightrope walk."

"But . . ." There was nothing I could say. I had told him the story, after all. And I had done exactly the same thing when I was a kid. Maybe I had been a bit older, but I shouldn't have been surprised by Daniel's tenacity. It made me wonder what other escapades he got into without my knowing about it.

"Never again," I whispered against the side of his sweet head, my mouth all but kissing the curved chrysalis of his ear.

He shrugged. "Okay."

Daniel was more than happy to let me slip out for a moment while they prepared his cast. Though it was next to impossible to leave him, I knew that Simon and Parker were beside themselves with worry. They were pacing the hallway outside the ER, waiting for a shred of news, for some indication of how Daniel was doing. When I caught sight of their faces, I knew that the vigil they kept was as tense and anxious as the hours we had spent here with Grandma. I broke into a grin when it hit me that our two emergency room experiences couldn't have been more different.

"He's going to be fine," I croaked.

Simon let out a whoop, and Parker looked as if he was about to collapse. I reached for him, and for the span of one uncertain breath, he wavered there in the hallway, weak-kneed and quivering as he stared at the tile floor. But then he looked at me, and his gaze was so intense, I almost took a step back. He didn't let me. My hand was still outstretched, and he grabbed me by the wrist and pulled me to him. Parker clung to me, pressing his face into my neck, and before I knew what I was doing, my arms were around him, too.

I don't know how long we held each other, but it was like surfacing from a fathomless, foreign sea when Simon asked, "Can we see him?"

Parker's hands released me slowly, and I swallowed hard before I said, "Of course, Si. Let's go see him."

While they prepped Daniel's ankle for a fiberglass cast, I called Grandma to let her know how we were doing. We felt terrible leaving her behind, but our frantic race down the hill was filled with such horror that we had left the farm in a flurry of gravel and despair. I called the house from my cell phone as I lunged into the backseat, and she had assured me, "Go! Just go."

By myself in the sparkling hospital hallway, I filled her in on the situation in minutes, and she alternated between chuckling softly and murmuring praises. Hearing her voice put the entire experience into perspective, and suddenly everything that had seemed so dark and serious such a short time ago was almost funny. Almost. From my bet with Parker to Daniel's spaceship ride, this would be the sort of story that would be told and retold. A favorite chapter from our family history, if only because the ending was so happy.

After Grandma and I hung up, I hurried back into the emergency room, where I found that Parker and Simon had already helped Daniel pick out a lime green cast. It was so obnoxious, I was sure it glowed in the dark. The doctor already had it halfway on and was cheerfully telling Parker about the benefits of fiberglass when the break wasn't too serious as he rolled wet coils of lizard-colored casting on Daniel's lower leg.

"Can I sign it?" Simon wondered.

"Sure." The doctor smiled. "Your mom and dad can pick up a Sharpie on the way home. They work the best."

My mouth gaped a little, and Simon's eyes darted between Parker and me so fast, I could hardly keep up with their riotous pace. But he didn't say anything, and as I fumbled for just the right words myself, I felt Parker take my hand. He gave it a tight, quick squeeze, a secret embrace that was laced with meaning. *Let it go,* I almost heard him whisper. *Just this once, let it go.*

We did stop at the store for a Sharpie marker, and before we even made it home, Simon had signed Daniel's cast. He spelled out his name in block letters across the very top rim, a statement of ownership. His name on Daniel's leg seemed to bind them together.

The fishing plans were abandoned for obvious reasons, and though I half expected Parker to leave for home by midafternoon, he elected to stick around. Daniel napped a little, and while he slept the dreamless sleep of the drugged, Simon and Parker and I started on the project that had flitted through my mind earlier that morning. It was probably an exercise in futility, but I blamed myself for misunderstanding the needs of my boys. Maybe if I had paid closer attention, Daniel wouldn't have found himself crumpled in a heap on the barn floor. Besides, I had to do something.

The leaning chicken coop was in better shape than I imagined it would be. Grandpa had taken meticulous care of his farm, and when he passed away, everything seemed to simply fall asleep too. Though we had all entertained grandiose plans of running the farm together—of filling the coop with chicks in the spring or buying a pony for me to ride—our plans never materialized. Once we realized that none of us had the time or energy to look after the farm the way Grandpa did, Dad and Grandma and I sold the half-dozen milk cows and mucked out stalls for the last time. And except for a few hens that wandered the farm, the chickens were already gone, so we just swept out the coop and closed the door. We lived on our pretty acres but slowly let the farm go dormant.

Standing in the middle of the sunny henhouse, I questioned why. It felt like we had squandered our chance. Wasted the opportunity for a life that was now lost to us.

"This will be great for the boys," Parker told me as we surveyed the small building. He handed me one of the brooms we had carried from the garage. "Once we get through the dust and clean up the debris, it'll be an awesome hideout."

"Awesome!" Simon agreed from the far corner. He was inspecting the brooder room, a ten-by-ten enclosure that used to house our spring chicks. Grasping the thin chicken wire of the half walls in his fingers, he rattled the flimsy cage and let out a mock cry of distress. "Help! I'm trapped!"

"That's the perfect place for you," Parker said, crossing the concrete floor to kick the door closed with his foot. "Can't get into much trouble there."

"Oh yes I can." There was a mischievous glint in Simon's eye.

We worked for an hour or more, sweeping dust into piles that Parker loaded into a grain shovel and dumped out the door. The broken glass went straight into our metal garbage can, and Simon got so carried away with our impromptu renovation that he took it upon himself to fix gaps in the netting with lengths of old wire he found curled in the corners. The roosting boxes were cleared of moldy hay, and Parker even brushed off the front steps. When we were done, the little building looked ready. Expectant. I could only imagine what my boys would hide in the stacked boxes or how they would utilize the corner room with its stone water trough.

"It's great," Simon declared when we were all done. And it was.

"I think we need to celebrate." Parker leaned his shovel against the wall and turned toward the door. "I'll go get us some juice. A toast is in order."

The chicken coop was quiet with Parker gone, warm and almost dreamy as the tranquil air trembled with a million amber dust motes. Simon still wore a soft half smile that lit his face from within. I watched him for a few moments, loving the peaceful way he absorbed the small universe around him, the way he looked his age again. It was beautiful to me.

In one smooth movement, I stepped behind my brother and wrapped my arms around his shoulders. I fully anticipated his rejection, and I waited cautiously for him to pull away. But instead of shrugging me off, Simon turned and slid his arms around my waist. He hooked his chin over my shoulder, and my heart skipped a beat at his obvious growth. We stayed there for a few precious seconds, and then Simon remembered that he was too old for hugs and backed away.

Before he could disappear and make everything go back to the way it had been, I caught him just below the elbows and held him at arm's length.

"I want to be your mom," I whispered. He stared at me, and my heart lurched at the realization that I had said those words aloud. I had thought them a hundred times, a thousand, never quite believing that I would be able to share them with my troubled brother. But I just had. And I couldn't pretend it was a slip of the tongue.

Tears filled my eyes so fast, I didn't have time to blink them away before they slipped down my dusty cheeks. "She's gone," I breathed, my voice wavering. "I don't think she's coming back. And I don't want you to be Simon Wentwood anymore. You're a part of our family. You always have been."

Simon didn't say anything.

"I've looked into it," I continued, reckless in my desire to make him understand. "We can do it legally. She's been gone so long that . . ." But I couldn't finish. I couldn't tell him that he was essentially an orphan. A child abandoned by his mother with little hope that she would ever return.

The truth was, ever since the night when God laid His plan on my heart like a gift-wrapped surprise, I hadn't been able to stop thinking about the possibility. We had given Simon a home, and we had given him a family, but I longed to give him a name. Not Wentwood, not his negligent mother's maiden name, a meaningless tag that tied him to no one and nothing. I wanted to give him our name. A name that we would all share, a name that would unite us as one.

As I wrote postcard after postcard to Janice, as I penned every fear and frustration or railed against her and what she had done, it became more and more obvious to me that she was finally, irrevocably, gone. My last postcard to her contained three short words:

He's mine now.

But what if he didn't want to be?

"Simon?" I asked, his name an appeal.

My brother, the boy who was a son to me, wouldn't look me in the eye. He stared at the toe of his sneaker, scuffing it gently against the cracked concrete of the henhouse floor. The hem of his jeans was frayed, the white fibers gray with dust from our afternoon endeavor. For some reason the sight of his dirty jeans and the large loop of his double-knotted shoelaces nearly broke my heart. I wanted to bend over and make a neat cuff, to retie the laces that were drooping beneath the soles of his shoes.

I didn't say another word, didn't raise my eyes from the ground until he pulled away from me. Then my gaze shot to his face, searching the depths of his dark eyes for some indication of whether or not he still loved me after I betrayed the woman he probably still considered his mother. I saw no answers in his fixed stare.

But after a moment that seemed to stretch into infinity, he gave me a slight, almost-imperceptible nod.

Something inside me broke open, a mighty dam that held back a flood of hope and doubt and pain and grief. I didn't really even know why he had nodded, or if I misinterpreted the inclination of his head, but before I could ask him anything, Simon whirled on his heel and raced out of the chicken coop. I was left to ponder the sharp crack of the slamming door and the way the light in the small room seemed to bathe me in hues of saffron and gold.

I wanted so much for us, for our little family of four. And though I had spent the last five years trying to make it all work, I wondered as I stood alone in the henhouse if all of my striving was for naught. Maybe, just maybe, the Lord had laid a path. And maybe, just maybe, my job was to walk it, to put one foot in front of the other the best way I knew how. I couldn't prevent Grandma's heart attack or stop Simon's heart from aching. I couldn't even protect Daniel from a fall. But I could love them with every ounce of my being. I could keep walking forward, believing that God would continue to make the pieces fit.

Maybe family was simply whom you loved and home was where you found it.

When Parker opened the door to the chicken coop and poked his head inside, I was sitting cross-legged in the middle of the crooked floor and probably looked like I was meditating. Or praying. Which I suppose I was, though I couldn't have formed a coherent word if I tried. I gave Parker a weak smile because he looked concerned, and when I didn't make a move to stand, he came into the little building and let the door fall shut behind him.

"I just saw Simon . . ." He trailed off, motioning in the direction of the grove. "Everything okay?"

I nodded.

"You look . . . Are you sure you're okay?"

"Yeah," I managed.

My feeble answer didn't wipe the worry from his brow, and Parker cast around for a moment, looking for a place to deposit the container of juice and stack of three plastic cups he was carrying. In the end he set them on the floor and came to stand over me. He offered me his hands, but I wouldn't take them. So he shrugged and plunked himself down across from me so that we were sitting knee-to-knee.

"Did something happen with Simon?"

I considered Parker's question for a moment. Yes, something had happened with Simon. And with Daniel and Grandma and Michael and even him. But mostly this was about me. "Something happened to me," I said, repeating the words running through my head as if I were reading them off a prompter.

"Are you all right?"

I smiled. "Yeah."

"Julia, you're acting really weird."

"I'm feeling a little weird."

"You want to talk about it?"

"I don't know," I said, trying to gather up every thought and feeling so I could put them in some sort of logical order. "I don't think that I can right now. But it's good."

"It's good? You're sure?"

"I think I know what God wants from me. I think I know who I am."

Parker grinned at me. "I know who you are too."

"You do?"

"I have for a long time now."

I cocked an eyebrow at him. "Really? Who do you think I am?"

"An amazing mother," Parker said without pause, "a devoted granddaughter, a loyal friend, a hard worker. You're selfless and patient and kind. You aren't afraid to sacrifice. You don't step down from a challenge."

"You think I'm all those things?"

"Oh, there's more. You're smart, talented, and beautiful."

There was something in his voice that made color rise in my cheeks. I studied my hands in my lap, wishing he would stop, but Parker went on.

"And I think I know what God wants from you. You know all those things I said? They're nice, but I don't think any of that captures the essence of you, Julia DeSmit."

"No?" I whispered.

"Not even close. At the root of it all, at the deepest center, the most secret place, you are *pursued*."

He was right. I knew Parker was right because I had seen it myself. God chased after me, and I ran stumbling in the dark, ignoring His advances. I pined for lost mothers and fell from dizzying heights. I never stopped long enough to turn and look Him full in the face. To see that everything I was looking for had been right there all along.

I was surprised when I felt Parker's finger lift my chin—and even more stunned when I realized that we were face-to-face. "You're going to be just fine, Julia," he whispered.

There was something about the way those words fell in the stillness of the warm afternoon sun that made me catch my breath. But not because they encompassed a dream or a hope, a desire I had for myself and my family. Parker's quiet assertion carried the weight of a promise because it was more than just a passing wish.

It was the truth.

unbound

PARKER SPENT THE NIGHT that night.

I know how that sounds.

And believe me, even in the split second that the invitation spilled out of my mouth, I fully grasped the fact that a casual sleepover in our living room would likely only intensify the rainbow of colors and hues that comprised our already-complex relationship. But it wasn't my fault. Not really. I blame it wholly on Parker. On the look in his eyes as he studied Daniel's face, on the way I could almost see his heart break while my tough little boy tried to hold back tears of pain.

The ER doctor had informed us that studies had proved painkillers could delay or even hinder bone healing. After the quick injection of whatever miracle drug the nurses administered, we were told to avoid pills altogether and give Daniel children's Tylenol only when absolutely necessary. I was so relieved at my son's less-than-fatal diagnosis that I didn't bother to push the issue. But when he woke up in a fog of pain, I regretted my lackadaisical acceptance that a broken bone was a bearable sort of suffering.

One look at Parker's expression as he descended the stairs at suppertime with Daniel cradled in his arms told me he felt the same way. He looked helpless, grieved, as if the creases in his son's forehead were marks that cut him to the bone. Daniel was making little mewling sounds, breathless gasps that indicated just how much his swollen ankle throbbed in its fiberglass cast, and with each one, Parker cringed. It was obvious that he felt Daniel's pain at the deepest part of his being.

"Stay," I said softly.

Parker just nodded.

We curled up on the couch and watched movies, our ragtag family shoulder-to-shoulder as we tried to keep Daniel's mind off the ache in his ankle. I held my son in my lap, but his legs were propped up on a pillow in Parker's lap so that without even knowing it, Daniel was embraced by both of his parents. For an instant I longed to tell him, to whisper the truth in his ear, but the timing wasn't right. I felt like the moment was coming, I could see it approaching on the horizon, but it wasn't quite here. Not quite yet.

On my other side, Simon had tucked himself under my arm so that he could whisper to Daniel as we tried to focus on *Up*. It was a movie the boys had seen a dozen times, but Daniel was still afraid of the dogs, and the only thing that calmed him down was the steady stream of Simon's made-up narrative. Whenever the snarling pack of canines appeared on-screen, Simon launched into a rapid-fire monologue, a story line that I couldn't make out but that made a thin, pained smile appear on Daniel's face.

I was so proud of Simon, so grateful for the distraction of his private game with Daniel, that I carefully laid my arm across his shoulders. He didn't shrug me off.

It wasn't until about halfway through the movie that I realized Grandma was watching us. She was in her favorite chair, the same chair where she had knitted more blankets than I could count. The same chair where she suffered a heart attack and we almost lost her. But when I felt her watching us and turned my gaze, I found Grandma looking healthy and whole. Radiant.

She beamed at me.

Grandma wasn't the sort to beam. Her joy was a steady sort of happiness, the kind of contentment that comes from understanding who you are and where you fit. As a smile grew on my own face, I realized that my grandmother was the most joyful person I knew. Satisfied. And yet it buoyed my soul to see her look at me like this—as if nothing could please her more than the sight of her family together.

I wasn't sure how Parker fit into the picture, and I wasn't sure that I was ready to know. But as Grandma and I grinned at each other wordlessly, another sort of realization settled over my shoulders. I twisted a little, wishing the weight would lift. It didn't. And though it cleft my heart to admit it, I knew what I had to do.

Parker and I took turns trying to settle Daniel down after the movie, and in the end I gave him a dose of Tylenol and a cup of chamomile tea that was half warm milk with a heaping teaspoon of honey. It made him drowsy enough to let me cuddle beside him in bed, a luxury that I hadn't experienced since he "grew up" and became a kindergartner. I cupped my hand against his cheek and told him stories until his breathing was slow and even. Then I held him against me and prayed over him until I ran out of words to say. I prayed for safety and health and healing. And contentment and love and holiness.

When I finally descended the stairs, everyone but Parker had retired to bed. He was sitting on the couch in the living room, looking for all the world like a lost little boy. He looked vulnerable. Forlorn.

"It's hard seeing your child hurt, isn't it?" I asked from the doorway.

Parker glanced up and gave me a somber nod. "I want to take it away from him."

"I know. But it doesn't work that way."

"Tell me about it," Parker sighed. "I've been praying all afternoon that God would let us switch places. Hasn't happened yet."

I laughed a little. "It's not going to. But I think that's okay. Maybe a painless life isn't all it's cracked up to be anyway."

Parker tilted his head and regarded me. "That's either very wise or just a bit sadistic."

"I trust you're familiar with the Beatitudes?" I teased.

"Yeah, but that stuff doesn't apply today, does it?" By the way his mouth curled up at one corner, I knew that Parker was playing along. It felt nice to find that we were on common ground.

I sat in Grandma's empty chair and leaned forward with my elbows on my knees. "I have to ask you a favor," I said carefully, hoping he wouldn't question my motives or drill me for answers that I wasn't ready to give.

"A favor?" Parker crossed his arms over his chest and sat back, but he smiled at me when he said, "Name it."

"If you can—I mean, if it's not too much trouble and if you can make it work—"

"Julia," he interrupted, "whatever it is, I've already said yes."

I gathered a breath and released my request in one quick, unemotional outburst. "I need you to stay here tomorrow with Daniel. Maybe even tomorrow night. I need to go somewhere and I don't know when I'll be back."

"Where are you going?" Parker asked calmly.

"Iowa City."

Parker knew that Michael lived in Iowa City, but he didn't ask me why I felt compelled to make a sudden, unplanned trip across the state. He merely dipped his head in accord. "No problem. Maybe I'll just stay through Monday to give you a hand? I never take time off—it won't be a problem at all."

His offer surprised me, but I nodded.

"And tomorrow I can join Grandma and the boys at church. I've always wanted to go to your church."

"If Daniel's up for it," I reminded him.

"Of course."

We stared at each other for a few seconds until I couldn't meet his gaze anymore and suddenly found my own fingers fascinating. As I fidgeted with my hands, I said, "Thanks. I really appreciate it."

"No worries."

"You'd do anything for Daniel, wouldn't you?"

Parker didn't answer right away, and I raised my eyes just enough to meet his. "Yes," he finally agreed. "I would do anything for Daniel. But I'm doing this for you."

Although it killed me to leave Daniel the day after his first major injury, I knew that I didn't have a choice. Something had changed; my world had shifted. And I was heartsick to imagine the fallout.

Grandma gave me a knowing look when I descended the stairs on Sunday morning, and she didn't seem the least bit surprised when I told her that I needed to make a last-minute road trip.

"We'll take good care of Daniel, I promise," she said.

I didn't tell her why I was going. I didn't have to. But I did want her blessing. "Am I doing the right thing?" I asked, holding her by the shoulders with just a little more force than necessary.

She smiled and put her hands on my wrists. "You know the answer to that question, Julia. You don't have to ask me."

It wasn't what I wanted to hear, but it did give me the confidence to walk out the door. The time had come for me to make my own decisions, to stop relying on everyone else to guide me in the way that I already knew, deep down, was right. It was my path to walk, however hard it may be.

Daniel woke up soon after I was dressed and ready to go. He shouted from his rumpled bed, and Parker took the stairs two by two to rescue our son from his tangled sheets. I was startled when Parker entered the kitchen with Daniel in his arms. The transformation was incredible. Daniel seemed much better in the lemony light of morning: clear-eyed and smooth-faced as if the pain of the night before was nothing but a bad memory.

In a flash I remembered his toddler years, that magical

time when he went to bed with a bruise and woke up with unblemished skin. Cuts healed overnight, bumps disappeared in hours. Childhood was nothing if not miraculous, and I marveled at the way his sweet body healed itself so effortlessly. Daniel was going to be just fine.

"Do you care if I leave for the day?" I asked him solemnly when he was seated at the kitchen table.

Daniel's brow furrowed.

"Parker is going to stay."

The shadow left his face as if blown by a sudden, mighty wind. "Sure, Mom! See you tomorrow!"

I had sort of hoped he would argue—that someone would try to make me stay—but nobody seemed to care much that I was leaving. Either that or they were all in support of my spontaneous road trip. After a round of hugs and kisses, and an awkward, one-armed embrace from Parker, I hit the road.

It felt strange to be driving away, to just leave my family in the care of the man whom only months ago I had loathed. No—I never loathed Parker. But I resented him. I distrusted him. And I believed I had every reason to.

That's the extraordinary thing about people. They change.

I spent the six-hour drive to Iowa City in silence. Maybe I should have prayed or tried to arrange my thoughts so that when I saw Michael face-to-face, I would be prepared to say all that I had to. But my stillness wasn't idle. I was listening.

Waiting. Hoping that all the wishes and wondering I had sent heavenward would not come back to me empty. I thought I remembered hearing something like that in Scripture. It was in regard to the Word of God, but I had faith that maybe it could also apply to my outstretched hands. I believed that He would fill them.

When I stopped at a gas station on the outskirts of Iowa City, I finally took out my cell phone to call Michael.

He answered on the first ring, a smile in his voice. "Hey. Aren't you supposed to be taking a Sunday afternoon snooze?"

"You know I don't nap," I said, trying to keep my voice light. "Actually, I have a surprise for you."

"A surprise?"

Maybe it was the wrong word to use. *Surprise* insinuated fun things, happy things. "I'm here," I blurted out before Michael could begin to imagine the exciting possibilities.

"What? What do you mean, Julia?"

"I mean I'm in Iowa City."

"What?"

I couldn't tell if his shock was pure delight or irritation at the absurdity of my last-minute, six-hour drive. "Yeah," I said softly. "I'm *here* here. *Where you are* here."

Michael waited a few seconds before he responded. "Honey, you haven't made the trip to Iowa City in nearly a year. What in the world made you decide to come down now?"

I didn't want to get into it over the phone, but I could

tell that Michael was more than concerned about my unannounced visit. A spur-of-the-moment trip of this magni-
tude was totally out of character for me. His apprehension
was warranted, and I had no desire to torture him.

"Can I see you?" I asked timidly.

"Of course you can. Come over to the apartment. You
remember where it is, don't you?"

But his apartment didn't feel like neutral ground to me. It
was too comfortable, too familiar, even though it had been
a long time since I'd snuggled with Michael on his sagging
love seat. I didn't want to see him there and lose my nerve.
Or remember that I was soon supposed to be the queen of
that particular castle, however small it might be.

"How about we meet at a park?" I posed the question
casually, but even I could hear the undertone of significance.
"It's such a beautiful day, and I'd love to stretch my legs after
being cooped up in the car."

"Sure," Michael said after a second of hesitation. "There's
a park around the corner from my apartment complex. Take
a right at the light and you'll more or less run right into it.
I'll meet you there in . . . ?"

"Ten minutes?" I guessed. "I'm at the Cenex just off of
I-80."

"See you soon."

We hung up without our customary good-byes and without a single mention of how eager we were to see each other.
It was like he knew.

The park in question was small and wooded, the sort of place that bespoke a history we could only picture in black-and-white photos, snapshots of a time gone by. Michael was pacing a sidewalk near the street, and I parallel parked as close to him as I could get. My heart was thumping out a staccato beat against my rib cage, and I worried that my face was flushed with the sick fear that I felt. As I turned off the car and sat for a moment in my hot bucket seat, I fought an urge to throw open the door and fling myself into his arms. To forget all that I felt and believed about Michael. About us.

But I couldn't do that.

Why had I never noticed Michael's subtle indifference? the way he tried to reach out to Daniel and Simon on his own terms but wasn't much bothered when they rebuffed his halfhearted advances? Why had I never detected the way Simon was quick to roll his eyes in Michael's presence? or how Daniel busied himself with solitary pursuits instead of seeking out his future stepdad's attention? I could remember a time when Daniel at least tried to win Michael's favor by soliciting games of catch or hide-and-seek. But the more I had thought about it in the weeks after I told my fiancé about Parker, the more I realized that Michael had rarely taken the opportunity to play with the boys, and they adjusted their expectations to account for his lack of interest.

Then there was our inability to coordinate our lives—my reluctance to give up Mason, our farm, our comfortable little existence. And Michael's attachment to his lifelong dream.

I didn't resent him for wanting to be a doctor. Quite the opposite. I was awed by his brilliance. I admired his ability to persist on a road that seemed so difficult. But the truth was, whether or not his imminent profession was estimable, he chose it over me. Over us.

And all of that was just the beginning. I was a factor too.

I knew now that I lusted after Michael. I relished the feel of his arms around me and his lips on my skin. He was perfect, a hero, something to be worshiped and adored. For years I had believed that I didn't deserve him, and he had patiently and persistently tried to prove me wrong. He was a wonderful man. A generous, good, and thoughtful man. I loved him, just not the way I was supposed to. And I believed that Michael loved me. But there would always be parts of Julia DeSmit that he didn't understand. Or worse, that he tried to ignore.

I gathered a shuddering breath and tried to steel myself for all that was ahead. But I was well past any pretense of bravery, and when I stepped from the car, I was already crying.

Michael crossed his arms over his chest and watched me come.

Each step toward him felt like it took an eternity. And as infinity seemed to stretch itself between us, I carefully uncoiled each strand of our relationship. It was five years of unraveling, five years of memories and hopes and wishes that should have culminated in every little girl's dream: a masterpiece of white from wedding dress to sugared cake to the unlined pages of our yet-to-be-written future. The loops of our shared history pooled at my feet, and when I finally faced Michael, I was sobbing and bereft of a life I had spent hours and days and weeks planning for.

I was unbound.

doxology

THREE THINGS HAPPENED in June that changed my life forever.

One thing did not. I did not marry Michael Vermeer.

When the date of our wedding came and passed, my heart suffered with the sort of throbbing, relentless grief that assured me my relationship with him was a wound that ran deep. It would leave a scar—and not one of those faint, near-invisible things. I would bear the mark of our ruined dreams, of the foolish youth that convinced me we were enough for each other just because neither of us had anyone else. How was I to know then that comfort did not equal love?

The morning after the canceled nuptials, I woke with a sense of finality. There was a somber edge to my acceptance of the U-turn my life had taken, but beneath the quiet acknowledgment of my own failed love, I could feel something else unfurling in the soil of my heart. It was little more than a seed, a freshly planted hope spreading a single, soft green root at my center. Testing. Wondering if I would reject or accept the promise that maybe there was more to come.

I didn't just accept it. I welcomed it. Watered it and coaxed it to grow with songs that my soul was just learning to sing.

And when the first life-changing event happened in June, my little seedling burst out of the ground with a new sort of vigor and curled the tip of a single leaf toward the cloudless blue sky.

On a quiet Tuesday in the middle of June, Simon Eli became my son. A local lawyer took the case pro bono, and since Janice had been out of the picture for so long, it wasn't much of a case at all. A lot of paperwork. A veritable mountain of paperwork. My name on so many documents that I contemplated getting a stamp of my signature made. But when we showed up for our court date on a sunny, early summer morning, the judge grinned at us like we were the highlight of his month and made us promise to love each other always. It was almost like a wedding.

We even had a little celebration when it was done. Grandma whipped up a from-scratch chocolate cake with homemade fudge frosting that curled in glossy swaths. There was sherbet punch and fresh strawberries that we'd bought from a pickup truck on the side of the road . . . and lots of laughter. It was gorgeous outside, so we ate on the porch, the sun slanting on the whitewashed boards and kissing our bare feet with afternoon light.

I could hardly take my eyes off Simon. He had transformed in the weeks since Daniel had fallen from the barn rafter. Or rather, since I had held him in the chicken coop and told him I wanted to be his mom. We didn't talk about it much, but I knew that he wanted it too. And why wouldn't he? I had whispered to him the words we long to hear above all else, even if we don't always realize it: *I want you.* Of course, there are a million different ways to say it. *I love you. Will you marry me? You are mine.* But it all comes down to the same thing: belonging. I think that's why when God invites us into His family with arms wide open, we aren't just honorary children. We're adopted. We belong.

I thought about sending Janice one last postcard, but it was time for me to let that particular dream go. Those heartfelt scribbles were lost to recycle bins or garbage cans or wherever undeliverable mail found a final resting place. Never once had I included a return address, and though I had sent each rendering of my soul with the fervent wish that it would find its way into her hands, I knew when I dropped every postcard into the mailbox that neither of us would ever see it again. I was okay with that. Janice wasn't coming back, and if she did, she would find us a whole and happy family. Wherever she was, whatever she was doing, I wished her well. Really, I did. After all, how could I fault her for all she had given me? Simon was more than enough recompense for everything I had endured.

The second thing that pitched the orbit of my world happened the same night that Simon officially became a DeSmit.

Parker had come down for the festivities, and even though it was a Tuesday night and he had to get back for work the next day, he stayed late. We tucked the boys in bed, washed the plates side by side, and sent Grandma to rest after she gave us a beatific but exhausted smile.

We found ourselves outside, beneath the stars that shone down on the farm where my boys would grow up. I loved that thought, savored the idea of our lives unfolding here with the sort of delight that accompanied rare candy. Sometimes I popped the unfinished dream of our twined futures in my mouth and let it melt on my tongue. It was so sweet, so perfect and beyond my imagination, that I could have cried at the beauty of it. Often, I did.

I think Parker knew that something had shifted in me. Not just my breakup with Michael or my adoption of Simon, though both of those things were enough to alter someone for always. It was something deeper. Maybe it was maturity. Or growth or understanding. Maybe it was just one of those nebulous things that you could never quite put your finger on even if you knew beyond a shadow of a doubt that it was there.

Whatever it was, it caused Parker to look at me differently. I knew because I watched him watching me, and I was confused by what I saw.

We had set off in the direction of his car, but for some reason our feet kept shying from the driveway and we found ourselves walking in circles. We ambled around like we had all the time in the world, like we cared for nothing more than the rhythmic sound of our own steps and the way we seemed to roam in harmony.

"Stop looking at me like that," I told him as we wandered toward the grove.

"Like what?" Parker stopped in the little clearing by our night tree and took me gently by the elbow. "How am I looking at you?"

"I don't know." I shrugged. "But you're making me nervous."

"Nervous? I make you nervous?"

"No, that look makes me nervous, and—"

But apparently Parker didn't much care to hear what I had to say, because before my lips could form another word, he cupped my face in his hands and covered my mouth with his own.

I didn't even know I wanted him to kiss me until it was happening. But once I got over the shock of it and could feel the gentle press of his lips, the way his fingers traced the line of my jaw and the slight weight of his thumb against the fluttering pulse in my throat, I couldn't stop myself from kissing him back. My arms went around his neck, and he took my yielding as an invitation to draw me to him.

It was the last thing I ever expected, though when Parker laughed a little against me, his chest vibrating with the pleasure of finally finding each other, everything seemed to fit. Looking back, I could see it all play out like the separate scenes from an epic movie. There was our first meeting in statics class. Our first date and kiss. The colossal mistake that gifted me with the purest joy I had ever known.

"I thought everything was about Daniel," I murmured, surprising myself. "The boys."

"Me too," Parker agreed. He gave me one last insistent kiss and then touched his forehead to mine so that when I exhaled, he breathed me in. "But it's been about you for a very long time."

"It has? Since when?"

"Oh, I don't know. Since I put my coat over your shoulders?"

"That was the first day!"

Parker brushed his lips against my nose. "I guess I'm a good secret keeper."

"I don't want to keep secrets anymore," I whispered. "I want your son to know who you are."

"Our son," Parker agreed.

"Sons," I blurted. "I have two sons." Suddenly I was terrified. Maybe Parker didn't realize that we were a package deal. That if he loved me, he had to accept me, and my family, as we were. Grandma, Daniel, Simon . . . we belonged together. I put my hands on Parker's chest and pushed away, desperate to search his face, to see his reaction to the reality of who I was.

Though I feared the worst, Parker was smiling. He took me gently by the wrists and lifted my hands to his lips. Kissing each of my palms in turn, he said, "I know. I love them equally, Julia. I have from the beginning."

I believed him heart and soul.

But there was no rush. No wild ride down a road that left us confused and dizzy. Instead, after our kiss in the grove, he was content to let everything develop slowly. *In God's good time,* he seemed to say. And I heard the same still voice.

In some ways, it was as if Parker began the process of courtship, a slow and gradual coming together that was neither rushed nor rash. Nothing much changed between us except for the knowledge that there was more to come. It was agonizingly delicious, a sweet ache. And if anyone noticed the shift in the air between us, they never said a word. Except Grandma.

A few days after the kiss that once again changed the trajectory of my life, Grandma cornered me in the kitchen and gave me as crushing a hug as she could muster.

"What's this for?" I laughed, holding her close and drinking in the warm, clean scent of her skin.

"For answered prayers."

"You've been praying?" But that was a ridiculous question. When didn't my grandmother pray? I modified my inquiry. "What have you been praying for?"

Grandma looked at me and smiled. All at once, I was certain that she knew about Parker and me. But instead of digging for details, she answered my question. "I've been praying for many things. But even though I've asked for a lot, God has seen fit to give me more." She backed away from my embrace and held out her hands, palms up. "It spills out, Julia. I can't contain it."

I placed my hands beneath hers, cupping her wrinkled fingers so that every blessing that leaked from her grip fell onto me. Grandma turned her eyes down for a minute, studying the way our hands folded together. Then she looked me full in the face and twisted her wrists. She emptied it all over my outstretched hands, passing on gifts and promises and hopes and dreams that were a heritage I didn't deserve. But that was what love did. It made you generous and reckless. It made you give of yourself without pausing to consider the consequences.

The seed that had been planted in my heart became a sapling that day. Grandma whispered it forth, and it uncurled generous leaves to bask in the warmth of her sun. She made it strong. Ready to face the third thing that happened.

Nellie DeSmit passed away in her sleep on a near-perfect summer morning in June.

I was up early because the birds were singing outside my window, a predawn symphony that was too pretty to ignore. Warblers and orioles and thrushes made nests in our grove, and their liquid songs lent a magical quality to a morning that was robed in mist like a gossamer veil. I could have snuggled in my bed and listened to them for hours, but something prompted me to swing my legs out from under the sheets and descend the stairs in my pajamas. I was called, really. Nudged forward by a voice that pulled me. That lured me to come. *Come.*

It wasn't like me to open her bedroom door. I never did it unless she had asked me to wake her at a certain time. But the urge was inescapable; I didn't even knock before I turned the handle of her door and stepped into the smoky, predawn light.

"Grandma?" I called.

She didn't answer.

"Grandma, it's such a beautiful morning. You should hear the birds . . ."

The realization came almost delicately, like a blanket placed across my shoulders and wrapped tight. There was something missing in the room. *She* was missing in the room.

I crossed the floor carefully, almost as if I trod on holy ground. And maybe I did. Her hand was warm yet when I took it, and there was a feeling like heaven in the air. This place was consecrated, if only for a moment. I felt like we had passed each other—one coming, one going—and in the breeze our souls stirred up, the presence of God still lingered.

Grandma's funeral was a quiet affair, even though the church was packed with people. Everyone appeared to know her and love her, to remember her generous spirit and sacrificial life. They came out of the woodwork to honor her. But there was no weeping or gnashing of teeth. At least, not in public. Her life was a cause for celebration, and so, it seemed, was her death. A homecoming.

But I missed her.

Oh, how I missed her.

The farmhouse was bigger without her in it. Hollow, as if she had filled the space with her presence, and now that she was gone, we were left to fully grasp all the ways that she had so graciously, so selflessly filled our days. We cried for want of her in the beginning, and when we started to get used to her absence, we cried because she was becoming a memory.

And yet Grandma didn't leave us empty-handed. Everything she had prayed for was a parting gift to us. Daniel and Simon and I discovered patience we didn't know we had, endurance beyond what we thought was possible. If we were woven together before, the three strands of our lives were braided into an unbreakable cord when we found that we had no choice but to cling to each other. We clung.

I even found I had the dignity to let Parker care for us. He didn't swoop in and rescue our drowning trio, for he could plainly see that we were far from drowning. But he did come alongside us; he walked with us in our pain. I knew that his role in our lives was a piece of the puzzle that Grandma had wanted in place for a very long time. And I was finally content to admit that it fit. That he fit.

By the time summer was dry and spent, the grass browning and the leaves starting to turn colors at the farthest tips, I could accept that Grandma's legacy was more than just one of family and belonging and home. It was something that stretched far beyond the day-to-day to the deepest, most furtive desires of our hearts. It was a heritage worth more than even her presence, her spirit, her endless words of wisdom.

I had once believed that Daniel sang preludes in his sleep. Preparatory songs that tuned my heart for praise. I now knew that Grandma sang too, hemming in our days with a doxology that echoed in a round without end.

I could hear her singing over us.

My children, may you grow in grace.

discussion questions

1. It has been five years since we last saw Julia in *Summer Snow*. In what ways has she changed? How has she stayed the same?

2. Although she is only twenty-four years old, Julia is essentially the single mother of two young sons. Do you think she is a good mom? Why or why not?

3. How do you feel about Michael at the beginning of the book? Does your perception of him change as the story unfolds? Do you think he is a good match for Julia?

4. When Parker reenters Julia's life, it turns her world upside down. Do you think he has a right to intrude after more than five years of silence? Why or why not?

5. Julia's relationship with Nellie seems to be the cornerstone that holds their unorthodox family together. In what ways has that relationship changed since *After the Leaves Fall* and *Summer Snow*? In what ways has it stayed the same?

6. How do you feel about the scrap of paper that Julia finds in her grandmother's Bible? Do you agree with Nellie's "life list"?

   I don't want Julia to be happy.
   I don't expect her life to be easy.
   I don't insist that it be painless.

But I do want her to be content.
I want her to love and be loved.
I want her to be holy.

7. On page 243, Julia says, "Our searching souls pursued happy endings. And the heart was capable of great and deceiving beauty." Do you think she's right, or is she being too pessimistic?

8. In what ways, subtle and obvious, is Daniel like Parker? In what ways is he like Julia?

9. Why do you think Julia sends Janice postcards when she knows that her estranged mother will never read them?

10. Were you disappointed when Julia broke up with Michael, or do you think she made the right decision?

11. In the final chapter Julia muses, "It all comes down to the same thing: belonging. I think that's why when God invites us into His family with arms wide open, we aren't just honorary children. We're adopted. We belong." Why do you think it was so important to Simon that he belong? Do you think things will change for him now that he is legally a part of the DeSmit family?

12. How do you feel about the ending of *Beneath the Night Tree*? Are you satisfied with how Julia's story has unfolded? Why or why not?

About the Author

NICOLE BAART was born and raised in a small town in Iowa. She wrote and published her first complete novel, *After the Leaves Fall*, while taking a break from teaching to be a full-time mom. *Summer Snow* and *Beneath the Night Tree* complete the series. Nicole is also the author of *The Moment Between*.

The mother of three young sons and the wife of a pastor, Nicole writes when she can: in bed, in the shower, as she is making supper, and occasionally sitting down at her computer. As the adoptive mother of an Ethiopian-born son, she is passionate about global issues and is a founding member of One Body One Hope, a nonprofit organization that works with an orphanage in Monrovia, Liberia. Nicole and her family live in Iowa.